THE
VATICAN'S
VAULT

BARRY LIBIN

MILFORD HOUSE

an imprint of Sunbury Press, Inc.
Mechanicsburg, PA USA

MILFORD HOUSE

an imprint of Sunbury Press, Inc.
Mechanicsburg, PA USA

For information about special discounts for bulk purchases, please contact Sunbury Press Orders Dept. at (855) 338-8359 or orders@sunburypress.com.

To request one of our authors for speaking engagements or book signings, please contact Sunbury Press Publicity Dept. at publicity@sunburypress.com.

ISBN: 978-1-62006-163-3 (Trade paperback)

Library of Congress Control Number: 2019932101

FIRST MILFORD HOUSE PRESS EDITION: January 2019

Product of the United States of America
0 1 1 2 3 5 8 13 21 34 55

Set in Bookman Old Style
Designed by Crystal Devine
Cover by Riaan Wilmans
Edited by Erika Hodges

Continue the Enlightenment!

To my grandsons: Jacob, Noah, and Elliot.

If they are the future,
then the world will find peace.

ACKNOWLEDGEMENTS

I would like to acknowledge the help given to me in writing this book. To Professor Lawrence Schiffman, professor of Hebrew and Judaic Studies at New York University, for sharing his knowledge and his graciousness in guiding me through the secret wonders of Rome. To Danelle McCafferty and Ted Gilley for their assistance, and a special thanks to Erika Hodges, my editor, for her insightful input and gentle critiques. To Lawrence Knorr of Sunbury Press for his publishing acumen. And finally, I would like to thank my wife, Margery, for her perceptive advice and continuous support throughout the project.

Our ultimate end is that of Voltaire and of the French Revolution—the final destruction of Catholicism, and even of the Christian idea. . . . The Pope, whoever he is, will never come to the secret societies; it is up to the secret societies to take the first step toward the Church, with the aim of conquering both of them. The task that we are going to undertake is not the work of a day, or of a month, or of a year; it may last several years, perhaps a century; but in our ranks the soldier dies and the struggle goes on. . . .

—THE PERMANENT INSTRUCTION OF THE ALTA VENDITA (circa 1820)

BOOK ONE

Even a man whose life entails death was not prepared for what was being witnessed. It wasn't the acrid smell of smoke or the ominous silence of blue-uniformed police and brown-suited detectives that proved so disconcerting, rather it was the body of a thin young man dressed in priestly black cloth wholly saturated with blood. Across his mouth was stretched a broad piece of silver duct tape, and through his heart was thrust a wooden stake that penetrated the wall behind—a body hanging as lifeless as Christ on his cross.

Dr. Jeffrey Moss considered the scene, fixing on a thin strand of cord suspended about the slumped neck, tied at each end to a piece of rotted wood on which was scrawled in large bloody letters the words *Soli Deo Gloria*. He took a deep breath, sparingly releasing the air to clear his mind, unable to avert his eyes from the sight before him. As a detective, physician, and assistant medical examiner of the City of New York, he had seen death in many forms and from multiple causes, yet this was different. Perhaps if it had occurred within the darkest reaches of the city where life can be valueless and survival an ongoing drama, it would have eased his senses, but not at 452 Madison Avenue. The building is a magnificent neo-gothic four-story structure adjoining St. Patrick's Cathedral in the heart of Manhattan, one of the city's most gracious homes, and one of its most sacred, for it is the official residence of the archbishop of New York, His Eminence, Patrick Cardinal Healy. Anthony DePalma, chief of Manhattan detectives, was directing the investigation with several of his officers when he recognized Jeff's tanned six-foot athletic frame clothed in a well-fitting dark blue suit and white dress shirt open at the collar.

"Apologies for the late call. Disturb anything?"

Jeff broke his gaze. "*Tosca,* at the Met."

"Sorry."

"No worries, the ending never changes—there's always an execution."

DePalma glanced at the victim. "Same here. Thirty years with NYPD, never saw anything like this."

Jeff combed his fingers through his light brown hair as he surveyed the third-floor room, one of several that led from the narrow hallway. The scene seemed as staged as the opera he had just left, yet filled with a horror that no librettist could dare conceive. The place was in disarray, lamps sprawled on the floor, empty dresser drawers flung open, mattress overturned, clothing scattered, a bloody hammer lying on what was once a pristine thick-piled taupe carpet now singed from flame, and an empty red overnight carrying bag with an ID tag that read "Air Italia."

"Who is he?"

DePalma took out a small notepad. "According to Monsignor James Quinn, the cardinal's secretary, his name is Alonzo Fabrizzi, a young priest, just arrived from Rome to meet with the cardinal tomorrow. Quinn stated he had never met Fabrizzi and assumed it was a personal matter. It appears that the request came from Rome, but not through official Vatican channels."

"And the cardinal?"

"Out of town until morning."

"Motive?"

"Not money. His wallet was found with three hundred euros."

"Then why?"

"No idea, but whoever did this tried to burn the place down."

Jeff stepped aside, allowing the police photographer to complete capturing the crime scene. "Nothing random about this."

DePalma nodded in agreement. "Any ideas?"

"Wooden stake through the heart, body hung as if crucified—that's how you kill a vampire."

DePalma scribbled a note onto his pad. "And the sign?"

"I figured you'd know."

"I was never the altar boy type."

"*Soli Deo Gloria?*" Jeff shook his head. "Only took Latin 101. Something about God's glory, but why here?" He removed several business cards from his wallet and placed them on the table. "Maybe we'll get lucky."

Jeff walked to the body and examined the wounds, as if trying to appreciate what the young priest had experienced. "He was alive."

"What do you mean?"

"When he was hung."

"How can you tell?"

"His eyes—they're raised toward heaven, as if praying to his God."

DePalma looked up at the crucified priest. "Wonder what kind of prayer?" He paused before adding, "Wonder what kind of God?"

"What do you mean?"

He looked back at Jeff. "I'm not a good Catholic, but what God could allow this to happen?"

"That's always the question, isn't it?"

Jeff made a final survey of the room before getting back on point. "Bring him down to the morgue. Once we do the autopsy, I'll know more."

JULY 1

The weather in Rome had been threatening, but the dire prediction would only shortly be realized. The sturdy figure of Cardinal Secretary Ludvik Jarogniew, wrapped in a loose-fitting dark cloak that overlaid his black clerical garments, made his way through the great doors of the Palazzo Apostolico, the Papal Palace. He gave a bare nod to the Pontifical Swiss Guards uniformed in red, blue, and yellow, colors of the Medici worn since the Renaissance, and took the private elevator to the third floor, where the new pontiff resided. Jarogniew's seventy-plus years still carried broad shoulders and a thick neck upon which balanced a squared cranium. He had a set jaw and a defined noble nose that revealed a violent history—features more often associated with a football linebacker than a God-fearing priest.

Jarogniew had held the position of cardinal secretary for the previous two popes, continued during the recent *sede vacante*, the election period, and agreed to remain until this new pope could choose his own. The cardinal secretary is the Vatican's Secretary of State, the head of its government, responsible for Vatican finances, and the pope's principal advisor. To veteran Vatican observers there was little doubt, nor to Jarogniew himself, that he would be reappointed for a third tenure.

But tonight was an inopportune time for such a visit. Jarogniew had more pressing business than to assist the new pope acclimate to his recently elected position. What possible emergency could have warranted his being summoned to the papal apartment at so late an hour—and with a forecast of such inclemency? Did the Holy Father have more questions about Vatican protocol? Did he seek advice on what activities the pontificate should be involved with? Surely these queries could wait until the day, regardless of how difficult it must be for this unknown cardinal from a poor country to be called to such prominence. The fact was, such concerns were minor compared to the issues that preoccupied Jarogniew, for tonight he was to learn if a mystery that has challenged man for over three thousand years had been solved.

Jarogniew glanced expectantly at his cell phone, awaiting the outcome of the intense but covert search that had taken place within a massive chamber, secret to but a few, whose only entryway was to be found within the depths of the Vatican itself, depths that history had christened the Vatican's Vault.

The Vatican's Vault. The name alone brought forth centuries of fear, suspicion, and myth attendant with the tortuous passageways and ancient crypts lying in the bowels of the Holy See. *Secretum* was how the mysteries that echoed inside its walls were described.

The search of the Vatican's Vault was more than a modest quest to discover papal documents stored in the Archivum Secretum Apostolicum Vaticanum, the Vatican secret archives. Those archives, many dating from the eighth century, had already revealed such significant matters as a letter to Pope Clement VII requesting the annulment of Henry VIII's marriage to Catherine of Aragon; letters from Michelangelo and Martin Luther; the official documents of the fourteenth-century heretical trials of the Knights Templar; and the seventeenth-century proceedings against Galileo for suggesting the earth, and its Church, was not the center of the universe. Such searches were conducted by religious scholars who devoted their lives to seeking holy truths and who considered their tasks as sacred as seeking the place where God himself dwelled.

But this exploration of the Vatican's Vault was of a different nature. It demanded greater discipline within a strict time restraint and was carried out by those with less holy intentions, whose heavenly obligations were subordinate to a craving for earthly power. Their purpose was explicit: to uncover an enigma that could be traced to the pyramids of ancient Egypt and earlier, a long-lost treasure so placed as to never be found yet containing a source of power greater than any other in the ancient world. To those trusted few who understood the significance, its discovery would unravel the Final Mystery. Ludvik Jarogniew was foremost of those trusted few.

The cardinal walked the stately third-floor hallway lined with priceless furnishings, sculpture, tapestries, and paintings by

Raphael, da Vinci, Fra Angelico, Caravaggio, Titian, and an endless list of the world's finest artists. He well knew that should
all the world's greatest art be destroyed, the Vatican's collection
alone would preserve the ultimate achievements of man's cul-
ture. Yet, tonight, with his hand tightly clutching his cell phone,
he had no inclination for gallery exploration. Rather, his concern
was with an abducted object transported to the vault in the midst
of the first century.

As Jarogniew approached the elegantly carved double walnut
doors at the hall's end, his phone vibrated. His heart contracted
with anticipation as he viewed the digital dispatch, its subject
succinctly written: *Il Vault del Vaticano*—the Vatican's Vault. Finally, the moment had arrived, the culmination of all that he had
devoted his adult life to. Impatiently he scrolled down to read the
remainder of the disclosure: *Abbiamo fallito, maestro. Non siamo
riusciti a trovare il Tesoro.* We have failed. There was no treasure
to be found.

Was this possible? Perhaps he had misunderstood. Jarogniew
focused again on the simple message, but the letters remained the
same. There was no misunderstanding. There was no treasure.

A crushing feeling swept over him, and an avalanche of
thoughts filled his mind: Was this all for naught? Was it only
myth? Was there no Final Mystery, no ancient power that would
enable him to achieve what he and those who came before him
had sought for so long? The cardinal forced a deep breath and
pounded his fist against his chest, punishing himself for failure
while calling forth the strength for renewed dedication. There
could be no mistake. The treasure had to be somewhere, he was
certain of it, but if not in the vault, then where?

* * *

Jarogniew powered off his phone and entered the imposing papal apartment overlooking St. Peter's Square. As he crossed the
threshold into the richly appointed drawing room, he was greeted
with a raised hand by a modest appearing, cherubic-faced man
with probing blue eyes and an engaging, unsophisticated smile.
To Jarogniew, the new pope seemed out of place in his opulent
surroundings. He was seated in an oversized wingback chair covered in acid-green velvet. He was wearing a white skullcap and a
crisp white cloak over which hung a large gold cross. On his right
hand, he wore the newly received piscatorial ring, the pure gold

ring of the fisherman presented to each new pope that recalled the original Holy Father, Peter the fisherman.

Jarogniew bowed and sat opposite the pope, considering how prudent a choice it had been to orchestrate the election of this unassuming priest. Without the papal regalia, the man before him could well have passed for a common fisherman concerned only about netting his day's catch. The cardinal secretary already envisioned being handed the keys to the kingdom.

"Thank you for your presence on such short notice and especially on a most threatening evening."

Jarogniew settled confidently into the richly upholstered chair's scarlet cloth. "Of course, Your Eminence, how may I be of service?"

The broad smile and sweet tones of the humble priest unexpectedly took on a declaratory demeanor. "It is time to convene an Extraordinary General Assembly of the Synod of Bishops."

Jarogniew was taken by surprise, and few events within the Catholic world had ever taken the veteran Vatican leader by surprise. He leaned forward, momentarily uncertain. Had he heard correctly? *It's time?* The cardinal was trying to understand what was being called for. This pope, in office but two months, wanted to convene an Extraordinary General Assembly? He knew well that a synod was only called to consider matters of extreme urgency and then only for questions of faith and morals. What circumstance could be of such great concern?

Jarogniew struggled to regain his composure. "For what purpose, Your Eminence?"

"Because I fear, Ludvik, that the direction the Church has taken since the Second Vatican Council has been lost, and unless we redirect it, it will challenge our very existence."

"And what challenge is that, Your Eminence?"

"Modernity. In the spirit of the Second Vatican Council, we must find a means to make a life of piety and prayer acceptable to our new age."

Modernity? The word rang like an alarm through Jarogniew's mind, his piercing sanpaku eyes constricting reflexively. So this was why he was called? The seasoned cardinal knew well what the code word meant: a liberal's call for the Church to conform to the invading pluralistic society, to modify tradition so that it would be acceptable to modern man. *And why?* Was it not true that every generation of church fathers had to deal with such concerns? And hadn't time proven that as long as the Church continued steady on its path of custom and ritual it always survived? Then why now?

"If I may say, Your Eminence, you are just learning our ways, how we function, how we oversee our canon, our liturgy."

"I can assure you, my dear Ludvik, I've been here long enough to know when it's time for change."

Change. Another alarm. Another word not to be tolerated.

"As you say, Your Eminence. I will summon the synod in accordance with current law, *moto proprio Apostolica Sollicitudo,* but it will take time."

"Time is one thing we don't have. It is to be convened by the month's end."

"But that is not enough—"

"That is all we have."

It had been a long time since Jarogniew had been silenced, even by a pope. He sat stunned.

"Our Church has lost its guidance, our world is in upheaval, authoritarian governments are challenging the rights of their people, the plague of poverty encompasses our children, and our flock knows not its direction. We are living in a new age, one in which the concept of family has been transformed and the definition of marriage redefined. No longer is it the joining of a man and woman but simply the uniting of two people. The demand for our Church representatives to perform same-sex marriages reverberates across the globe, gay couples ask to be blessed, gay priests choose to be recognized, and the deadly sins of child molestation that have cursed our houses need a response."

A sudden chill ran through the cardinal. With caution, he replied, "Of course, Holy Father. And has it been determined what that response will be?"

"Interpreting our faith in a new world will require input from Catholic leaders across the globe. It is time for a doctrine of inclusion."

Inclusion—a word that threatened the very position of power that Jarogniew had cultivated over the years. Democratization, equality for all—had these indulgences not resulted in today's chaos? Was it not the lack of authority that had occasioned the rise of terrorism, the vulnerability of nations, and the waywardness of their citizens?

"Does that mean, Holy Father, that you are questioning Church doctrine?"

"That is precisely what I am doing."

"If I may speak frankly, Holy Father, the papacy has traditionally relied on those of us here in the Vatican, men of long experience in Church matters, to provide such counsel."

"That must also change. Did not Pope John the Twenty-third say it was time to open the windows of the Church and let in the fresh air?"

"Of course, Your Eminence, but—"

"Did not Vatican Two teach that a pope is to share his papacy with bishops under our Principle of Collegiality?"

"Yes, but—"

The pope raised his hand and calmly continued.

"I've selected eight bishops, yourself included, with whom to meet before the full synod convenes, men of experience and repute, as you say, throughout the Catholic world to help guide us through this maze. Now when shall that meeting be?"

Jarogniew's response reflected how the past forewarned the future. He knew precisely what day was to be selected. "The sixteenth of July."

The pope smiled. "Perfect. Then we have two weeks to prepare."

The cardinal shifted uneasily in his chair. "Yes, Your Eminence, but to reinterpret our faith that casts aside tradition—"

Again, he was silenced. "We must deal with the world as it is, not as it was!"

This was a side of the pope Jarogniew was not aware of. It was all he could do to control his rising anger. "There will be opposition."

"Never fear opposition, Ludvik, when you walk in the ways of God. Perhaps you are familiar with a passage in the Siddur, the Hebrew prayer book that Jews read every day. It is found before the Shema, the holy prayer that declares their faith in the One God. In Hebrew it reads: *Oseh Chadoshot, Baal Milchamot.* It means, if you wish to make new things, you must be a master of war. It is worth remembering, Ludvik, for if opening the windows of the Church requires war against those who resist, then war it will be."

Jarogniew did not have to be reminded. He had been taught long ago that to achieve one's destiny, one needed to master the art of war. He had been preparing for years, and now he had but two weeks to demonstrate his mastery.

Jarogniew rose, bowed, and took his leave. Yes, Your Eminence, he thought as he checked the time and hastily retraced his steps through the long hallway, then war it will be.

* * *

11:30 p.m., Vatican City

There was an anonymity to the starless night, the driving rain blinding the cardinal secretary as he hurriedly exited the Papal Palace. The prediction had proven true, echoed in the ominous clashes of thunder and cosmic bolts that caused the earth to tremble and the heavens to burn. Those within the Vatican's walls who possessed a more prophetic nature would interpret the inclemency as a warning from on high, while those of a more satanic inclination would call it a foreboding from below. Regardless, it was a night that kept all but those with a mission of greatest import secure in their shelters.

Ludvik Jarogniew was on such a mission, and he was late. Sparks painted the sky as he rushed across St. Peter's Square and exited the Holy City. He tightly drew in his outer cloak, already saturated from the torrential rain. He adhered closely to the line of buildings along the Via Giulia, finding a moment of shelter within the shallow entrance of a bistro closed for the night. If anything, the meeting with the new pope had made him realize how significant tonight's mission would be.

Jarogniew girded himself with a deep breath, trying to determine what was to be done. Time was no longer an endless commodity; only fourteen days remained, and the hope of a painless transition to a new world was proving more difficult than planned. He realized the need for power was essential, one that not even the Vatican could resist. To Jarogniew, such power could only be found by unraveling the Final Mystery. As he concealed himself from the elements, Jarogniew realized there was now only one course left to take, though one that carried considerable danger. Yet, wasn't reward always proportional to risk? Hadn't Caesar jeopardized everything when he led his army across the Rubicon? And in matters of such great importance, do not the ends always justify the means, regardless of what those means dictate?

Jarogniew's mind ran through the final considerations. Only a decision was needed to put the plan in motion, for once the instruction was sent there would be no turning back. Was there really a choice? With purpose decreed his fingers pressed the keys of his phone. *Alea iacta est,* he thought, The die is cast.

The wireless transmission was sent. It consisted of one word: *adesso!*

Now!

* * *

5:40 p.m., New York City

It was a hot and humid day in New York when the lone passenger in the rear seat of a stretch black limousine read his cell's message: *adesso!* It took but a moment to offer a forbidding smile as he interpreted the terse instruction: *Now!* The passenger flexed his grip on the handles of the large black duffel bag he held beside him, impatient to carry out his assignment.

"Four fifty-two Madison," he told the driver. He knew exactly what was to be done.

* * *

Midnight, Rome

Well past the appointed time, Jarogniew rapidly snaked through the narrow, rain-swept vias, his furtive glances finding only the innocence of darkness. Satisfied he was alone, he turned onto a dimly lit street and halted before a time-worn, soot-covered building of three stories almost hidden within the density of its gloom. Once again, he scanned the environs before descending the ten steps below street level to a secure wooden entry. His triple knock was answered, quiet phrases were exchanged, and a door without a number opened to sounds of monotonous meditative incantations—prayers not readily recognized by the Holy See. He removed his rain-soaked cloak, threw on the black cape handed to him by the door warden, and entered a large windowless room.

The space was faintly lit by tall white candles placed strategically throughout, giving an unnatural glow and flicker of shadows amidst the amber light. As Jarogniew entered, the noises abruptly ceased as those present turned to face the newcomer. He made his way to the front of the underground chamber as the silent, seated figures observed his path. A small square table covered with a black cloth was positioned at the room's head, and on it lay a Bible, a carpenter's square, and a compass. To the right of the table stood what appeared to be an altar upon which was set a thickly bound manuscript containing a number of loose pages yellowed with time. Jarogniew took in the tome's burnt leather cover, his eyes familiar with the faded inscribed title, *The Permanent Instruction of the Alta Vendita*. As he stretched out his hand, a thunderous roar from the storm above invaded the cellar room like the vibrating bellow of a tympani, causing Jarogniew to hesitate and the assembled to shudder.

"My brothers, forgive my lateness, but there remains great disharmony in the world this evening, and it has not spared us."

His attempt to control his anger was palpable. He came straight to the point.

"Those of us who believe in *authentic* Christianity have been put on notice by those wishing to reinterpret Church theology to advance their own liberal agenda. That, my friends, must never be allowed."

Voices of assent rang through the room.

With two hands, Jarogniew raised the old text as if he were Moses raising the stone tablets of the Law. "Yet, within the pages of the *Alta Vendita*, written over two hundred years ago, lies our response, for it foretells that cataclysmic events are about to occur, and those of us present tonight are at its epicenter."

He carefully returned the timeworn volume to its place.

"Its authors knew it would take decades to accomplish and its fulfillment only secured by future generations of the initiated. And, my friends, we are that future generation."

A voice was heard from the looming shadows of the room.

"I thought the *Alta Vendita* instructed the propagation of liberal ideas to influence the church? Was it not written to promulgate progressive principles?"

Jarogniew smiled, as if looking forward to responding.

"I see that you know your history, and yes, you are correct. But what was then used as an attempt to destroy our traditional values, we are now using to enhance them. Our fathers, and those before them, have wisely appropriated the *Alta Vendita* for their own purposes, our purposes—for its strategy remains as astonishing in its boldness and genius today as when it first appeared.

As the book says, 'In our ranks the soldier dies and the struggle goes on.'"

Jarogniew paused and looked out at the transfixed faces that stared back at him like facades under a spell of stone. "My brothers, the struggle that our mentors taught us generations ago is soon to be over, the future to which we and those before us have dedicated lives is no longer, for we have but fourteen days for that future to arrive. Now is the time to grasp the seat of power, now is the time to declare a new world that will make order out of the chaos that runs amok! Now is the time for true leaders to come to the fore and guide their followers to a better, more structured life, one that honors the values of discipline, tradition, and direction." Jarogniew paused, regarding them, letting his words be fully understood. "Tonight begins the final destruction of the Catholic Church as we know it."

If a passerby happened to be near at that moment, the cry of men preparing for battle would have sounded like the call to the first crusade. When the shouts seeking glory abated, a voice was heard from another darkened corner.

"Does that mean you have uncovered the Final Mystery?"

Jarogniew smiled, slowly raising his hand. "Almost, my brother, and when secured, it will contain a boundless power. one that will allow us to achieve our destiny."

Again, the voice questioned. "What do you mean, almost?"

The cardinal responded evenly, "The signal was sent. All that remains is its execution."

Only a few in the room appreciated the irony of his statement.

"And when will that be?" asked another.

Jarogniew raised his arm and glanced at his watch. "I suspect presently."

"Where?" questioned a third voice.

The speaker hesitated before responding. "New York."

"And will we be informed of its success?" inquired a fourth.

The cardinal's cell phone buzzed and he lowered his eyes to decipher the simple but concise transmission crossing the Atlantic: *Mutatis mutandis.* The necessary changes have been made.

The voice repeated the question. "I asked if we will be informed of its success."

The shadowed smile reappeared as Jarogniew stayed the moment. His heart pounding, he returned his attention to those before him.

"You have been so informed. The angel of death never fails."

* * *

11:50 p.m., New York

It was close to midnight by the time Jeffrey Moss made his way out into the moonless evening. Word of murder spreads quickly, even in the big city, and reporters and camera crews were already stationed outside the Madison Avenue entrance that had by now been cordoned off by police. He stepped around the yellow crime scene tape and metal barriers, trying to avoid questions. The medical examiner is only called after the deed has been done, but some deeds are worse than others. This was one of them.

A gentle rain started to fall, giving New Yorkers the false but pleasant hope of cooling temperatures and, with time, the bright colors from the city's neons began to dance off the wet pavement. He walked west on Fiftieth Street, oblivious to the display of the new fall fashions in the windows of Saks, trying to make sense of the unholy act he had observed. Head down and shoulders sagging, he felt as if the weight of the world was upon him, a feeling that settled as slowly as the invasion of an ocean fog. Regardless of the number of times he had witnessed the aftermath of brutal murder, the price on his psyche had to be paid. It was more than a personal response, it was a human response. Why such evil? How is it that when man is good he can reach the angels, but evil can deliver him to the depths of hell?

Jeff's mind continued to grapple with the thought when, from out of nowhere, a car horn trumpeted its warning. He gave a startled look, then realized he was about to cross Fifth Avenue against the light, and quickly retreated onto the sidewalk. As he scanned his surroundings, he noticed the huge bronze sculpture rising before him, as if guarding the entrance to Rockefeller Center, one of the most recognized figures in the world. It was the Greek titan Atlas, arms stretched overhead, sentenced by Zeus to forever lift the heavens. Jeff allowed a broad smile of self-recognition to appear, the cloud of despair evaporating with the appreciation that Atlas had heavier responsibilities to deal with.

* * *

It had been three years since Jeff left the practice of medicine to join the ME's office. After graduating from Harvard's medical school, then Mass General for cardiothoracic surgical training, he was hired to upgrade the Cardiac Surgery Department at New York's Metropolitan Hospital. After fifteen years of mitral and aortic repairs, and complex emergency surgical procedures for heart failure at all moments of calendar and clock, the stress had finally taken its toll. At first, he thought it was only occupational fatigue resulting from the intensity of the work, the concern for his patients, the stimulus of success trying to balance the disappointment of failure. Surely a few weeks off was all that was needed. But when the stay in Florida, with its endless rounds of golf, films without interest, and novels whose lack of novelty refused to satisfy, he grew restless. The phone calls from colleagues requesting his return were increasing, yet something within him resisted. After long hours of reflection, he came to understand why: medicine had changed. Jeff would say it wasn't he who left the practice of medicine, but the practice of medicine that left him. Politics had made its inroads, and the role of physician was increasingly being defined more as employee than healer, more concerned with examining the bottom line than examining the patient. Treatment was planned by insurance guidelines rather than by diagnostic protocols, and patient care was dictated by statistical outcomes and predetermined time slots rather than individual needs.

Einstein wrote that coincidence is God's way of remaining anonymous, and so it was that Jeff received a call from Stan Galvin, his friend and former med school classmate. Stan was in his third year as New York City's medical examiner and had already accomplished a great deal toward making the largest ME office in the country both efficient and effective. Yet, there was so much more to undertake in the new age of computer-based analytics, and recruiting top personnel was the key to success.

"Heard you're wandering the Everglades, chasing wayward golf drives and even more wayward women. Better get back to New York a-sap. We're introducing forensic medicine into the twenty-first century, and I need you with me. And, by the way, if we're going to truly develop a seamless investigative team, all my Assistant ME's are going through law enforcement training."

"What does that mean?"

"You're going to the police academy."

"You want me to be a cop?"

"No, a detective. We're going to bring modern technology to finding the bad guys."

The thought of finding the bad guys made its mark. And it was personal. Jeff had lost someone he loved to bad guys and found himself helpless to seek retribution. The words of Edmund Burke resounded within him: "All that is necessary for the triumph of evil is that good men do nothing." Jeff understood himself well enough to know that he was no longer capable of doing nothing. Perhaps he needed a new direction. And so, the decision was made. With no ties to bind him, he packed his bag and took a late flight out the following evening, ready to accept Stan's offer.

* * *

The stillness of the night surrounded him as Jeff continued walking down a deserted Fifth Avenue. A lonely taxi slowed, hoping for a fare, but he waved it on, recent images needing time to clear his mind. After all, this was a priest, a man of God, gruesomely murdered in one of the most beautiful churches in the world. Who would commit such a crime? And why?

JULY 2

The early morning stars had not yet evaporated into their heavenly home when a little-used cell phone rang in the privacy of an apartment in Rome. Ludvik Jarogniew, half asleep, reached across the night table and fumbled for the intruder. As he raised himself from his bed he managed to slide the interface to answer:

"Si?"

"The angel will soon be arriving. He was instructed to bring the holy vessels with him."

A smile of success briefly crossed his lips. Jarogniew clicked off the cell and let it drop onto the carpet. Within moments he fell back onto the comfort of the welcoming pillow, closed his eyes, and dreamed of a treasure about to be found.

* * *

The pages of the morning papers were filled with the story. Jeff glanced at the headlines as he walked past the Third Avenue kiosks crowded with candy bars, magazines, and newspapers. "MURDER IN THE CATHEDRAL!" trumpeted the front page of the *New York Post*, including close-up photos of the crucifixion. Similar coverage was given by the other city tabloids: "ST. PAT'S MASSACRE" announced the *Daily News* under the gruesome image, and even the *New York Times* reported, with rather more circumspection, the death on page one. How had they obtained the photos? Jeff realized that the ethics of reporting these days had not improved since the beginning of headline-selling newspapers: If it bleeds, it leads.

He stopped for a paper cup of coffee at a corner deli before climbing the granite steps to the Milton Helpern Institute of Forensic Medicine at 520 First Avenue. Helpern had been New York

City's chief medical examiner from 1954 to 1973 and was largely responsible for making the facility the most modern in the country. But until Stan's appointment, the department had fallen into disorder, misplacing DNA samples, losing evidence, and falling behind on drug cases.

On the surface, it appeared that the roles of surgeon and forensic sleuth were similar: both involved knowledge of anatomy, biology, physiology, clinical experience, and instinct. But Jeff's decision to change careers was influenced by more. It was an opportune time. As the role of physician was constricting, the role of the medical examiner was expanding. What once focused only on autopsies, dissecting the deceased to determine cause, the office was now being assigned broader responsibilities. Under Stan Galvin's guidance, New York's ME's office had become an integral part of the investigative team, and with Jeff having completed police academy training, he was able to smoothly transition between pathologist and local and federal authorities to determine not only the cause of death, but who caused it—and how. DNA analyses and software-based outcomes had become the smoking gun of the new century, providing evidence that could not be refuted. It was this expanded role of forensic medicine that Jeff found intriguing, allowing him to use both sides of his brain: the left for the analytical aspects that good medicine demands, and the right for the intuitive insights a good detective needed to integrate the parts.

Security let him through, and he waved to the receptionist sitting behind a counter under a sign with the ME's motto: Science Serving Justice. He walked the long, narrow fluorescent-lit hallway and peered through the open door of Stan's office. The ME's office was always a busy scene, responsible for investigating all manner of deaths.

Since Jeff joined the staff, it had become routine for he and Stan to take their morning coffee while reviewing the day's schedule, but today would be anything but routine. After looking in, he continued on to the stairs that led down to the lower level morgue. An instant of emotion swept through him as he recalled the moment he'd walked these same steps to confirm identification of the woman he loved.

Dr. Sebastian Gogoli, the chief coroner, glanced up from his work when he heard Jeff come in. "Well, if it isn't our own doctor detective. Heard you had a tough case last night."

"Worse if you saw him."

Gogoli picked up the file. "Yeah, the photos were sent over. A priest impaled at the church. What the hell happened?"

"That's precisely what happened, but this time it invaded the gospel." Jeff looked down at the cadaver lying on the narrow table. It had already undergone Gogoli's internal examination and Jeff followed the familiar Y-shaped incision from both shoulders to the sternum and continuing down to the pubic bone. The skin and underlying tissues had been flapped open and the rib cage and abdominal cavity removed along with the underlying neck and chest anatomy, allowing examination of the deeper organs.

Jeff turned to his colleague. "Find anything?"

"Yes. External examination indicated he was tortured." He pointed. "Deep bloody whip marks made with tough leather penetrated the dermis throughout the torso. Poor guy couldn't even cry out with his mouth taped."

Gogoli was a short, bespectacled man in his early sixties with thin gray hair and a belt size two notches larger than it should have been. Jeff knew him as a conscientious physician, dedicated to his craft and a stickler for details. Everything you would want in a scientist whose chief role was dissecting bodies for evidence of the minutest pathology or hint of toxins that could influence death.

Gogoli recited the details from the file: "Victim, five feet five inches tall, one hundred and thirty pounds. Primary cause of death: severance of the right internal carotid artery at the level of the third cervical vertebra, just above the bifurcation to the internal and more superficial external branches. Once the carotid was severed, blood supply to the brain was cut off, leading to instant death. Postmortem: a thirty-inch wooden spike was hammered or otherwise pushed through the thoracic cavity, puncturing the left ventricle and exiting the dorsal skeleton."

Jeff shook his head. "What a way to die."

Jeff took a final look at the priest. "Okay, you know the routine. Any personal property that wasn't found at the crime scene needs to be inventoried and safeguarded."

Gogoli placed the sheet back over the body. "There was something."

"Really, and not noted at the initial investigation?"

"The shoes."

"What about them?"

"Their size. The heels and soles appeared thicker and wider than normal."

"Five-five, maybe he wanted to look taller."

"That's what I figured, but it wasn't just for height."

"What do you mean?"

"The sole of the left shoe could be slid forward in a track, and under it was a space that was five inches wide, eight inches long, and a depth of two inches."

"That's interesting."

"And that's not all. The heel could be unscrewed, resulting in a space two and a half inches wide and two inches deep."

"That's even more interesting."

Gogoli put on green latex gloves, placed a sterile white towel on his desk, and picked up a large plastic evidence bag, which he opened. Enclosed was a white envelope, a polished thin U-shaped metal container, and a scrap of paper.

"Take a look."

Jeff scrubbed, gloved his hands, and with forceps removed the paper, on which was written several numbers.

"16/7?"

"At first, I had no idea, but then I recalled that since he was European it might refer to a date, July 16. And take a look at this."

From the envelope Gogoli removed two large round polished gold coins. He placed the coins on the towel and gently snapped open the U-shaped container as if it were a CD case, from which he removed a thin U-shaped gold band that brilliantly reflected the overhead examination lights.

"Already checked for prints, there were none. By the way, it's pure gold—twenty-four karat."

"Expensive jewelry."

He handed Jeff a magnifying lens and continued. "What's ingenious is that the victim's foot rested within the arc of the U-shaped band, and the coins were encased in layers of soft rubber within the oversized heel."

"So the pieces were never damaged."

Gogoli nodded. "Exactly. The coins are identical in size and contain images on each side, which I don't recognize. There are inscriptions written in Latin, but the dates are in Roman."

Gogoli handed Jeff the U-shaped band. "Looks like three small holes through it, one at each end and one in the center."

Gogoli nodded. "Correct, but check out the engraving."

Jeff studied the engraving: "Hebrew letters."

"Yes, but what's unusual is that the letters are raised, not pressed."

Jeff returned the pieces to the towel. "Why would he be hiding these?"

"I don't know, and he sure didn't want anyone else to know either."

"Could he have given up his life for a few gold coins?"

"That's what I was wondering."

Gogoli replaced the pieces in their containers. "But why the effort? I mean, torture by flagellation, then the carotid, then postmortem lifting of the body and finally driving the stake into a wall? Rather ritualistic, don't you think?"

"Agreed, but why?"

Jeff's cell rang, and he recognized Chief DePalma's voice. "Autopsy show anything?"

"He was tortured before he died. And something else. Dr. Gogoli found three gold pieces in his shoe."

"In his shoe? No wonder we missed it. OK, then you're the impounding officer. I need an inventory of the evidence, where it was found, and a full description."

"Already done.'

"Good, then I want the package transported to my office immediately. Maybe we can start to make sense as to what this was all about."

"Yes, sir."

Jeff ended the call and Gogoli handed him a small USB flash drive. "Figured you'd need this. I loaded it with several high-power images of the pieces."

Jeff signed for the evidence, placed the flash drive and container of gold pieces into his briefcase, and started to leave when Gogoli called after him.

"What's happened?"

Jeff looked back at the coroner. "What do you mean?"

"This is ugly business, Jeff. What's happening to this world?"

Jeff's expression reflected his thoughts. "I wish I knew, Sebastian. The world has changed. It's no longer enough to just shoot someone—now you need to sever their heads or crucify them."

Gogoli paused for a moment. "Find the bastard."

Jeff felt a familiar wave of anger. This time, however, it lasted but a moment, for there was no sense of helplessness. Gone was

the incapacity to respond to injustice, for now he was in a position to do something about it.

"I'm going to try."

* * *

10:30 a.m.

Jeff exited the ME's office and crossed First Avenue, making his
way west to Lexington where he took the number 4 subway down
to City Hall Station. The train was crowded with morning commuters, and it was evident that the temperature would soon defeat the
train's air conditioning. His station appeared, and he stepped off,
then hurried up the stairs to street level, feeling the slight comfort
of a gentle breeze coming off the choppy waters surrounding lower
Manhattan. He tightened his grip on his briefcase and walked down
Park Row, past City Hall, until he reached One Police Plaza, the
thirteen-story inverted pyramid–shaped building familiarly called
One PP that headquarters the New York City Police Department.
After being checked by security he proceeded to the bank of eleva-
tors that would take him to the eighth floor. Upon arrival, he made
his way down the hallway, glancing through the walls of glass that
enclosed rows of computers comprising the Real Time Crime Center. It was the detectives' brain center, an anticrime technology
network that contained the building's huge search engines and
data storage systems. He entered room 814 and was ushered into
the office of the chief of detectives by a pert uniformed officer.

"Darlene Thomas, without you I wouldn't even bother to come
up here," he said with a contagious smile that came as much
from his light blue eyes as his lips.

"Dr. Moss, you're always welcome," she said, smiling.

Anthony DePalma stood up to greet him. The oldest of three
brothers, all of whom, like their father and uncle before, had
joined New York's finest and worked their way up the ranks, De-
Palma was a former Marine and a veteran officer, popular with
the men he commanded, with a reputation as a demanding but
effective leader. He worked the twenty-four-seven stressed hours
with a calm exterior and had overseen many of the city's high-
profile murder cases. He had a defined prognathic jaw that suggested respect and a full head of black hair still worn in a military
cut. He kept his six foot, two hundred and ten pounds in trim

condition. He spoke softly, was a man of few words, but when heard, conveyed an air of authority.

"So, you found something?"

Jeff removed the sealed envelope from his briefcase and placed everything on the desk. "Gogoli found them in the victim's shoe which contained an ingenious sliding mechanism."

DePalma examined the pieces. "What are they?"

"No idea—yet."

DePalma sat back in his chair. "Must have been worth a great deal to someone."

Jeff looked at his colleague. "Seems like it."

"You have digitals?"

"Dr. Gogoli already took them."

"Prints?"

"Found nothing."

DePalma called in Darlene. "Better deposit this in the evidence room. We may need to reexamine it."

"Anything on your end?" DePalma shook his head. "Nothing. No prints, no DNA, nothing. The perp must have worn gloves, left nothing to go on, a real pro. The security cameras have proved worthless, as if he knew exactly where the cameras were placed. All we see is the back of a large man in a black hoodie."

"Any other residents on the floor besides the monsignor?"

"Only one, a Father John DeSantos. The monsignor said most of the priests were out for the evening or away on summer holiday. Even spoke to the cardinal when he got in this morning. He was shocked that this could happen but seemed to have no knowledge of the young priest or what he was scheduled to speak to him about."

"So, all we know is how he died."

DePalma stood up. "That's not what the mayor wants to hear. I'll speak to Monsignor Quinn again. Maybe he can remember something else."

"And maybe an old friend can help me figure out what these gold pieces are."

* * *

As Jeff entered the Seventy-Seventh Street entrance of Pierre et Fils, Conservation and Restorers of Fine Art and Documents, he realized it had been over a year since he had last been there. He asked for the director, Francois DeLordet, and within minutes a young woman escorted him to his second-floor office.

"Well, if it isn't M. Docteur Jeff, welcome."

Jeff gave a genuine smile and a hearty handshake to the man who had helped him find Keith Jessup and solve the mystery of the Milton Manuscript.

"Am I to believe that you are here to solve another mystery?"

Jeff laughed. "I'm afraid so."

"Well, we did it last time, *n'est pas, mon ami.* Who would have known that the murder of an Oxford English literature professor would be traced back to the real meaning of John Milton's epic poem, *Paradise Lost.* That was real detective work on your part."

"It was my first big case, and I couldn't have done it without your help."

Jeff took out the flash drive and handed it to Delordet. "But here's the new case. Take a look at these images. Pure gold pieces that I need identified."

Delordet studied the screen before commenting. "Artistically they are beautiful, but I am no expert in this area. However, with your permission, I know someone who is."

* * *

July 2, 10:30 a.m.

At One PP, Chief Anthony DePalma's phone did not stop ringing. From the mayor's office to the commissioner, from members of the city council to reporters, the questions all concerned the murder of a young priest in a bedroom located on the same floor where the archbishop resided. *Who's responsible for security,* they wanted to know. *What was being done to catch the perpetrator?*

"Chief, the commissioner's calling, for the third time."

"Ten-thirty and only three times? Must be his busy day."

Darlene Thomas had already proven her smarts when dealing with people, especially difficult ones. "You'd better take it. Sounds angrier than usual."

DePalma hesitated before picking up the phone. "Yes, Josh, sorry, been a little hectic with this whole thing."

Joshua Fleck had been police commissioner for six months, ever since José Arroyo, the newly elected mayor of New York, appointed him. Arroyo ran on the campaign promise, "It's time to share equally," and "sharing" turned out to be "sharing everything." If Arroyo had his way, he would take from the rich and give to the poor until everyone had equal amounts to spend. That was how you eliminated income disparity. And with his victory came the election of his handpicked nominees for the city council. Arroyo was given free rein from the previous administration to turn the city around. Equality, to that administration, had meant what it had always meant in U.S. history: equal opportunity, not equal results. It was, basically, the age-old dichotomy of a socialist versus capitalist philosophy of interpreting what true democracy really means.

Fleck, as police commissioner, assumed he was given the same blank check as the mayor. He had been one of Arroyo's closest associates, and no one helped push the mayor's election by "the people" more than Joshua Fleck. A born organizer and agitator with a tall imposing figure, his eloquence as a Baptist lay minister kept his flock spellbound on Sundays. But his total resume of police experience consisted of twenty weeks of One Station Unit Training for the military police, eighteen months of law enforcement service at Fort Hood, and following an honorable discharge, several days spent in a New York City jail for instigation to riot. This latter item was not lost on the police union nor the city newspapers, certainly not the conservative *New York Post*, whose page one headline read: "IS THE CITY'S SECURITY SECURE?" Even the liberal *New York Times* had to agree that "power to the people" required some limits. The more conservative city voters claimed that Arroyo was elected by a coalition of liberal-minded white and minority leaders whose quest for equal sharing of power and profits had no basis in reality. There was, however, one reality that conservative voters had found difficult to accept: the minority population of color was no longer the minority. As a result, DePalma now found himself having to deal with an inexperienced administration that demanded action through the only outlet they knew: the media. And so, each day, dozens of calls came into the eighth-floor chief's office demanding that something be done, although what could be done, and how it could be accomplished, they had no idea.

"Damn it, Anthony, I've been calling all morning."

"Just got in. This St. Patrick's thing is taking up all my time."

"It better, I'm under a lot of pressure. The mayor wants to know how this could happen when we're supposed to be protecting the place. The Latino community is up in arms and wants to know why."

"Josh, I'm working on it, but I'll have to get back to you. I'm in the middle of something." DePalma hung up before another word could be spoken.

"Darlene, I need to meet with Monsignor Quinn. Someone must know something about Father Alonzo Fabrizzi."

"Yes, sir."

* * *

It was noon by the time Jeff and Delordet reached the American Numismatic Society, at 75 Varick Street. The building housed a museum and research institute devoted to the study of coins from all periods and cultures. Professor Antonio Siglione, a tall, thin, slightly bent man whose facial topography suggested a long history, was at his desk in his third-floor office examining a coin through his vintage optical light microscope when he heard the expectant knock on his office door.

"Please, come in."

As Jeff and Delordet entered, Siglione started slowly to rise.

"Antonio, my dear friend. Stay right where you are."

Siglione sat back, and the two old friends shook hands. "It's getting more difficult."

Delordet smiled sympathetically. "I know what you mean. Antonio, this is Jeffrey Moss. Jeffrey, my good friend Antonio Siglione. We have known each other since, what was it, eighty-one, when we were both at the Louvre? Antonio was the curator of Greek coins and I was curator of impressionist painting."

Antonio nodded to his friend, "Ah, *si il mio amico*, and we were both younger then."

Delordet turned to Jeff. "But now we have become rather sedentary in our work, except that Antonio runs this place with the precision of a Swiss clock and is probably the greatest authority on coins in the world."

"My friend is very kind," Siglione said. "I am not certain about the greatest, but what is great is the numismatic collection this building contains. I'd say we house about 800,000 coins, which makes it second only to the largest state collections of Europe."

Delordet said, "And he knows every one of those 800,000."

Siglione smiled. "Please, sit down."

The visitors sat in the two chairs facing the desk.

"You mentioned you have something to show me?"

Jeff took out the flash drive. "I came across some gold pieces that Francois thought you might help identify. I know very little about coins."

"Of course. So perhaps I should begin with a primer on coin collecting."

Siglione glanced at his watch. "In ancient times there were no printing presses, no newspapers, no way of disseminating information. Instead, coins were issued by the powers that be, with words or images that represented what the king or emperor wanted communicated to his subjects. To those who understand coins, it often provides the keys that unlock our past."

Jeff handed Siglione the flash drive and as he inserted it into the USB port of his computer, he continued. "Originally, barter was the principal means of obtaining products, similar to how Abraham in the Bible purchased the cave in which to bury his wife Sarah. However, as man learned more about metals and appreciated the value of gold and silver, the making of coins that were portable and in constant demand came into practice and that is when—"

Siglione stopped in mid-sentence, totally absorbed with the images that had appeared on the screen. After a moment, he turned to his visitors. "These are not coins but medals, carved by Benvenuto Cellini, the great Renaissance artist, in 1534 for Pope Clement the Seventh. As far as I know, Cellini only made the pieces in gilt silver, not in gold. I wasn't aware that more than one set had been made, and that remains in the collection of the Museo Nazionale del Bargello in Florence. You have shown me something I was not aware of."

Siglione enlarged the images on the screen.

"Notice how the two medals share a common obverse portraying Clement in profile, the first pope to ever wear a beard, and

clad in a richly embroidered cope closed with an oval button."
Siglione moved to the second set of images.

"Notice how the versos differ on these images. The image to
the right bears a female figure personifying Peace, holding a cor-
nucopia in her left hand and a torch in her right as she is about
to set fire to the alms placed before the temple dedicated to Janis,
to which a male figure representing Fury is chained. But the image of the left medal is of Moses striking the rock with his rod to
quench the thirst of the Jewish people."

Siglione continued to study the images. "These are astonishing pieces of workmanship, revealing Cellini's outstanding ability.
Just look at his attention to detail. No one has ever achieved finer
artwork, in my opinion—and I have 800,000 pieces to judge by."

The two guests remained attentive as Siglione continued.
"What is interesting is that the pieces were cast as part of an artistic competition of medal making between Cellini and Giovanni
Bernardi. Cellini, whose personality and ego were larger than life,
often found himself at odds with a great many people, including
Pope Clement. He had hoped that by fabricating these medals
for him he could resume his friendship—and the papal commissions that came with it. Yet, in spite of the brilliance of his work,
the pope never resumed his interest in Cellini, and Clement soon
died. The end of the story was that Cellini soon murdered a rival
goldsmith whom he blamed for his failure."

"A rather pathological sense of self."

Siglione smiled at Jeff. "You have no idea. On a number of
occasions when Cellini felt someone had slighted him, he would
murder or beat them close to death. He nearly killed a woman
modeling for him by dragging her around his workshop by her
hair. Anyway, let's get back on subject; otherwise, we could talk
about Cellini all day."

Jeff, making notes, said, "There's one more piece I'd like you to look at."

Siglione returned to the screen and viewed the image of the gold band.

"Now, what do we have here? A gold diadem?" Siglione asked.

"It's twenty-four karat gold. Pretty expensive jewelry."

Siglione focused on the piece. "Jewelry would be unusual. High karat gold is a relatively soft metal, and therefore easily damaged. To make it more usable some alloy would have been added. Historically, twenty-four karat gold is not used for dress-up affairs but rather for ritual use or for preservation in a museum. Today, most gold items in stores have a karat rating in the range of nine to eighteen, and if an item is to be sold as jewelry in the United States, there must be a minimum karat value of ten." Siglione returned his focus to the diadem.

"Wait, what is this—Hebrew words engraved?"

"What does it mean?"

Without taking his eyes off the screen, he replied, "Holy unto God."

Jeff continued. "Is there some significance to it?"

Siglione hesitated, "I'm not certain . . . unless . . ."

He looked back to Jeff. "Where did you find this?"

Jeff realized that what had begun as a light-hearted intro to Coinage 101 had suddenly turned into more serious conversation. "All the items were together."

"Together? But where? How?"

He handed the professor his card. "I'm with the medical examiner's office and what I'm about to tell you is to be kept between us. Is that okay with you?"

"Of course. Much of what we do here is strictly confidential."

Jeff spoke cautiously. "This involves a case of an individual who was murdered."

Siglione thought for a moment. "A recent murder?"

"Yes."

"I see. And would this have anything to do with the reports of a young priest found dead in the cardinal's residence?"

"Correct."

Again, Siglione was silent for a moment. "And he was carrying these pieces?"

"Yes, hidden in custom-made hollow insets within his shoe."

"So, he took great pains to avoid their being found." As he enlarged the image he began to explain: "What you have here could be . . ."

The sentence was never completed. Siglione stared at the screen as if transfixed by what he saw. Suddenly he braced his arms on the desk and with effort lifted himself from his chair, then took hold of a rubber-tipped metal cane leaning against the black file cabinet alongside his desk. With difficulty, he walked to a corner window that overlooked the street. The two guests looked at each other without saying a word. Finally, Siglione walked back to the desk and returned his eyes to the screen. "Is this possible . . . Shimon?"

Jeff couldn't make out the comment. "Did you say, 'Shimon'?"

"No, just thinking out loud."

"But what is it? Could there be a connection to the Cellini medallions?"

"You mean, why were they found together? To answer that you would need an archeologist, one who specializes in ancient biblical scholarship."

"Do you know someone?"

"Perhaps I do. Let me think about that. Do you mind if I download this for further study?"

"Sure, if it will help—but please remember to keep it confidential."

When he had finished the copy, Siglione removed the memory stick from the USB port and returned it to Jeff. "Why don't you call me later? Perhaps I will have a name."

* * *

July 2, 1:00 p.m., St. Patrick's Cathedral

Monsignor James Quinn was a large, heavyset man in his early sixties. His dark graying hair was neatly trimmed, in contrast to his jet-black eyebrows that overhung his intense gray eyes. Though big, he was more muscle than fat, and his grip was firm when DePalma met him in a small office in the church.

"I already told the officers that I know very little about Father Fabrizzi. I met him for the first time yesterday upon his arrival. The call came from the Vatican, that I know, and a message was left that it was imperative for him to meet with the cardinal today. I returned the call to Rome, but the administrator would only say that Father Fabrizzi was employed there. Seeing that there was such a priest at the Vatican, I made the appointment."

"When did he arrive?"

"About five in the afternoon. I showed him to his room, where he asked if he could rest and clean up before dinner. That was the last time I saw him—alive."

"And who found him?"

"Apparently, Father John smelled smoke and ran into the hall. It had been a long day and I was taking a nap when I was awakened by a shout. I immediately went into the hall and found Father John distraught. The door to the guest room was open, and the smoke detector began its whining siren. I looked inside, and when I realized what was happening I grabbed the fire extinguisher from the hall and put out the fire before it could spread. I called 9-1-1 and within minutes the fire department and police were here."

DePalma checked his notes. "Yes, we received the call at 6:42 p.m." He thought for a moment. "And what do you make of the wooden sign that the young priest had around his neck, *Soli Deo Gloria?*"

"Meaning 'glory be only to God'? It's the work of a madman."

"Anything else?"

"Nothing I can recall."

"And where can I find Father John?"

Quinn hesitated. "Father John? I believe he's on personal leave."

DePalma hid his surprise as he studied Quinn. "But you said he was here last night?"

"And left early this morning."

DePalma instinctively reacted to the glibness of the remark. "Let me remind you this is a murder investigation, and anyone who was here last night is to remain available for questioning. I need you to get in touch with Father John immediately, I want to speak with him."

DePalma handed Quinn his card.

"Of course."

"And you're sure there was no one else on the third floor?"

"Not that I know of. Most were away on summer holiday."

DePalma said his goodbye with the gut feeling of questioning someone who knew more than he revealed—much more.

* * *

Quinn brushed his fingers over DePalma's card as he sat at his desk in thought. After several moments he scrolled through the contacts on his cell phone until he reached the name of John DeSantos. It took several rings before the call was answered.

"Yes?"

"Father John, it's Monsignor Quinn. I'm calling to see how you are feeling."

"A little better, Monsignor. I just need some rest. I can't believe what happened."

Quinn sensed the anxiety in the voice. "It must have been a terrible shock."

John continued. "I'm sorry that I acted as I did, but when I saw the man running out of the guest room –"

Quinn interjected. "You saw someone running out of the room?"

"Yes, sir, as I smelled smoke, I ran in to see what happened. That's when I saw a man rushing out of the guest room, and when I went in I saw the priest just hanging . . ."

Quinn gently responded. "I understand, it was terrible, and you should take as much time off as you need."

"Thank you, Monsignor."

"And you say you saw a man."

"Yes, sir. Big fellow. Never saw him before. He was pulling a hoodie over his head, but he's someone I'll never forget."

Quinn hesitated, as if contemplating the significance. "Tell me, Father, where will you be staying?"

"I'm leaving tomorrow for my brother Phillip's home in Washington, Connecticut. It's a nice quiet spot, and the walks through the forest will help take my mind off what happened."

"That sounds good, John. Whenever you feel up to it, we'll look forward to your return."

Quinn hesitated before ending the call, as if a decision was to be made.

Finally, he removed a piece of plain paper and wrote a short note without signature and placed it into a nameless white envelope.

* * *

It was early afternoon when DePalma had Darlene contact Air Italia to determine when the priest had arrived in New York. It took an hour for Darlene to report back.

"He didn't fly Air Italia, at least not yesterday. In fact, he didn't fly on any airline from Rome yesterday."

DePalma looked up from his desk. "Then how did he get here?"

"I asked my cousin at TSA to look through all of yesterday's arrivals. An Alonzo Fabrizzi landed yesterday at JFK at 3:20 p.m."

"But not from Rome."

Darlene handed him a paper. "Correct. He arrived on El Al flight LY7 from Tel Aviv."

DePalma looked up. "So he flew to Tel Aviv first."

"Yes, on Air Italia, but two days before."

"OK, at least we're getting to know something about this priest. And Darlene, get me some background on Monsignor Quinn. I've got a bad feeling in my belly about him."

****

In a phone call Jeff brought DePalma up to date regarding the meeting with Siglione.

"The medals were made by Cellini in 1534, but to link it to the curved band would take a Bible scholar. He said he may have a reference for us."

"Fine, I'll call him. And by the way, we just found out that Father Fabrizzi's flight came from Tel Aviv. Apparently, he had left Rome on Air Italia, stayed overnight in Israel, then boarded an El Al flight for JFK."

Jeff was surprised. "What was he doing in Israel?"

"That we don't know."

"And Chief, one more thing. I'd like to run this case."

DePalma hesitated before responding. It wasn't his concern about how effective an investigator Jeff was, that had already been proven in his ingenious uncovering of a manuscript explaining the meaning of *Paradise Lost*, written by Milton himself. But to lead this case, DePalma sensed it had become personal, a cry that begged to avenge a similar cruelty from the past.

"Let me think about it."

* * *

4:00 p.m., One PP

"Here's what I have on Quinn." Darlene glanced at her notes as she reported to DePalma. "All agree Quinn's a strong defender of the Catholic Church and its traditional teachings, especially on birth control, abortion, and homosexuality. He calls abortion murder. It's been reported, but not confirmed, that he even criticized Rome for being too accommodating to modern influences. But one thing all agree on, he runs the diocese for the cardinal like a tight ship—very tight."

DePalma clasped his hands in thought. "So he's got some rebel in him. Good to know."

* * *

It was late afternoon when Joshua Fleck took the elevator down from the fourteenth floor and entered DePalma's office as the chief was getting off the phone.

"Commissioner, how good to see you."

"I bet it is. Look, Anthony, I need to be kept up to speed on this. The mayor's all over me. Tell me you've made some progress."

"So far we have very little. We have no motive and no idea why the priest was even here. Without that we can't get started."

"Well, you better. I don't care if you have to go to Rome to find out who he is, as long as it appears that we're doing something. That's all people want from their officials—to think we're doing something."

* * *

July 2, 4:00 p.m.

The long black limo made its way down busy Fifth Avenue before pulling alongside the curb between Fiftieth and Fifty-First Streets, coming to a stop in front of a massive white marble neo-Gothic structure with two spires rising 330 feet from street level. The building was constructed with the intricate designs that make St. Patrick's Cathedral not only the largest Catholic Church in the country, but one of the greatest and most recognizable architectural landmarks in the city. The uniformed driver stepped from the car and opened a rear door to allow a thick-set, muscular individual of average height to exit. His head was shaved, and when he removed his tinted glasses, one could see eyes as black as midnight. His well-tailored dark suit sculpted his toned body. After a few words with the driver, he walked, with a noticeable limp, up the entrance steps. For a moment he stopped, turning to glance behind as if looking for someone, and then continued on through the huge bronze doors that led into the cavernous interior saturated with streaming sunlight diffused through the prisms of stained glass windows. He withdrew a roll of hundred-dollar bills from his pocket, tossed one into the collection box, and walked down the long center aisle, surrounded on either side by pews that could seat more than two thousand people. When he approached the altar he knelt, said a few words under his breath, and made the sign of the cross. He stood, once again scanning the vast room behind him, checked his gold Rolex, then walked into the third confessional along the north wall. As he sat on the hard seat, he bowed his head in silence.

"May I help you, my son?" the priest prompted.

The penitent suddenly looked up into a dark anonymous screen, as if being released from the reverie of his prayers. Quickly he made the sign of the cross and recited, "Bless me, Father, for I have sinned. It has been three months since my last confession. Father, I have committed a mortal sin, so terrible in the eyes of God."

"And you know well the difference between mortal and venial sins?"

"I do, Father. Mortal sin is so severe that it destroys the life of grace in the soul."

"And did you understand what you were doing?"

"I did, Father."

"And when was this sin committed?"

"Last night, Father."

"And what does your God tell you about this sin?"

"That human life is sacred, but the life of the Church is the most sacred."

"Yes, that is true. Above all, we must give honor to the life of the Church, even if that requires extreme sacrifice. Do you wish absolution?"

"I do, Father. My God, please forgive me for my sins, for both what I have done wrong or failed to do good. I have sinned against you, you whom I should love above all things. If I have sinned, then, with your help, I will do penance, will sin no more, and avoid whatever leads me to sin. Amen."

The dark screen that separated one compartment from the other suddenly rose, like the firmament that divided the earth from heaven, and two envelopes, one white and thin and one manila and thick with content, was passed to the penitent.

"Thank you, Father."

"And the holy vessels?"

The penitent paused for a moment. "I could find no holy vessels."

The silence on the other side of the confessional was solemn. "There were *no* holy vessels?"

"No, Father. I looked carefully. I found nothing."

Again, a momentary pause: "I see. Well then, if you have sinned in the eyes of God, then you are truly forgiven. If not, then may you continue to do what is right with the Lord. Go in peace."

The man responded, "*Soli Deo gloria.*" As he left the confessional, he placed the envelopes inside his right jacket pocket, and walked out to the waiting limousine, an absolved man. How easy it was to be freed of sin when the sinner need not face the sinned. As the car pulled away, he removed the envelopes. He opened the white, thin nameless envelope and read the short note without signature: Father John DeSantos will be staying at his brother Phillip's home in Washington, Connecticut. The man smiled and placed the note into his pocket. He then opened the filled manila envelope, and with the utmost deliberation, sat back into the cushioned leather and tallied the generous contribution inside. *The Lord is mighty in all his ways and gracious in all his works.*

* * *

July 2, 11:45 p.m., Rome

Midnight was nearing in Rome when the call came through on a private cell. "The angel insists there were no holy vessels."

The response cut like a knife. "My information suggests otherwise. Find them." What remained was the deadly sound of a dial tone.

* * *

4:45 p.m., New York

Joshua Fleck's iPhone lit up with a number that he readily recognized. The police commissioner quickly ended the call he was on, thought for a moment, and then answered his cell.

"Monsignor Quinn, I was about to call. We are all so disturbed by the terrible violence that happened last night at the cathedral. I can assure you that we're doing everything we can to find the perpetrator."

"I know you are, and that's why I'm calling."

"Yes, monsignor how may I be of service?"

The fact was, there was little service that the new police commissioner would not provide for the monsignor, seeing how instrumental he had been in delivering the large Catholic Latino vote for Mayor Arroyo.

"Commissioner, it's most important that the archbishop be kept informed of the investigation's progress."

Joshua Fleck swiped a handkerchief across his moistened forehead. "Absolutely."

"Perhaps you might have information regarding certain artifacts found during the investigation?"

"You mean something is missing?"

"We can't be certain, and the church certainly would not want to falsely accuse anyone."

"Of course not."

"Should you hear of anything, I know you will contact me directly."

"Most certainly, Monsignor."

"And, Commissioner, I know you will treat our discussion with great sensitivity."

"You have my word."

* * *

The chief of detectives brushed his fingers over the evidence bag containing the gold pieces and picked up the phone.

"Professor Siglione, this is Anthony DePalma at police headquarters. You mentioned to one of my detectives, Dr. Jeffrey Moss, that you might know a biblical scholar to help us."

The response was long in coming. Siglione was hesitant to give out the name of a young archeologist whose father had been a dear friend. His concern was that if the gold band was what he thought it was, it could bring danger to whoever pursued its source. And yet, identifying that source could be one of the greatest archeological finds in history. Should he deny that opportunity to another because of his personal fears?

"Professor Siglione, are you there?"

DePalma heard a raspy reply. "Yes, I know of one, but not in New York."

"Well then, where?" DePalma was already thinking about his minimal travel budget.

"Israel, at the Israel Museum, and you would need to bring the pieces."

"And who is this biblical scholar?"

"Danny Teller. Professor Teller has a PhD in ancient Jewish history and archeology, a special interest in artifacts of the period of the Dead Sea Scrolls, and a close family friend."

"I see."

"There will be no danger, will there?"

DePalma heard the tremor in Siglione's voice and replied routinely, "I'm sure everything will be fine. Just need to ask a few questions."

"I don't think you realize what you may have found."

As DePalma was about to ask what Siglione meant, the call was ended. He scribbled Danny Teller's name on his pad, realizing that Fabrizzi's last known stop was Israel, and now this expert is in Israel. That means someone has to go. He was thinking about who to send when Darlene entered.

"Chief, the commissioner."

Now what? DePalma took a deep breath and picked up the phone. "Yes, Josh, how can I help you?"

"I got roped into a five-thirty press conference that's going to make the six o'clock news, and I promised the reporters I'd meet them on the second floor. I've got to give them something, so what do you have?"

"Well, I'm not sure what we should go with at this—"

"Look, either *I* go and tell them something or *you* go and tell them you have nothing."

Fleck knew DePalma would try to avoid the second-floor press conference room at all costs. "The Shack," as the room was called, was inhabited by reporters on the police beat representing most of New York's press and TV stations. The name had been brought down through the years from the original venue, probably a crowded tenement shop across from police headquarters back in 1910, where newsmen would get their stories.

"Well, we're taking your advice and tracking the victim's itinerary to New York."

"Good, that sounds good. And who are you putting in charge of the investigation?"

DePalma knew the chief wanted a name.

"Well, this is an unusually complex case that may involve a number of disciplines, so we need someone who has a broad background."

"Yes, that would be my choice also. And who will that be?"

DePalma thought about how his staff was deployed. All were in the midst of major criminal investigations, and to call any of them off now would jeopardize their progress. He thought for a moment longer.

"Chief?"

DiPalma knew he had to answer. "Ah, Moss, Dr. Jeffrey Moss, the one who solved the Milton Manuscript murders."

"Perfecto, that was a big case, the reporters will like that, plenty to write about. And when is Dr. Moss leaving for Rome?"

DePalma smiled. "You mean Israel."

"Israel? I thought the victim was a priest from Rome."

"We're checking everything."

"Anything else? You must have found something."

This was the problem of not trusting your police commissioner. DePalma realized that Fleck deserved to be in the loop, at least enough to prevent his being charged with not keeping the commissioner up to date.

"Oh, yeah, a few old coins were found at the scene. We had the Numismatic Society take a look. Doesn't look to be of much value."

"Coins? And the Numismatic Society checked them out? Well, thanks for your help. I think we've got enough to keep the sharks fed."

* * *

There is no overtime pay for the chief of detectives, but the real downside of being chief is political. DePalma was used to speaking his mind in short and simple sentences, but editing his thoughts had not been a priority when he joined the force thirty years ago. Working with the new commissioner was testing his self-control and patience, but he had a media-hungry case to solve, and this was no time to get sidetracked. He picked up the phone and called Stan Galvin, the ME. Galvin, like DePalma, was a reformer, not afraid to step on toes to make needed changes to enhance service to the community.

"Stan, Anthony DePalma. I need a favor. We've run into a wall on this St. Patrick's murder, and the commissioner's getting on me. I was being pressed, and I gave them the name of one of your assistant ME's as being the lead detective on this."

Stan smiled. "I suppose you're speaking of Jeff."

"I am."

"He already gave me a heads-up on the autopsy. Some mean bastard sure's not going to heaven. Where you going to use him?"

"Israel."

"Does he know?"

"Thought I'd check with you first. Looks like that's where the victim had come from prior to arriving here. It's also where we might be able to figure out the meaning of those gold pieces your man, Gogoli, found."

"Yes, I heard. This is becoming quite a story. Well, it's up to Jeff. How long?"

"Hopefully not more than a few days, but he'll have to take the pieces with him."

"What about security? I mean, Jeff can handle himself, but it seems like whoever killed the priest will stop at nothing."

"I'll take care of it. Listen, Stan, he wants this."

"Yes, I guess he would. Remember, Jeff and I have been friends since med school and through a lot, especially with Kate's murder."

"I know. He still blames himself. So what do you think?"

Stan pursed his lips in thought. "To be honest, if anyone can get a handle on this, he can. And like you say—he needs it."

"OK, I'll let him know."

* * *

6:15 p.m.

Antonio Siglione had no one to go home to. He sat alone at his desk viewing the digital images of the gold pieces he had saved to his hard drive, his hands slightly trembling. He was one month away from celebrating his sixty-eighth birthday and his physician had warned that unless he strictly followed the prescription of diet, exercise, pills, and easing work habits, he might not reach his sixty-ninth. He had already suffered a cerebral stroke that resulted in his right leg being partially compromised. Physical therapy and exercise had helped muscle tone, but reducing stress was easier said than done. It wasn't just the work. If anything, it was work that kept his mind free from the personal strains he had to endure. He had lost his wife years before to multiple sclerosis, but having to raise his troubled son, Angelo, by himself was a constant source of worry. From what he had seen, the gold artifacts, at least the gold band, could be the missing link to one of history's greatest mysteries and one he wished he could participate in. Yet, he knew it was too much for him. What he and so many others had been looking for their entire professional lives would never be realized, for he no longer had the physical capacity to endure the search—a search that would be fraught with danger. Hasn't it always been that the race for riches and power often leads to the worst in man? Already a priest had been killed in a most horrible way. Would that be the fate of anyone seeking the ultimate prize?

As he reflected, a growing sense of fear overcame him, for he had given out Danny's name. Had he put his most promising student in danger? It wasn't just any student, but family, for Danny's father had been Siglione's colleague and friend for years.

His thoughts were interrupted by the ringing of his phone.

"Monsignor Quinn, what a surprise."

"How are you, my friend? I hope you are feeling better."

"Mezzo, mezzo."

"I need your help. I understand that a few old coins were found in the archbishop's residence where that blasphemous murder took place and were brought to your attention. Can you tell me what they were?"

Siglione felt a tightening in his chest. He had promised to keep this confidential and wasn't aware that the information had been made public.

"I'm not certain . . . but they seem to be some early medals."

The monsignor continued. "How early?"

"Probably early Roman. Nothing too spectacular."

"I see, and where are they now?"

"I'm not sure. I only saw pictures."

"Who showed them to you?"

"I believe it was someone from the medical examiner's office."

"You mean Dr. Moss?"

Siglione looked at Jeff's card on his desk. "Yes, that was his name."

"And what did he tell you?"

"Nothing, really."

Quinn paused for a moment. "My dear Antonio, we've been friends for a long time, no? Do you remember when your son, Angelo, had his problems and how you came to me for help?"

"Yes, Monsignor."

"What was he accused of? Oh, yes, distributing drugs, armed robbery, even rape, and what did I do? I brought him into the church, vouched for him, fixed it with the authorities, didn't I?"

"*Si*, Monsignor."

"Made certain those scandalous allegations against your son were excused as frivolous."

"*Si*, Monsignor."

"Exactly. Even paid off the young lady and arranged for her therapy, I believe that's what they call it."

"*Si*, Monsignor."

"And now he's grown up, has become a respected individual, has a most important and well-paying job and travels in style."

"And I am most grateful, Monsignor."

"I know you are. So, what I need to know is, where are those medals now?"

When there was no response the monsignor continued.

"Come now, I tell you what. You tell me about the medals and I will continue to keep Angelo's past hidden."

Siglione reached for the bottle of water on his desk. He felt he was being asked to decide between his son and Danny, the child of his dearest friend.

Finally, he spoke. "The police, they have the medals, they were gold medals."

"Tell me, Antonio, where did the police find those gold medals?"

Again, there was silence.

"Antonio? Are you there? I want to know where those medals were found."

"In the shoes the priest was wearing."

"I see. Quite ingenious . . . By the way, Antonio, you wouldn't have any images of those medals, would you?"

The professor responded without thought. "No, Monsignor. They didn't give me any."

"You're sure? You mentioned pictures just now."

"Yes, but . . . no. They did not give me those."

"And what are the police going to do?"

"They're seeking a second opinion."

"And where is that?"

"Jerusalem." Siglione's voice was almost a whisper.

"Jerusalem? Why?"

Again, a silence.

"Antonio!"

"To have the Israel Museum evaluate the pieces."

"The Israel Museum? You mean Shimon Teller's kid?"

"I . . . I don't . . ."

"Come now, Antonio, we don't want the kid to end up like the father, do we?"

An alarm sliced through the older man. "What do you mean?"

"Nothing—I just want to be certain that is who we are speaking about."

A soft *"si"* found its way across the cellular maze.

"Thank you, my friend. That's all I wanted to know."

Siglione sat in his chair staring at the picture in front of him. "I'm sorry, Danny."

JULY 3

3:00 p.m., Westhampton Beach, NY

The long Fourth of July weekend was hot and humid, and Main Street in the usually placid village of Westhampton Beach was busy with summer residents and cash-laden shoppers. The beach was crowded with sun worshippers, and after emerging from a long ocean swim in the sparkling blue waters, Jeff made his way back to his blanket, athletically avoiding children's sand pits, teenagers tossing footballs, and the multishaped frames of the newly wed and nearly dead. As his well-toned body soaked up the rays, his mind willed someone to come forth who had witnessed what happened the day of the murder. He was falling into a deep sleep under the solar emissions when he felt a tap on his shoulder.

"Your cell's ringing."

He reached for the phone, his voice not fully awake. "Jeff Moss."

"Dr. Moss. This is Monsignor Sean O'Reilly. I found your card on the third-floor residence of four fifty-two Madison, where I live. We need to speak." The voice was subdued, yet revealed a sense of urgency, if not fear.

Jeff immediately came to life. "Of course, at the parish house?"

"No, that would not be good. We need to meet elsewhere." Jeff heard a pause and then a hurried whisper. "Someone's coming. I'll have to call you back."

What could that have been about? Jeff grabbed a towel, dried himself off, and looked out to sea, waiting. Twenty minutes later, his phone sounded its familiar call.

"It's me. When can we meet?"

"I'm leaving town tomorrow."

"Then it will have to be today. There's an indoor parking garage on Fifty-Third between Third and Lex, north side. I'll be in a green 2008 Mazda at the entrance. Can you make it?"

Jeff looked at his watch, figuring drive time on a holiday-packed Long Island Expressway. "Be there at seven."

* * *

7:00 p.m., East 53rd Street

Monsignor Sean O'Reilly did not look like a man of the cloth. Indeed, he looked more like a rural gardener in khaki pants, a short-sleeved dark shirt partially covered by a lightweight blue jacket, and dark sneakers.

"Dr. Moss, I presume?"

Jeff opened the Mazda's passenger door. O'Reilly was a short, wiry man with a pale complexion and receding light blond hair.

"Let's go for a ride."

They drove up to Seventy-Second Street and crossed through Central Park to the Upper West Side, parking on a quiet residential street between Broadway and West End Avenue.

"What I am to tell you must remain between us. I was there the night of the murder. I had just entered the residence and began walking up the stairs when a man came hurrying down and brushed into me, almost knocking me over."

"Do you recall what he looked like?"

"He wasn't that tall, but he sure was solid. I mean, it was like a truck had just rushed by. He was wearing dark clothing and a hoodie that fell back when we collided."

"Then what happened?"

"I held onto the rail so I wouldn't fall, and looked back as he rushed out. I continued up to the second floor when I heard a loud scream from above. When I reached the third floor I began to smell smoke. That's when I saw Monsignor Quinn running from his room and into the guest room. When I entered, he shouted to get the fire extinguisher. By the time I returned, the smoke alarm had gone off. He grabbed the canister and put out the fire. Father John was already there, but he seemed completely dazed, just staring at the far wall. I glanced up to see what he was looking at, and that's when I saw what had happened, a young priest hanging, blood splattered all over. Quinn picked up his phone, called 9-1-1, and told me to help Father John. I brought him a glass of water and when he regained his wits, helped him back to his room. By the time I returned to the scene, the firemen and police were already arriving."

Jeff had read in DePalma's report that Quinn said only he and Father John were present.

"So, you were there?"

"Absolutely, like I told you. Ask Father John."

"We're trying to locate him. And the person who ran into you coming down the stairs? You said his hoodie came off. His hair, what color was it?"

"His hair?" O'Reilly thought for a moment. "Why he didn't have any—completely bald, you know, like men who keep it shaved clean." O'Reilly paused before adding, "And one more thing. When I looked back as he was rushing down the stairs I noticed something else."

"And what was that?"

"He was holding a large black bag, like a duffel."

"Would you be able to identify him if you saw him again?"

"I think so."

"Good. And the sign around the victim's neck. Does it mean anything to you?"

"*Soli Deo gloria*? It's the murderer's signature, and has been for almost eight hundred years."

Jeff looked at him, puzzled. "What do you mean?"

"What do you know about the Inquisition?"

"Enough to know the Church killed a lot of innocent people."

"That's only the start." O'Reilly unclasped his seatbelt and opened his door. "There's a bar around the corner. We have a lot to talk about."

* * *

The Emerald Stone was an ideal place for someone wanting both drink and solitude. Dim and almost empty, the room had an old wide-planked oak floor and was divided lengthwise by a low wood-paneled wall. To the right was an area containing about a dozen small square tables; the other side contained a long oak bar with a mirrored backbar reflecting a row of liquor bottles that extended for the mirror's entire length. Two men were sitting on barstools, chatting with the bartender and watching the Mets game on the big-screen TV.

"What'll you have?" the bartender said as O'Reilly and Jeff crossed the divide and took seats at one of the tables at the far end.

"Whatever's on tap."

The bartender brought over two half pints. O'Reilly took a long, thirsty drink. Then in a lowered voice, he began to talk.

"The Inquisition was the most systematic attempt by any religion to force people to convert their spiritual beliefs to those of the Catholic Church. Under the penalty of death, the Church developed an entire legal system to terrify people into obedience."

"Sounds like Germany in the thirties."

O'Reilly looked intently at Jeff. "Where do you think the Nazis learned it from? Trials were not held to save souls but to fill people with such terror that it would lead to unquestioned obedience."

"And they were judged by the inquisitors?"

"Judged? There was no judgement. If they didn't like the answers, the inquisitors were ordered not to argue, but to thrust their swords through the interrogated."

"So the inquisitor was both prosecutor and magistrate?"

The priest took another drink before responding, "Correct, and the job requirement was simple: whoever could find the most unbelievers, regardless of evidence, was awarded the position. And that included forcing children to incriminate their parents."

Jeff leaned forward in thought, his elbows on the small table, hands resting under his chin. "And the pope allowed this?"

The monsignor responded quickly. "Allowed it? It was his idea. Pope Gregory the Ninth, in 1231, set up an independent court whose inquisitors were beholden only to him. Then, Pope Innocent the Third declared that any individual whose view of God conflicted with Church dogma would be put to death."

"I'm impressed that you know so much about this."

"I have a doctorate in religion, concentrating on the Middle Ages. The fact is, there was no way for the interrogated to prove their innocence, no counsel, no evidence offered, not even what heresy they were charged with."

Jeff drummed his fingers on the table. "Pope Innocent appears to have been misnamed. Everyone was guilty."

"Unless the bribe was adequate to fill the inquisitors' pockets."

"So the inquisitors grew rich."

"More so by taking everything the accused owned."

The priest paused and took another drink, as Jeff tried to put the information into perspective.

"Who were the inquisitors?"

"Mostly men from the Dominican and Franciscan orders."

"I thought they took vows of poverty?"

The priest smiled. "So much for vows. And, by the way, every punishment included flagellation."

Jeff's eyes widened. "That's what happened to the young priest."

"And if they refused to confess, they were burned at the stake."

"Like what happened, or almost happened, here."

"Yes, and one more thing, just like the fellow who almost knocked me over, inquisitors wore black robes with black hoods."

Jeff took a long drink and sat back in his chair. "And the sign around his neck?"

"Yes, the sign. That was most telling. You see, the inquisitors developed crude machines of torture, devices that would tear apart bodies to extract confessions, regardless of truth, all with the pope's blessing. And inscribed on the machines were the words *Soli Deo Gloria*." O'Reilly paused before adding, "And by the way, the Church never officially delegitimized torture until 1917."

Jeff edged closer to the table. "Are you saying that what happened on the third floor was a continuation of the Inquisition?"

"That's exactly what I'm saying."

Jeff finished his drink. "So, that's what this is about."

Monsignor O'Reilly leaned forward and lowered his voice. "Yes, my friend, for whatever reason, someone deemed Father Alonzo Fabrizzi a heretic and sentenced him to death—to be tortured and burned at the stake."

Jeff stood and paid the tab. "By the way, what happened on July 16? Was there something special in Church history on that date? Supposedly that was what Fabrizzi was to speak to the archbishop about."

"July 16? Church history?" The monsignor arose from his chair, trying to remember the date. "Perhaps the Great Schism in 1054, when the Catholic Church split into the Eastern Orthodox and Roman Catholic divisions."

"What happened?"

"When Cerularius, the patriarch of the Eastern Church, refused to accept the pope's decree that Rome had authority over all Christians, the pope sent the three legates of the Western Church to Constantinople. In the middle of a Saturday mass, they walked into the Cathedral of the Hagia Sophia and, while the patriarch was speaking in front of a packed congregation, marched up to the altar and placed a papal Bull of Excommunication against him. In response, Cerularius immediately excommunicated the papal legates. That's what led to the schism."

"But why would the young priest want to speak to the archbishop about that?"

O'Reilly shrugged. "A schism? I have no idea."

As they walked out, Jeff asked, "Where can I reach you?"

Jeff could see the fear on the other man's face. "You can use the cell number I called you on. If Quinn ever knew that I spoke to you, I would be in grave danger. He rules that enclave with an iron hand. Nothing happens without his knowledge. I'm afraid to be here any longer."

* * *

O'Reilly returned to his car and drove onto the West Side Highway, crossing the Hudson River via the lower level of the George Washington Bridge, the one called Martha. Staying hidden, several cars behind, was a black Esplanade. The driver, whose shaved head reflected the shining bridge lights, picked up his cell. "He's heading over the GW to New Jersey."

After a pause a voice gave instructions. "I heard he had a place somewhere in upstate New York. Follow him, see where he's going, then return. Do you understand? Do not make contact with him."

* * *

9:30 p.m.

Jeff reached his apartment and texted DePalma. *Met with O'Reilly. Possible he ran into the murderer coming down the stairs. Might be able to ID. Leave for Israel tomorrow.*

Moments later a return flew back. *Great. Enjoy the trip and be careful. If you need help, call this number. The name's Zvulen Rosen, an old acquaintance. We worked a case finding a terrorist who wanted to set off bombs in Times Square. Zvulen's a good man.* Jeff made a note and saved the message.

He packed a few changes of clothing into an overnight bag and placed the gold pieces into a briefcase and locked it. He tried sleeping but sleep was difficult to come by as the picture of the priest and the thought of his torture interfered. Finally, he succumbed to fatigue, but appreciating their first break: O'Reilly may be able to identify the murderer.

JULY 4

The distinguished men wearing nonliturgical black simar-like vestments with scarlet silk piping, buttons, and matching skullcaps were seated about a round polished poplar table cut from the forests of sixth-century Italy. Their meeting place was a large circular Florentine room filled with lavish tapestries, hand-woven wool carpets, and finely carved sixteenth-century beech furniture. It was the first gathering of the pope and his new advisors before the full assembly would meet. Each had received, like other invited leaders of the Catholic world, an envelope containing the summons, written on official Vatican stationery and sealed with the mark of the papal office:

> THERE WILL BE AN EXTRAORDINARY GENERAL ASSEMBLY
> OF THE SYNOD OF BISHOPS
> REGARDING AN EXISTENTIAL CHALLENGE TO THE CHURCH.
> THE TITLE OF THE SYNOD WILL BE
> "JESUS CHRIST RESPONDS TO MODERNITY"
> TO BE CONVENED ON WEDNESDAY, JULY 16,
> THE SISTINE CHAPEL

Each man understood the implications. A general assembly of the synod of bishops is "extraordinary" only when dealing with matters that demand, according to the Code of Canon Law, immediate attention for the good of the entire Church. The Extraordinary Assembly would end with proposed declarations that would go to a full Ordinary General Assembly of the Synod of Bishops and then receive papal approval for a final synod document.

Would the document recommend a reaffirmation of traditional Catholic values, or would it alter the course of the Church with a more liberal interpretation of Church doctrine? Either way it would be a teaching that many called for and as many opposed.

The new pope had not yet officially declared his agenda, but whatever it was, it would guide the Church for the coming decades.

The invited eight included a bishop from each continent. Already the group had been dubbed by Vatican observers the "pope's cabinet."

* * *

The door opened and Cardinal Jarogniew strode in. "His Eminence asks your forgiveness, but he has been delayed due to the circumstances in New York. As you know, several days ago a young priest from Rome was found dead at Cardinal Healy's residence."

As the concerned responses abated, Jarogniew continued. "His Eminence was advised that Cardinal Healy would not attend today as the situation required his full attention there."

"The news reported that the man arrived in New York from Rome, is that correct?" asked Cardinal Dunajski.

"As far as we know, and he was scheduled to meet with Cardinal Healy."

Dunajski followed up: "There was no cause of death reported. Is there any information on how he died?"

"He was murdered."

An abrupt silence remained until the pope entered the room. The assembled rose as he walked to the scarlet-covered chair and motioned them to be seated. He was aware that this first meeting would be a test of his leadership. He would need their support if he was to succeed in the furtherance of his policies.

"My brother cardinals," he began, "in twelve days we will be meeting to deal with a most difficult question: Can the Church survive in this new age of instant communication, where man has a front seat to the horrors of a world torn by poverty, crime, and war? Is it no wonder that so many believe their faith in God and Church has not been justified?"

He walked to a window overlooking St. Peter's Square.

"Our Church is in crisis. Attendance, except for the poor nations of South America, is dwindling, and the number of priests who choose to service their flock has diminished. God is not a popular topic these days, and the clamor for change is loud and clear." He paused and turned to face Caravaggio's painting *The Entombment of Christ*, as if wishing for a second reappearance. "Even the challenge to holy marriage is as great today as when

John Milton, almost four hundred years ago, insisted that divorce be allowed for emotional reasons. As Milton said, 'Would you rather have the sin of divorce or the sin of infidelity?'

"But it is not only the family that must be reinterpreted, it is our own house. If the Church is to lead the world in moral action and social justice, we must be certain that we, ourselves, have been cleansed of the plague of scandals with which our Holy See has been implicated. Now is the time to make our bureaucracy more transparent and accountable, and this includes the Vatican Bank."

All eyes shifted to Cardinal Jarogniew, for he, more than anyone, was responsible for overseeing the Curia's administration, and who by consolidating his power, gave him control of the bank and its assets. Jarogniew's face reddened as the pope continued.

"It is time to become more critical as to who we really are. It is like looking at a peacock; it may be beautiful if you look at it from the front, but if you look at it from behind, you discover the truth. The fact is, nothing must be as it was."

Jarogniew kept his silence reluctantly, swallowing his anger, and quickly appraised the situation. As he looked into the faces of those at the table, he realized that the majority agreed that change was needed—these men were more concerned with their immediate local issues than with understanding the historic role of the church. They spoke of their loss of priests, and the need to attract new ones by challenging the rule of celibacy. Others decried the large number of women leaving the Church, demanding that it was time for women to be given a pastoral role, if not the privilege of priesthood itself.

Jarogniew also realized that these grievances could continue for hours, unless it was stopped. He gave a faint nod to his one ally, sixty-five-year-old Cardinal Emanelle Estefaz, archbishop of Santiago, Chile, who rose to speak.

"Pardon me, Your Eminence, but what we are hearing are cries for change, allowing priests to marry, women to become priests, the condoning of homosexuality, the expansion of annulments. Where does it end? The idea of changing dogma at the whim of the public reminds me of a lesson my mother used to teach about leadership. Watch the dog, she would tell us, see how it walks in front of its owner as if leading the way, but observe how it is always looking back. Why? To see what happens when the owner changes direction. And then, Your Eminence, what does the dog do? It quickly runs in front of the owner's new path to again lead the way. Is that how we also lead? Can the doctrine taught by Christ two thousand years ago simply be redirected because it becomes inconvenient for the masses? Are we a religion that caters to anyone's belief? Have we finally become simply stewards of 'cafeteria' Catholicism, selecting what we find convenient and dismissing what is not?"

Estefaz took a sip of water and brushed his hand through his black hair before continuing.

"Your Eminence, God calls us to follow him unconditionally, and faith calls us to believe even when we may not understand."

The others at the table had no response, either because the retort was reasonable, or because they were not able to debate the argument. But the argument could not be left unchallenged, and it was Bronislaw Dunajski, the tall, stately Polish scholar, who realized that if the pope was to effect change, now was the time to come to his defense. In his rich and gracious voice, Dunajski responded.

"Your Holiness, I too am concerned with the shortage of priests, the declining number of parishioners, and the cry for participation from those we have scorned and cursed for two thousand years. But I also believe that as the world has changed, so must the Church. If the sheep have been lost then the shepherd must follow. I have asked myself, shall we reach out and lead them back into the fold or simply wait for their return? And who is this flock? Are they not ours, regardless of their background, their lifestyles, their preferences? Should not all who reach out their hand asking for love not be given the same love our Lord has given us? Are we to deny them Christ? Are we to deny them revelation? Are we to deny them salvation? Did not Jesus die on the cross for all mankind?"

The pope surveyed his advisors, waiting for further counsel, but there was none. Following Dunajski's eloquence there seemed to be nothing left to say: *Res ipsa loquitur.* The thing speaks for itself.

Jarogniew fought to hold his tongue. It was against his nature to see his persuasions not followed. Did not his given name, Jarogniew, define who he was: *yaru*, meaning fierce, and *gnyevu*, meaning anger? Throughout his life, he had never been a man to trifle with. A superb athlete, competing with him was like entering mortal combat. To the cardinal, those around the table were like sheep at pasture following blindly, and this warned of a danger to come. Even this meeting, allowing the pope global input, he perceived as a personal attack, seriously reducing his hard-earned papal influence. The pope might be the figurehead of the Church, but in terms of governance, he was the head of the Vatican, and nothing in the Vatican happened without his approval. In the Catholic world, he who has the ear of popes wields enormous power, and Jarogniew, for almost a quarter of a century, had that ear. As the ultimate Vatican broker, he had made certain no one else would obtain it.

Indeed, the whole idea of reform troubled him, for once you begin to change long-held traditions, where do you stop? And besides, if reform was required, shouldn't it be under his direction? For years he had worked at consolidating his influence and making changes that would advance his agenda, an agenda that he believed would alter the world. But now he felt resistance, and he would overcome it.

Jarogniew had carried out the strategy precisely as instructed in the *Alta Vendita*. Year by year he increased his authority, and each year he aided the advance of certain individuals, brothers to the cause, directing them into positions of influence within the Church hierarchy. He had patiently waited for the day when all decisions would rest in their hands, when the moment of critical mass would be obtained.

He recalled his mentor's words when he was but a young man, words that he was never to forget:

> God's foes gained entrance to his church many years ago,
> trying to alter the Gospel of our faith. Their plan was to
> entrench themselves within the uppermost places of power
> from which they were to mislead, misguide, and destroy
> until they were able to emasculate our religion. For that,
> they are never to succeed, never allowing them to redirect
> our faith, and we will do that by using their own strategy,
> ensconcing ourselves within the uppermost places of power,
> just as they did, but we will do it better. I have spent my
> life in the service of such achievement, and now, my dear
> Ludvik, now that I have grown too old to lead, it is you who
> must prevent this Church from departing its original path.

Jarogniew had carried out the directive better than his mentor could have imagined. He administered the Holy See to advance his objectives in undetectable ways, aided by his control of the vast Vatican assets and the brilliant use of bribes, financial enticements, and shifting of funds into secret accounts, all to consolidate power into the hands of one man: himself. How ironic, he thought, that the strategy of the *Alta Vendita*, originally used to liberalize the Church, was now being used to return it to its original doctrine.

And yet this pope, who was to be part of that plan, was not playing by the rules. Did he not owe him? Was it not he, Jarogniew, who had been instrumental in influencing his election? And yet, in spite of all that he had done, he now realized that his power and his ambitions were being challenged—and he was ill accustomed to losing.

With no further comments, the pope closed the meeting. "My friends, I thank you for your concerns and pray that the Lord help us guide our Church to the changes that are demanded of us."

Jarogniew realized that he need only curb his anger for ten more days. One thing was clear, he and the pope were in complete agreement that *changes were being demanded.* Yet, more than the pope, it was Cardinal Dunajski who carried the sway of the others; it was he who needed to be challenged. As the attendants left, Jarogniew approached his lifelong nemesis.

"My dear Bronislaw, I fear some of us have misinterpreted the last Vatican Council's changes as license to engage in untraditional directions. The Church must guard its sacred teachings against secularism and modernization. Christianity would dissolve itself if it allowed its revealed content, handed down in tradition, to be replaced by contemporary theories. And it is people like you," he caustically added, "whose thoughts are born with the devil's blessings. If I were you, I'd be very careful before you criticize the canon law that has guided this Church for two thousand years. Many have been excommunicated for less."

Dunajski looked into Jarogniew's eyes and recognized hate. Without a word, he turned and followed the other cardinals out of the room, leaving only Estefaz behind. Jarogniew walked to the door, locked it, and turned to Estefaz.

"I erred in assuming that once we installed this new pope his ideas would conform to ours, that he'd understand the importance of adhering to the strict traditions of our fathers."

"But your plan goes well beyond adhering to traditions."

"Only that I demand absolute adherence. It is simply a matter of degree. Lead and they will follow."

Estefaz looked at the cardinal secretary with both admiration and fear. "And how will that be done?"

"In the name of Catholic unity, as taught in the *Alta Vendita*. The masses simply seek a path—and someone to lead them."

"But the pope has already forged his path. The synod will follow his path, not ours."

"Then he will have to redirect his path."

"Redirect how? You don't have the votes."

"Then there will be no vote."

Estefaz seemed surprised. "So you unlocked the Final Mystery?"

"Not yet, but soon."

"And the power from that mystery will cause the pontiff to alter his belief?"

"If needed."

"A greater power than the pope's?"

"As great as the Lord's."

"And you would use such power?"

"If there's no other way."

"When will it begin?"

"It already has."

* * *

Ludvik Jarogniew returned to his opulent apartment, finely decorated with luxurious furnishings and priceless art. He poured a glass of claret and sat in his chair to think. How had he made such a miscalculation on this papacy? There was little from the new pope's past to suggest that he would be so liberal. It was one of the few misjudgments the cardinal had made on his steady rise to power from his humble beginnings as a parish priest in a small Polish church. As he drained his glass he understood he would never make the same mistake again. He pressed the numbers on his cell.

"I want the holy vessels—NOW!"

JULY 5

4:00 p.m., Israel

A thin, dark-skinned young man with short, curly black hair, a groomed beard, and wearing dark glasses kept his eyes on the large series of steel-framed glass doors at the entrance to the International Arrivals Building of Israel's Ben Gurion Airport. He held a cigarette in one hand and with the other a sign reading Dr. Jeffrey Moss, below which was the name Shalom Transport, ltd.

He took staccato puffs and nervously turned his head as if wary of being recognized. Suddenly the sounds of rolling suitcases and calls for taxis were heard as doors flew open and a multicolored throng appeared. The young man focused on the exiting passengers, raised the sign, and took a final drag on his cigarette before throwing it down.

"I'm Dr. Moss. You must be Moshe."

The man replied in broken English. "No, I take his place." He reached for Jeff's briefcase. "I help you."

Jeff instinctively tightened his grip. "I'll keep it."

They walked to an old, dust-covered Saab so dirty its dark color was difficult to identify. The backseat was filthy, with old magazines and newspapers strewn on the floor.

"Is this the car you always use?"

"No, limo being repaired."

Jeff's sixth sense raised suspicion. "You know where we're going?"

The grunt from the driver was affirmative as the car raced out of the airport and onto the highway that ran three lanes in each direction. There were signs in Hebrew, Arabic, and English.

Something seemed wrong. It was certainly possible that the driver was replaced, but this was supposed to be one of Israel's finest car services. Jeff recalled DePalma's last words: "Be careful." He quietly reached into his briefcase and removed the plastic evidence bag containing the gold pieces and tucked it into his sock.

They followed Route 1 to Jerusalem. The late afternoon traffic was heavy, and Jeff settled back for the drive, fatigue beginning to overtake his suspicions. As he gazed out the window, the miracle was readily apparent. A country the size of New Jersey, which only decades ago had been a dry, barren desert for thousands of years, had been transformed into a paradise of seemingly endless vital acres filled with fields of fruit trees and vegetables, serviced by life-giving irrigation.

He had visited once before—with her. He was to deliver a lecture at Hadassah Medical Center and Kate had accompanied him. As he dozed, his mind replayed how they had met. It was on Peter Island in the British Virgin Islands. When his date canceled at the last minute, he had gone solo. He was on line at the front desk and couldn't help but notice the woman in front of him. She was tall, well figured, early thirties, with long brunette hair spilling over her shoulders, and well-tanned from the sun. As it happened, she would be leaving the next morning, but their opening conversation soon led to a long dinner and longer conversation. They exchanged addresses, and he had the singular feeling that it was only the beginning. It was. If only it hadn't had to end.

* * *

It was a dream he'd had many times, but this time it came to an abrupt ending as the mesmerizing sound of rubber on evenly laid highway turned into the sudden jolts and noise of an unpaved, potholed surface. Jeff opened his eyes with a start, reorienting, realizing they were on an old dirt road leading up a steep mountainside into woods.

Alarmed, Jeff leaned forward and shouted, "Something wrong?"

"Need to stop."

"Why?"

"Check motor."

The driver pulled onto the side of the road, got out of the car, and opened Jeff's door.

"Out." In his hand was a short-nosed revolver. "Walk."

The driver pointed to an indistinct trail and Jeff began the ascent, the driver following. Suddenly, the world became a blinding light and then a darkness without memory. It was half an hour before rays of light entered Jeff's consciousness. Slowly, he picked himself up from the ground, his hand reaching for the source of the aching roar catapulting from the back of his head, aware of a molten sensation of clotting blood.

* * *

The Saab and briefcase were gone, and fresh tire marks suggested a hasty retreat. Reflexively he placed his hand along his ankle and felt the gold contents: his hunch had paid off. Jeff checked his jacket pockets. His wallet and cell phone were still there, and nearby he found his overnight bag unopened. This was no ordinary robbery—it was the briefcase that was wanted. As his strength returned and his mind cleared, he began the descent to the highway.

* * *

"Where are you?"

"The main road to Jerusalem. Across the highway I see old metal frames of small tanks and jeeps."

"Okay. I know where you are. Route 1, I'll be there in forty-five minutes."

* * *

Jeff was sitting patiently on a rock off the side of the highway when a black Toyota Corolla pulled onto the shoulder. The door opened and an authoritative voice said, "Jeff Moss?"

"That's me."

"I'm Zvulen. You okay?"

"Yeah, except my head feels like it's in a vise."

The man smiled in sympathy. "Let's see the damage." He checked Jeff's head. "Nice scalp wound, some dried blood. But you're the doctor."

"Yeah, I'll be fine. Thanks for coming. My boss gave me your name."

The man was built like a tank. Slightly shorter than Jeff, with closely cropped curly black hair and steel-blue eyes that seemed to lock onto Jeff's face like a missile tracking its target. He stood as straight as a gun barrel, and when they shook hands it was like pressing iron. He wore a blue blazer that barely stretched over the breadth of his frame, and when he unbuttoned it, Jeff saw the handle of a pistol in a shoulder holster.

"Yeah, your chief told me you might call, just didn't think it would be this soon. He told me about your trip. Did they get your cargo?"

"No, the guy who took my briefcase must not have bothered to look inside. Left everything else, wallet, overnight bag. Guess he took what he thought he wanted and raced off."

"Someone knew what you were carrying."

Jeff passed his hand gently over his head. "Sure sounds like it. I thought we were secure for this trip. I mean, the guy was waiting for me. Said he was a replacement for the original driver."

"Then you were lucky, but DePalma worries about you, so I've been assigned to be your shadow during your stay. I was told you have reservations at a quiet inn where you can get some rest. In the morning, you have a meeting at the Israel Museum, so I'll pick you up at eight. Here's my card."

It was a simple white standard stock card with small black print. Only the name, in English and Hebrew, was printed: Zvulen Rosen.

Zvulen opened the car's rear door and handed Jeff a package. "Better hold on to this during your visit."

Jeff opened the brown paper package to find a black Sig Sauer automatic in a shoulder holster.

Zvulen looked in the rearview mirror. "Familiar?"

"A semi-automatic. Only used it at the police academy firing range."

"Should be helpful. Easy to conceal, holds fifteen rounds."

"Thanks. After today, I may need it."

"Who knew you were coming to Israel?"

"I thought only a few trusted people." Jeff took some deep breaths and tried to relax. He looked across the road. "What's with those old tanks?"

Zvulen smiled. "Remains of the forty-eight War for Independence." Zvulen glanced at him in the rearview mirror. "They remind us of the courage it took to build a democracy in a neighborhood that doesn't like democracies."

As the car climbed the mountain curves, the distant hills of Jerusalem appeared, and soon the reflection of the sun's rays bounced from the rooftops.

"Jerusalem of Gold," Zvulen said, pointing to the scene before them. The horizon was filled with mechanical cranes that rose to the skies like graceful birds alongside magnificent high-towered structures. As they entered the city, the streets were crowded with cars and tourists wandered in all directions. It wasn't just vibrant, it was clean, a city where old meets new, where East meets West, where churches and synagogues and mosques dwelled together, where religion met the secular, where twenty-first-century malls, modern international hotels, and posh apartment buildings were made from the simple yet majestic blocks of glistening Jerusalem stone.

It was after six by the time Zvulen drove through Jerusalem's upscale German district. The winding, narrow streets with their blooming roses and colorful hyacinths bordered the properties of the gracious residences of an earlier generation. Zvulen explained how the German Colony was named for members of the Templar sect from Wurttemberg, Germany, who broke from the Protestant church and settled in the Holy Land.

"The British deported them during World War II because, as Germans, they were considered enemy citizens who supported the Nazis. Their homes were purchased by wealthy Christian Arabs, but in 1948 the Arabs abandoned their homes, being told that their armies would conquer the land within days, and then they could return. With Israel's victory they never returned."

Jeff was dropped off in front of a small but stately inn, and entered the ambiance of an earlier era, clean, quaint, and quiet. The young woman at the front desk welcomed him and arranged for his morning wake-up call. She rang a bell and a tall, thin, neat-looking teenager with a gracious smile and perfectly arched white teeth appeared. The name Amir was engraved on a shiny gold-colored plate pinned to the lapel of his jacket, and Jeff couldn't tell if he was Arab or Jewish; nor did it seem to matter.

"Do you have a first-aid kit?"

The young man noticed the dried blood, went to the desk, and returned with a small brown container.

"I can clean it up. Looks like quite a gash."

Jeff smiled. "If you know what you're doing."

Amir laughingly responded. "I better, I just finished my first year of med school." He cleansed the wound with peroxide, applied an antibiotic ointment, and smiled, announcing a job well done. Jeff thanked him and predicted he would have a great medical future.

Amir showed Jeff to his room and received a generous tip for his help. The room had an inviting double bed made up with fresh linens, and Jeff felt the exhaustion quickly close in. He locked the door, forswore dinner, took a long hot shower, placed his loaded Sig Sauer, under his pillow, and fell into a deep sleep.

JULY 6

Jerusalem

The wake-up call came at 7:00. Jeff shaved and changed into tan slacks and a white dress shirt left open at the collar. He strapped his holstered pistol under his blue sport jacket, and with the gold in his pocket, went downstairs. Amir escorted him to the veranda and did a quick check of Jeff's wound.

"Looks much better." Amir explained that he was an Arab, off from school for the summer, and held two jobs, bellhop and waiter. He proudly announced that he was studying at Hebrew University, and was the only son of eight children—and the first in the family to attend college.

Jeff sat at a table alongside a three-foot-high stone wall that overlooked the colorful summer garden blooming with yellow, white, and red roses. He was having a cup of coffee and a bagel with cream cheese when a message lit up his cell: his ride was waiting. He walked down the inn's front steps to the waiting Toyota.

"*Boker tov*, Doctor. We're going to the Israel Museum this morning for your meeting. It's going to be a hot one today, but you'll be cool indoors. Have everything you need?"

Jeff checked his jacket pocket and felt the envelope. "Yes, everything."

"Good. How's your head?"

"Better."

They drove through the twisting streets, and although the sun was only at eight hours in the clear blue sky, the day's dry heat was already penetrating. Jeff tried to put yesterday's encounter behind him. He took a deep breath, loosened his shoulders and immersed himself in the early morning peace of the quiet residential neighborhood. Soon, the car accelerated as it joined the morning rush onto a highway filled with the sounds of commuters driving to work and buses filled with kids going to summer camps. Below, nestled in a valley, lay a series of contemporary low-rise pavilions built along the gentle slopes of the Judean Hills. To his right was the Knesset, Israel's parliament building, an austere-looking structure with windows on all sides. Zvulen drove toward a contemporary building composed of a series of modular units reminiscent of an old Mediterranean village that could grow organically as the need arose.

"Welcome to the Israel Museum. Someone will be waiting for us at the front desk."

Jeff looked surprised. "You're coming with me?"

Zvulen smiled. "My instructions are to make sure that nothing like yesterday happens again, at least until we reach the lobby." As they walked, he told Jeff that the Israel Museum ranked as one of the world's leading art and archaeology centers. He led Jeff through the large glass doors where several security guards were stationed with semi-automatics slung from their shoulders. A young woman in an army-green uniform greeted Jeff's escort with a big hug.

"Zvulen, what a surprise."

"Good to see you, Dahlia. How's the family?"

"Thank God—hakol beseder, all's well."

"Dr. Moss flew in from New York to see Danny."

"Danny? Of course." She gave Jeff a broad smile of welcome that showed a dimple on each cheek.

"Welcome to Israel."

"Thank you."

"If you're carrying a firearm, we will need to hold it for you until you return."

Jeff handed her his pistol, and she placed it into a locked room.

"Zvulen, Danny's on the third floor. I'll take him up myself."

"Fine. I'll stay here."
****

Jeff followed Dahlia to the elevator. "So," he said, "I see you know Zvulen?"

"This is a small country. Everyone's family."

"He won't let me out of his sight."

Dahlia smiled. "That's why he's here."

"What do you mean?"

"Zvulen's Mossad. I guess your friends back home want you back safe and happy."

They exited the elevator and walked through the crisp, white air-conditioned hallways, passing displays of ancient pottery and contemporary sculpture, until they stopped outside room 304.

"This is where I say good-bye. Danny should be inside."

Jeff entered the office and found a tall, attractive, and well-proportioned woman, mid-thirties, wearing stylish glasses that fit over a slightly pugged nose and long brunette hair that fell down her back. She wore a soft yellow short-sleeved dress shirt, a light blue knee-length skirt, and her skin was tanned to a golden brown. She was reading a journal as she stood by a window overlooking the city. Jeff felt a sense of déjà vu, and he couldn't help but stare. It was almost as if . . .

Aware of his entrance she turned from her reading. "You must be Dr. Moss."

"Yes, Jeffrey Moss, here to see Daniel Teller. I believe he's expecting me."

The woman seemed surprised at the request.

"Well, Jeffrey Moss, I'm afraid there's no Daniel Teller here."

"Oh, I was told this was his office—"

"There's a Daniella Teller, often called Danny."

Jeff felt like he was back in grade school and had missed an easy spelling question.

"Daniella? So he's a she?"

"That's one way of putting it. Do you have a problem with women?"

He smiled. "I always have a problem with women, but I can adapt. Is she here?"

"I'm Daniella Teller."

Jeff realized this was not going well. "Sorry."

She smiled, with a mischievous look in her eyes.

"No need. It's happened more than once. My father called me Danny as a kid, and still some of the old family friends call me that. Now that I'm a little older I prefer Daniella, sounds a little more adult."

She extended her hand. "Anyway, *Baruch haba*, welcome to Israel."

They shook hands. Her grip was soft yet firm. She invited him to sit down. He glanced at the wall of plaques behind her: BA from Stanford, Rhodes Scholar at Oxford, PhD at Hebrew University, archeology fellowship at the Louvre.

"So, Professor Siglione gave you my name."

"With instructions not to get you into trouble."

Daniella gave an easy laugh. "He only says that because he was one of my father's good friends and my mentor in Paris."

She turned to the screen on her desk. "I've been reviewing the images that Antonio sent. Would it be possible to see the pieces themselves?"'

Jeff took out the plastic evidence bag and handed it to her.

She looked at the scrap of paper. "Why 16/7? Did something happen on the sixteenth of July?"

"In Catholic history, yes. It has to do with the Great Schism."

She laid the pieces out on a cloth. "You have identified the medals?"

"Professor Siglione did. Made by Cellini in 1534 for Pope Clement the Seventh."

She picked up a lens and examined the pieces. "They're in great shape for five hundred years. Wish I could say the same."

Jeff surveyed the well-contoured evidence, thinking. So far so good.

She placed the two coins back into their envelope and focused on the gold band. "This is what Antonio wanted my opinion on?"

Jeff didn't respond as she continued to examine the piece and read the Hebrew inscription.

She looked up, astonished. "How did you find this?"

"It's evidence for a case I'm investigating in New York."

"If this is real, it would be remarkable."

"It's real gold, if that's what you mean."

Daniella brushed her fingers through her hair and examined the piece through her lens. "Mind if I ask a colleague for his opinion?"

Jeff agreed and Daniella made a call. "Moshe, I think you should come to my office."

Moshe Katz, chief curator of the museum, was a short, rather rotund man in his mid-sixties with bushy gray hair and wearing dark slacks that needed a crease and a white short-sleeved dress shirt that needed an iron. Jeff observed that hidden behind the full gray beard whose ends could use a scissor's snip was a face too large for his body, a double chin, large ears, and thick lips that drooped at the corners. If he'd had a cask of whiskey hung around his neck he could've been a stand-in for a big, lovable Saint Bernard.

He greeted Daniella with a broad smile. "So, what's the emergency?"

Daniella pointed to the band on the desk. "Take a look—and read the engraving."

The curator's eyes settled on the gold band. "A gold diadem? 'Kadosh Ladoshem,'" being certain to avoid reciting the holy name of God as written on the diadem. "Is this real?"

"That's what I asked."

Katz looked at Jeff. "This is yours?"

"Yes, sir." He put out his hand. "Jeff Moss."

"Pleasure." Katz, clearly excited, turned to Daniella. "Get Mordechai down here—quickly."

Mordechai Keppler was tall, with a full head of graying hair. He was wearing an outfit similar to Moshe's, with one difference: his was a long-sleeved shirt but the right sleeve was neatly pinned back to hang just off the shoulder. He had lost his arm in the Six-Day war in 1967 when he was a young paratrooper in the IDF, the Israel Defense Force. After being introduced to Jeff, Keppler sat behind the desk and examined the gold medals, then focused on the gold diadem. "Where did you find this?"

Jeff explained the reason for his visit, how the packages were found hidden on the murdered priest, and how the priest had arrived in New York after leaving Rome to fly to Israel—a detour no one could explain.

"I'm investigating the case, trying to determine who he is and why he was murdered."

Mordechai looked up from the diadem, then placed his left arm on the desk to support himself as he rose.

"What do you think?" Jeff asked.

"I'm afraid to think."

"First Temple?" Katz asked.

Keppler walked to the window overlooking the Billy Rose Garden that displayed its full summer Technicolor bloom. "If it's original, way before."

Daniella said, "It's pure gold."

"Twenty-four carat? Well, that reduces potential forgeries."

Jeff followed their interaction. "Would there be any reason why the priest would go to such lengths to conceal these pieces?"

Keppler answered. "If this piece is real, it would be the oldest known artifact in biblical history, long before the Dead Sea Scrolls and long before the First Temple. It would be priceless."

"I'll give you a second reason," said Katz, "if this is real it could lead to the greatest treasure the ancient world has ever known."

"And that is?"

Daniella answered: "The Temple Treasure."

"You mean the one that's been missing for two thousand years? I thought that was fiction."

"Daniella's father didn't think it was fiction," Katz interjected. "He spent his life looking for it."

"And I believe that's what it cost him," Daniella quietly added.

Jeff wished she would clarify the statement, but Keppler quickly added, "And your murderer didn't think it was fiction."

Jeff said, "How much are we talking about?"

"Most historians speak of a rumored fifty tons of gold and silver. That's a lot of dollars."

"All in one place?"

Keppler laughed. "Like having the key to your own Fort Knox. But it's not only the monetary value that gives it worth, it's the historical and spiritual significance. That's why it's priceless."

Jeff quickly put it together. "So, if the murderer was aware of what the priest was carrying, he tortured him not just for the gold, but to lead him to the Temple Treasure itself?"

Daniella nodded. "The gold pieces by themselves would be worth pennies compared to finding the Temple Treasure."

"But I suspect that if he refused to give the murderer the gold, he also refused to tell him how he found it. That means one thing. We have to find it."

Jeff interpreted the bewildered looks. "What I mean is that if we find the treasure, we'll find the murderer."

"Why's that?" Daniella asked.

"Because if he wants the treasure so bad that he'll kill for it, and we have it, he'll come to us."

"That's a pretty risky bet," Katz said.

"And a little naïve." Keppler tried to mute any condescension. "Surely you realize that people have been looking for that treasure for two thousand years."

"But," Jeff replied, "you just told me that this could be the first substantial clue as to where it may be found. Tell me about the treasure."

Katz responded. "The short or the long version? If you want the short version it follows the treasure from Egypt to Jerusalem, then Babylonia to Persia, back to Jerusalem, and then to Rome."

"And the long version?"

"Thirty-five hundred years."

"Then shorten the long version."

As Jeff took out his notebook, Katz began.

"The Temple Treasure is from the First Temple, the temple King Solomon built here in Jerusalem."

"So, it really is Indiana Jones!"

Keppler laughed. "With one exception."

"And that is?"

"This is real. After the Israelite slaves left Egypt, Moses received the stone tablets containing the Ten Commandments at Mount Sinai, and a temporary ark was built to house them. For forty years, while wandering through the desert, the Ark traveled from one site to another until King David conquered Jerusalem. He moved it to Mount Zion, placed it in a tent, and planned to build a temple to permanently house it."

"Spielberg's lost Ark."

"No slight to Steven, but we prefer to call it the Ark of the Covenant, and David was to build an enduring house for it. But the prophet Nathan warned that it was to be his son, Solomon, who God had chosen to build the temple. And Solomon did, in about the year 900 BCE, and amassed an enormous treasure. Temple life and the Jewish people thrived for more than three hundred years until 586 BCE, when Nebuchadnezzar, the king of Babylonia, defeated the Jewish army. He destroyed Jerusalem, burned down the temple, removed the sacred vessels of gold, silver, and brass and took the treasure back to Babylonia, today's Iraq.

"We know that because Belshazzar, the last king of Babylon and presumably Nebuchadnezzar's son, gave a great party and displayed the temple treasures that were stolen. During the feast, according to the Book of Daniel, a large unattached hand appeared and wrote a message on the wall, only understood by the prophet Daniel: *God has numbered the days of your kingdom and brought it to an end . . . your kingdom has been divided and given to the Medes and Persians.*"

Jeff said, "So that's where the phrase 'to see the writing on the wall' comes from."

"Precisely, and sure enough, that night the armies of Medes under Darius, and Persia under Cyrus, invaded Babylon and conquered it.

"Then, around 530 BCE, Cyrus allowed the Jews to return to Jerusalem."

"Why?"

"The Book of Ezra states that the Lord ordered Cyrus to permit the Jews to return to their home and commanded him to rebuild the temple."

"So, God appeared to Cyrus in a dream?"

Keppler nodded. "And the sacred vessels and treasures were returned to Jerusalem."

Katz picked up the story line.

"And stayed there, right through to Alexander the Great and the Greeks, who defeated the Persians. And for the most part, in spite of the many wars between the Jews and the Greeks, the treasure remained in Jerusalem. At least until Rome defeated the Greeks. It was Rome who destroyed the temple and took the treasure, while it also conquered the world."

Keppler checked his watch, rose from his chair, and picked up a journal lying on Daniella's desk and handed it to Jeff. "We have meetings to go to, but to understand what happens next we leave you to Daniella, the true expert in this area."

Jeff glanced at Daniella's copy of *Archaeology Review*, and read its cover: "Where is the Temple Treasure? A New Analysis by Shimon Teller, PhD and Daniella Teller, PhD."

He stood as the two men gave him a parting handshake. "So now what?"

Keppler looked at Daniella. "First, see if the diadem is real. Check it out with Ephraim."

Katz nodded. "I agree." He turned to Jeff. "Ephraim Selzer is probably the most knowledgeable dealer in biblical artifacts in Israel, if not the world. A scholar's scholar, the one who helped find the Copper Script of the Dead Sea Scrolls."

Daniella said, "How do we get to him? Supposedly, he has two guards at the door, like the fiery seraphim protecting the Garden of Eden."

Keppler smiled. "Daniella's correct, no one gains entry without Ephraim's approval. I last saw him about six months ago at the reunion of the remaining members of the unit. Like all of us, he's aged, gained a little more weight, but he's as brilliant as ever. He received his doctorate in philosophy from Oxford, taught there for a while, but moved to Israel in the early sixties and joined the army, eventually becoming a colonel. After two wars, he called it quits and went into business, making a fortune knowing what to buy, when to sell, and most importantly, being trusted. If anyone can help you, he can."

Keppler wrote down Selzer's address and a brief note. "Here, give this to him. It may help."

Jeff took the note. "You think he'll see us?"

Keppler rested his arm on the desk to support his getting up. "I believe he will. He was the commander of my unit in sixty-seven. I stopped a bullet that was meant for him. I suppose, in a way, it saved his life and cost me an arm."

* * *

Jeff and Daniella returned to the entrance and found Zvulen reading the monthly museum newsletter. He greeted them, had Jeff's revolver returned to him, and they walked out to the car. The sun was not yet at half height in the cloudless sky, yet the radiance of heat rising from the asphalt surface appeared like rain rising to the heavens instead of falling from it.

"Where to?"

Daniella handed him the address. "Old City."

As the Corolla drove out, Zvulen checked his rearview mirror. Following them at a distance was an old, dark blue, dust-covered Saab.

"Jeff, what kind of car did you say picked you up at the airport?"

"An old dark-colored Saab."

"And the driver, what did he look like?"

"Thin, young, dark skinned, with short, curly black hair. Why do you ask?"

"I believe he's following us. There's two of them. Don't turn around, but it's my guess that someone wasn't happy when your briefcase didn't contain what it was supposed to."

Daniella looked at him, puzzled, and Jeff told her what had happened. "I thought your visit was confidential."

"That's what I thought."

As they approached the central city, the traffic almost came to a standstill. Zvulen, looking into the rearview mirror, noticed the Saab several cars back. Suddenly, Zvulen saw an opening and stepped on the pedal, turning into a narrow one-way side street followed by other narrow streets that appeared from nowhere. Within minutes, and ignoring stop signs, they approached the Old City. He came to a sudden stop and parked the Corolla two blocks from the Jaffa Gate, the busiest of the eight remaining entrances located on the western side of the city next to the Tower of David. The area was congested with pedestrians and crowded with taxis. Zvulen looked back: the Saab was nowhere to be seen.

"I think we lost them, at least for the moment."

As they left the car, Daniella asked, "But who else knows why you're here?"

"Only your friends at the museum."

Zvulen said, "You may have a leak back home."

They walked into the Old City, surrounded by the great wall built in the first half of the sixteenth century by the Ottoman Turk, Suleyman the Magnificent. As they walked, Jeff turned to Daniella.

"What did you mean when you said you thought the search cost your father his life?"

"My father had been fascinated with the Temple Treasure since grad school. The last time we spoke was a little over a year ago. He was in Rome, finishing months of research and was in great spirits. He told me that he had found several clues as to where the treasure might be and would tell me more when he returned to Israel in the next few days. Except he never returned. Two days later we were told that his body was found floating in the Tiber, a deep gash on his forehead, multiple wounds to the body, and a sky-high blood alcohol level. The police report assumed he fell into the river when he was drunk and drowned. All I can tell you was my father never drank anything more potent than tea. Somebody was covering up something, and our investigation was stonewalled at every turn."

Jeff remained silent. He understood what it was like to lose someone you loved.

They walked on and Jeff found himself in another world: streets narrowing to alleys and an atmosphere alive with chaos, music, and the strong fragrances of cumin, cardamom, sumac, and Baharat spices. They made their way through an endless maze of constricted passageways bordered by small shops crowded with Arabs wearing traditional clothing and tourists in shorts and tank tops. From either side, Arab shopkeepers hawked their wares: textiles and religious items and silver and copper water basins cluttered their stalls along with shiny trinkets, brightly colored shawls, and picture postcards. Anything that could command a price was being sold, and if you bargained well, for almost any amount.

Jeff absorbed the sights as they walked down the cobblestoned pathway to a security checkpoint, where Zvulen spoke briefly to the guards. As they passed through, they looked out to see the Temple Mount, where both temples once stood. Below was a huge square, one side bordered by a massive wall made of cream-colored stones polished smooth by three thousand years. Before the wall, hundreds of Jewish men and women were praying. Orthodox Jews and young yeshiva students in dark suits stood next to Hasidic rabbis wearing long black alpaca coats and black fur hats from a previous century, all swaying back and forth in dialog with their God. Jeff realized he was viewing the living history of a people in their holiest place, appreciating the joys that belief in the one God had given them, yet aware of the deadly price that had been paid. Now, where the temples had once stood was the Al-Aqsa mosque, revered by Moslems as their third holiest site.

"The mosque is on the site of the temples," Jeff observed. "How does that work?"

"Over the centuries," Zvulen said, "the Muslims, who took control of Jerusalem, built two mosques on the Temple Mount where the temples had been. It's a common Islamic custom to build mosques on the sites of other people's holy places, but although many Jews see it as a direct affront, the geopolitical reality is that any attempt to destroy these mosques would incite a jihad of global proportions. The fact is, the temple can only be rebuilt when our Messiah comes. But the Arabs have excavated huge amounts of material beneath the mount, trying to destroy any evidence that the temples existed, or that the Jewish people had any relationship to Jerusalem. They are denying history, and when you repeat a story enough, people will begin to believe it."

* * *

They came to a building with a stone façade that looked hundreds of years old. Affixed to the wall, adjacent to the heavy wooden door with its mezuzah, was the number thirty-six, beneath which was written: Ephraim Selzer, Appraiser of Antiquities.

Zvulen knocked, and two giant men dressed in street clothes appeared.

"Do you have an appointment?"

Zvulen spoke in Hebrew and handed them the note Mordechai Keppler had written. The men looked over the three petitioners, and one of them took the note and disappeared. Within a short time, he returned and escorted them in.

Zvulen scouted the area. "I better wait out here. Take your time."

Jeff and Daniella left the heat of the day behind and entered the air-conditioned building. They were led through a stark, limestone hallway to a wood-paneled wall that ingeniously slid sideways, then entered an elevator that silently lowered them to the floor below. When the door opened, they found themselves in a brightly lit huge rectangular room about fifty feet long and twenty feet wide, and two levels high. The air was filled with the soft sounds of orchestra and chorus that Jeff recognized as Brahms' Ein Deutsches Requiem. Placed throughout the room were a dozen mahogany and glass display cases and several Louis XVI–style tulipwood vitrines, all containing artifacts of various shapes and sizes: antiques of natural clay and glazed pottery, jewelry from gold and precious stones, sculptures of bronze and marble, and fine paintings. A separate section contained cases of Judaica, including silver menorahs and Kiddush cups fashioned with the finest hand craftsmanship. To Jeff, it was like being back in the museum.

From the far end a booming voice welcomed them. As they approached they saw a large, heavy-set man sitting in an oversized leathered chair. He had sparkling blue, deep-set eyes, heavy drooping eyebrows, high cheekbones, and a big smile lighting up an old but energetic face. His full head of white hair was tied back by a blue ribbon into a ponytail, and he wore a white shirt with wide-open collar and bright red suspenders holding up white slacks. He spoke the King's English in a deep, sonorous voice slowly and rhythmically. He reminded Jeff in both shape and sound of Sidney Greenstreet in *The Maltese Falcon.*

With a wave of his hand, Selzer motioned for them to sit in two carved mahogany library armchairs placed in front of an English walnut writing table. Holding the note, he greeted his guests.

"It is not possible to refuse to meet with friends of Mordechai. He and I go back a long way. I suppose it's because of him that I am able to meet with you today." He threw his head back and laughed—an infectious roar—and continued reading the note of introduction.

"So, you are Dr. Jeffrey Moss, and you must be Daniella . . ." He paused before saying, "Teller? You wouldn't have authored an article in this month's *Archaeology Review*?"

Daniella smiled. "Why, yes."

"And you worked with Shimon Teller?"

"Shimon Teller is . . . was . . . my father."

The big man seemed to study Daniella more closely before responding. "I see." He remained silent, seeming to appraise her, before continuing.

"I knew your father."

"He was a well-known archeologist."

"And a very good one. Many of our interests lie in the same area. But I knew your father outside of his profession."

Daniella's eyes widened in surprise. "How was that?"

"Your father was in my command in Lebanon. He was a courageous young officer, brilliant thinker, a good chess player, too. I was sorry to hear of his death. In fact, I believe I even met your mother."

Daniella leaned forward, easing her business-like demeanor. "You knew my mother?"

"Quite by accident. It had been about two years since I last saw your father following the war. I had just completed a business meeting and was to have a late dinner in a restaurant here in Jerusalem. From across the room I recognized your father with a young woman, his very pregnant young wife. That was in the spring of eighty-four. They invited me to join them, and I accepted. We had a wonderful dinner, discussing the work your parents were doing as archeologists, the progress being made in finding the Temple Treasure, and then we spent the rest of dinner discussing issues that affect most Israelis: life, death, God, and, of course, the hope for peace for the new generation your mother was bringing into our world."

Daniella smiled broadly. "Spring of 1984? Then, I would think I was also present."

"Yes, I suppose you were. If memory serves me correctly, you look a great deal like her. The same coloring and both very beautiful."

Jeff noticed Daniella's blush. "Thank you."

Selzer continued. "So, we are old friends." He glanced at Jeff. "And you and Daniella are also old friends?"

"Actually, I only met Daniella recently. We're working on a project together and thought you might help us."

Selzer smiled. "Forgive me for being too personal. You looked like a handsome couple."

He stood and walked to the marble-topped credenza and poured three glasses of iced tea, then placed one in front of each of his guests and returned to his seat.

"And may I ask what project that may be?"

Jeff removed the cloth pouch from his pocket and handed it to Selzer. "We were hoping for your opinion."

Selzer examined the pieces before turning to a microscope on the credenza. After a few moments, he looked at his guests. "I've seen these pieces recently."

The two visitors looked at each other in amazement. "Are you sure?"

"No question, these pieces were brought to me last week by a young man, a priest. May I ask how you happen to possess them?"

Jeff handed Selzer his card and explained that he was investigating a murder that took place in New York, and the only clue were these pieces cleverly hidden by the victim.

"I am most sorry to hear this. The young man was a gentle sort, deeply spiritual. He was working on his dissertation and mentioned that he was referred to me over a year ago by an older scholar who apparently was the one who found the gold pieces."

"An older scholar? Then, it wasn't Fabrizzi but someone else who found the gold?"

"That is what he told me."

Daniella followed up. "Did he give you a name?"

"I asked, but he was hesitant to say. So, I examined the pieces and gave him my opinion."

Daniella edged forward in her chair. "And may I ask what that was?"

Selzer was silent for several moments, his fingers tapping lightly on his desktop.

"Please understand there is a great deal of danger in discussing this. You see what happened to our young friend, and to . . . and to others."

"Others?" Daniella asked.

Selzer seemed to know he was on delicate ground. "There is great danger in dealing with anything of such immense value."

Jeff said, "I've already found that out. But, until now, we haven't met anyone who even knew the priest. That's why we need to know the context of your conversation."

"He explained that the medals were made by Cellini but was more concerned about the gold diadem."

"And what did you say?"

"I took out a copy of the Hebrew Bible and turned to Exodus, chapters twenty-seven and twenty-eight, and asked him to tell me what it was referencing. He said that God was commanding Moses to fashion eight sacred garments for his brother Aaron to be the high priest, including a gold crown. I asked him to examine the gold band he brought me and compare it with the biblical description of the high priest's crown. The crown, he read, was a thin plate made of one piece of pure gold shaped into an arch. It was at that point that he realized what his gold diadem might be."

"You mean the gold band could have been Aaron's crown?"

Selzer shrugged. "It matched the description found in the Bible. We even examined other texts with further descriptions, which explained that unlike a crown worn by kings and queens, the high priest's crown was to be worn stretched around the forehead and back to each ear. Maimonides described it as being two fingerbreadths wide, or about one and a half inches; and most important of all, the crown was engraved in Hebrew with the words 'Holy to the Lord.'"

Jeff and Daniella looked at each other. "The same as ours."

"Yes, and most telling was how the letters were engraved."

Jeff remembered his conversation with Gogoli. "You mean raised, not stamped."

"Exactly. The Talmud describes how the letters were made. Maimonides writes that they would pound out the letters in a mold until their shapes were raised on the other side. Furthermore, our sages tell us that the crown had three small holes, two on each end, and one in the center along the upper edge. Dyed threads were run through these holes and the ends tied behind the high priest's head to keep the diadem secure. The one you have is a perfect match."

"So, is it the high priest's crown?"

Ephraim glanced at his watch. "Perhaps we can answer that at lunch. To keep my girth, it is essential I stick to a strict diet." He put the pieces back into the pouch. "If I were you, I'd keep these very close."

* * *

They exited the building and walked up the slight incline of the narrow cobblestoned street with Zvulen and one of his men positioned several paces behind. The sun was strong, and Selzer was already perspiring when he stopped outside a small, run-down café with a sign above the entrance that read Sula's. As they walked in, Selzer turned to his visitors and said, "Don't be fooled by outer appearances. It's what's inside that's important."

The two security men sat at one of the outdoor tables, shaded by a discolored umbrella, while Selzer and his guests entered. Inside there were three square tables and a counter displaying food. An old man in wrinkled Arab robes was seated in the corner, smoking a cigarette and drinking coffee from a demitasse. He gave a quick nod to Ephraim.

The kitchen was in the back. They were welcomed by Sula, a soft-spoken Arab, who moved two of the tables together to seat them. He and a busboy set out plates, glasses, and utensils, then brought out a flask of red wine, a pitcher of cold water, warm pita that came directly from the oven, plates of hummus and *sabih*—a sandwich of fried eggplant—and tahini.

Selzer ceremoniously draped a large napkin, which looked more like a small tablecloth, over his chest. He poured wine for everyone and began partaking, breaking apart the pita and dipping it into the hummus.

"Now, doctor, what were you asking? Oh, yes, is your diadem the crown that Aaron wore over thirty-five hundred years ago?" He took a sip of wine before answering his own question. "Very possibly. Unfortunately, carbon dating does not help date an inorganic substance, so I suspect the only way to definitively know is determine its behavior."

"Behavior?"

"Yes, Dr. Moss. You see, our sages tell us that whatever was held in the Ark will hold a wide range of mystical powers. For example, the high priest's clothing could forgive sin while the staff of Aaron and Moses could even alter the rules of nature itself. I am not an expert on those powers, since I deal more with market values, but there are others who do. What I am saying is that someday, if you ever test those powers, you will know if it's real."

They completed the meal in silence, Selzer's guests pondering the information. The waiter cleared the plates, and Sula brought Ephraim another napkin before serving him *malawach*, a flaky round pastry with a sweet caramel topping, and an order of *knafeh*, a shredded pastry with soft cheese and sweet syrup.

"Dessert, anyone?" Selzer asked.

Jeff and Daniella ordered iced coffees, but their host didn't hesitate with his choice.

"Sula," he said, glancing at the old man who'd greeted him when they came in, "bring my old friend a dessert and another café. Just put it on my bill."

The old man nodded, filled his fork with the malawach, and washed it down with a cup and a thank-you smile that revealed tobacco-stained teeth. The desserts were served, and Selzer washed his down with a cup of *café hafuch,* an "upside-down" cappuccino.

As if defensively, he said, "I'm at an age where I must enjoy whatever is left."

Jeff, feeling the urgency of their mission despite Selzer's serenity, raised the last major question. "Did the priest say where the scholar found the relics?"

"He did not. It was as if he was concerned that giving out too much information would put that person in danger."

"Because of the monetary value?"

"I don't think so, Dr. Moss. I asked if he was interested in selling the pieces, advising him that they would have immense value on the open market, but he politely refused. At first his refusal appeared counterintuitive. You see, I've been searching for the Temple Treasure all my life and believed that the real value in knowing where he found the crown was that it could lead to the rest of the treasure."

"Then what's counterintuitive? Is not the ultimate prize finding the treasure? Isn't that what this murder is all about?"

"I assumed that was the case, but after speaking to the young priest, I'm not so certain."

Selzer checked the time. "You must forgive me, but I have an appointment and must return to my office." Sula helped him out of his chair, and Selzer slowly stood, placing a handful of shekels on the table. "Perhaps you will allow me to give this some further thought. May I suggest that we continue our discussion with you as my dinner guests this evening, say the King David at eight?"

When they agreed, he gave a last word of caution. "Be very careful, young man. What you have may be worth more than you realize."

* * *

Sitting by the doorway of a small café within sight of Sula's, was a thin, dark-skinned young man with short, curly black hair and a groomed beard, wearing tinted glasses. He smoked a cigarette and silently played with a short-nosed revolver as if nonchalantly passing time. Across from him sat a bull-sized figure in priest's clothes, his face hidden by a newspaper, which when lowered revealed a wild bearded older man with a large tear-shaped gold earring hung from one ear. He sipped a glass of lemonade. "Put that away, Abdul-Sabur. You already failed at one job."

"Not my fault. I was told to get briefcase, that's all. How was I to know the stuff wasn't in it."

"Yes, but you were told there was to be no harm to anyone."

"I had no choice. I had to make sure I could get away safely."

"I'm speaking about murder. The radio reported that the driver of the Shalom car service was found dead in his limo at the base of a cliff, with a bullet through his head."

"Yeah, well, he didn't let me rent car for few hours, so he had accident."

The big man studied his counterpart. "This will be your last chance. When I told our employer what happened, he wanted to get rid of you. I told them I would be with you this time. I hope your family didn't misunderstand your character when you were named. Abdul-Sabur means 'servant of the patient'—why don't you show a little more of it."

The younger man angrily crushed his cigarette into the ash-tray while the priest seemed more concerned with the discussion taking place up the street. He lowered the pages of that morning's *Haaretz*, one of Israel's daily papers, observing Selzer and his departing guests. As Selzer and his man continued down the street, the others started in the opposite direction. The observers remained seated until the trio made their way up the partially stoned surface. The older man was speaking on his cell phone.

"The meeting's over." He listened, then: "*Si, signore*, but I'm certain he has the gold, the meeting was with a famous antiques appraiser. . . . *Si*, the woman is with the American, but now there is another problem—Mossad." Once again he listened, then spoke: "*Si, faremo come si chiede*—we will do as you ask." He returned the cell to his pocket and threw several shekels on the table. "We are to follow, but must be careful. The American will surely recognize you."

"This time I get him."

The older man gave him a troubled look as they followed the threesome. The street soon narrowed, crowded with tourists, street vendors, and the typical traffic of a business day in the Old City. They quickened their pace, pushing their way through pedestrians, keeping pace. When the trio paused before a leather goods shop, they also stopped. Jeff tried on a sheepskin jacket, and modeled it before a mirror. What he saw reflected was of greater significance than what he was trying on: standing in a nearby stall opposite, looking directly at him, was a face Jeff could not forget.

He turned to Zvulen. "That's him."

"Who?"

"The driver from the airport, I'm certain of it. He's behind us."

Zvulen kept looking forward. "OK, let's find out who he is, and who he's working for."

They left the stall and made their way up the street.

"Jeff, you and Danny walk directly behind me, blocking his view. I'm going to slip into one of the stalls and when he passes, I'll follow."

"Then what?"

"Up ahead, the street forks off to the right into a private dead-end alleyway. Once he follows you in, I'll come up from behind and grab him."

Jeff shook his head. "Let me do that. This is the guy who gave me a headache, it should be my honor."

Zvulen, sensing Jeff's resolve, nodded. "Fine, then we'll let him follow us until we reach the fork. We'll try to conceal ourselves, and hopefully he will enter the alley. That's when you can follow him in. But, best be careful, this guy will do anything to avoid failing a second time."

The three set out through the narrow aisles, Jeff, crouching slightly, in front of Zvulen and Daniella, who walked as if joined by the hip. As they passed a stall selling clothing, Jeff slipped behind the colorful displays. His companions increased their pace, trying to stay together, blocking the view from behind. Abdul, seeing their quickened steps, followed, forcing his way through the crowded passageway, trying to keep up. Jeff waited for him to pass, then followed, unaware that the man with the gold earring realized what was happening. The man took out his cell and made a call, but there was no answer. He tried again, but Abdul never took the call.

Ahead, Zvulen saw a large cart filled with cartons at the fork, momentarily blocking the entrance to the side street. He and Daniella quickly hid themselves behind the cart. Jeff watched as Abdul, having lost sight of his quarry, pushed ahead, trying to see around the people jammed before him. When he arrived at the fork he paused, looked both ways as if deciding which path to take, and then turned to the right, entering the small alleyway that led into a dead-ended courtyard partially paved with old, unevenly laid stone blocks.

The courtyard was deserted except for several alley cats meandering along the shaded sides of the buildings, meowing with hunger. Abdul drew his revolver and looked around, puzzled, searching for his prey. How could they have just disappeared? The space was shaped like a keyhole, and at its far end was a church. To its left was an old four-story dark gray stone building with faded letters spelling St. Diamana School engraved over its portico. To the right was a six-story cement apartment building that looked abandoned, its broken windows covered with the dust of time and neglect.

Abdul, his eyes alert for movement, walked toward the school, then saw that it was padlocked. He walked across the courtyard to the apartment building and tried opening the front doors, but they also were locked. Finally, he walked toward the church and entered through the large wooden doors. From a distance Jeff followed, removing the Sig Sauer from its holster. Silently, he made his way into the sanctuary, greeted by a musty odor and dark shadows outlined by the dull spectrum emanating through the stained-glass windows. As Jeff's eyes adjusted, he cautiously walked down the center aisle until he heard inaudible echoes. He stopped for a moment, trying to make out sounds and shapes, his fingers gripping the handle of his revolver. With a few more steps, he relaxed his grip, realizing the voices were those of tourists sitting in the front pews, listening to a guide explaining how the St. George Church was named after the man who killed a dragon.

Suddenly the voice was interrupted by a loud gunshot, and Jeff felt the splintering of a wooden pew in front of him. Panic filled the visitors as they shouted in fear. Jeff tried to determine the origin of the shot, and, crouching low, made his way between the pews toward the right outer aisle. Then a second and a third shot was fired and Jeff marked it as coming from the right outer aisle. Several of the frantic visitors ran up the center aisle toward the front doors while the rest remained on the floor. Jeff made his way between the pews, trying to reach the outer aisle when he heard a nearby movement. Before he could react, he felt a cold piece of steel against the top of his head.

"Drop gun."

Jeff had no choice. He let the gun fall to the floor.

"Now give me gold, and this time no mistakes."

Jeff realized he had no options. A host of images flashed through his mind as he followed Abdul's command. He removed the gold pieces from his pocket and, as Abdul reached for the package, a single shot rang out, then a sigh as if air was emitting from a perforated balloon, and Abdul fell to the floor.

"Jeff, you okay?" Zvulen's voice resonated through the silence.

Jeff realized what had happened. "I'm fine."

Zvulen and Daniella ran toward the outer aisle and saw Jeff kneeling over the dying man. The sun's rays outlined the fallen body with a translucency that suggested he was already being transported to his final destination.

"He's lost a great deal of blood." Jeff put his hand under the man's head. "Tell me why you wanted the gold."

Abdul struggled to speak. "He send me."

"Who sent you?"

The garbled speech was difficult to understand. "Big man in Rome, pay me lots of money . . . lots of money . . . lots of . . ."

There was no further confession. The pulse had completed its lifetime assignment.

From the church entrance a heavy-set bearded man with a gold earring, seeing what had happened, quietly made his exit. As he walked away he left a short message on a rarely used cell phone in Vatican City: *Abbiamo nuovamente fallito*—we failed, again.

* * *

Within minutes the Israeli police arrived from the station located at the Western Wall, called by the tourists who frantically hid from the gun shots. Jeff and Zvullen gave statements about the incident and when the interviews were completed, the three returned to Zvulen's car.

"That was close. Glad you're a good shot."

"Actually, I was quite surprised that I hit him. Not much light. Guess I got lucky."

Jeff looked at Zvulen, trying to figure if he was being truthful or joking. Daniella put her hand on Jeff's shoulder.

"He was kidding. He's a real marksman." She looked at Jeff seriously. "How you doing?"

"I'm fine. I'm under more stress doing open heart surgery then I was in there."

"Maybe we should take a break for the rest of the day."

"Absolutely not. There's still a lot to do, so let's get going."

* * *

9:00 a.m., New York

"Chief, the commissioner's on the phone."

DePalma took a deep breath before answering the call. "Yes, Josh."

"Anthony, glad to see you're working early. I'm meeting with the mayor in an hour, and he wants a full update. Anything new?"

DePalma took the yellow tennis ball he kept in his top drawer and began to squeeze it in his right hand.

"Nothing yet."

"Listen, Anthony, everyone's clamoring for a bit of news, including the mayor who's getting his own heat. You sure those security cameras saw nothing?"

DePalma knew everyone was under pressure on this. "We have a possible break, but it must remain between you, me, and the mayor for the time being."

"Of course, of course."

"There was a witness at the cardinal's residence, one of the priests. He may be able to identify the murderer."

"A witness? One of the priests? So you found Father John?"

"Father John? Not yet. It was someone else."

A broad smile crossed Fleck's round face. "Now that's progress, wonderful work, Anthony, wonderful work. I'll let the mayor know."

"Remember, it's confidential. Only the mayor."

"Absolutely."

Commissioner Fleck ended the call and sank back into the comfort of his black leather chair, rhythmically tapping his pen to the sounds of John Coltrane's 1957 album *Blue Train*, wondering if he should make the next call. Surely no harm, and why waste an opportunity to show appreciation for the support the mayor and he received in the last election—and hopefully, the next. He pressed the automatic dial and heard Quinn's voice asking for the required message.

"Thought you should know; we have a witness who can identify the murderer. Apparently one of your priests. Who else was there besides Father John?"

If anything good could be said about Police Commissioner Fleck, it was his taste in music.

It would take several hours before Monsignor Quinn played back Fleck's message. He would replay it many times before it was determined how to respond. Was one of Quinn's priests truly a witness? If so, the situation must be dealt with, but who could it be? Surely, if not Father John, there could only be one. The monsignor made his decision and placed a call.

* * *

4:00 p.m., Mt. Scopus, Hebrew University

Zvulen parked his car at the entrance to the Rabin Building, Faculty of Humanities, Hebrew University and remained observing as Daniella led Jeff through the front doors and into a maze of hallways that brought them to an office that read: Daniella Teller, PhD, Professor of Ancient Jewish Studies. The office was decorated in a warm and cheerful combination of colors. There were two comfortable-looking tan leather arm chairs, and a walnut desk behind which was a soft brown leather swivel chair. A credenza was positioned against the wall showcasing family pictures of Daniella as a young girl on a pony, one photo of her parents in khaki shorts at an archeological site, and a third with two handsome young men in uniforms flashing large smiles with cigars in their mouths. Jeff glanced at the floor to ceiling bookshelves that lined the room on three walls.

Daniella stood beside him. "When I heard those gun shots, I was worried about you."

"To be honest, I thought it was all over, but glad Zvullen was there." He looked at her for a moment, then walked over to the large window that presented a spectacular scene overlooking the rolling desert hills of Judea.

She pointed out into the horizon. "It is peaceful, isn't it? Beyond those hills is where I've spent a great deal of my academic life—the Qumran Caves, the Dead Sea, Masada—all carefully carried out archeological digs. That's where the scrolls were found. Now archeologists are turning their attention to the Temple Mount, collecting scientific evidence to prove Solomon's Temple was there fifteen hundred years before Mohammed."

Jeff's mind quickly transferred from the crisis of the morning to the mystery at hand. "But isn't that historical fact?"

"You have no idea the extent our neighbors will go to revise historical fact."

"But, I thought no one's allowed to dig on the Temple Mount."

"We didn't, the Arabs did it for us. In 1999, the Waqf, the Muslim trust that manages the site, illegally bulldozed a huge pit in the Temple Mount to destroy evidence that the Jews had rights to Jerusalem. To dispose of their dig, they dumped about nine thousand tons of its soil into the nearby Kidron Valley. Israeli archeologists found the soil, moved it to a safe area, and are sifting through it to find evidence of the Temple Mount's history."

"Did they find anything related to the treasure?"

"Not the treasure, but certainly evidence of the Temple being there. These days, most scholars believe the treasure lies in Rome, somewhere in the depths of the Vatican's Vault. Even your evidence suggests everything was in Rome: Wasn't it the home to Cellini? The home to Clement the Seventh? The city where Fabrizzi met the scholar? And even where my father was last seen alive?"

"And you think the Vatican is hiding fifty tons of gold, silver, and sacred objects in its vaults?"

"That's not what my father believed, nor I."

"Is that the journal article that Ephraim alluded to?"

"Yes, it was just published."

"Tell me about Rome."

"After Rome defeated Greece, it took over Israel. As long as Israel paid taxes to Rome, it remained autonomous, but when the Jews refused to continue paying the increasing amounts, a full-blown revolution erupted. The fighting was heavy, tens of thousands were killed as the Jews overran the Roman garrison in Jerusalem and defeated the Syrian Legion with a loss of six thousand Roman soldiers. With Rome's losses mounting, the Roman general Vespasian was ordered to end the rebellion, and Titus, his son, became second-in-command. Vespasian invaded the Galilee in the year 67 and ravaged the countryside until, following months of costly fighting, Rome prevailed. The battle for Jerusalem ensued, and when Vespasian became emperor of Rome, Titus was given the order to destroy Jerusalem. It has been reported that one million Jews were killed and ninety thousand were exiled to Rome as slaves."

"And the treasure?"

"Titus brought it back to Rome." She walked to one of the bookcases and removed a volume of Josephus's *Jewish Wars*. "Josephus described how a certain Jewish priest named Phineas, to avoid being sold into slavery, aided the Romans in carrying away some of the sacred treasures, including the menorahs, tables, bowls, and platters, all made of solid gold. It is said that Phineas even helped the Romans find the high priests' vestments."

Jeff checked his notes. "Including Aaron's crown?"

"Appears so, and according to Josephus, those temple contents were brought to ships in the port of Caesarea and transported back to Rome."

"And you believe this to be true?"

Daniella nodded. "I've been to Rome, and his description mirrors the events portrayed on the huge victory arch that was completed following Titus's death in 81 CE. Those engravings clearly depict Roman soldiers carrying the golden menorah, the silver trumpets, and the table filled with jewels on their shoulders, all of which, according to Josephus, were displayed in Rome's Temple of Peace. Apparently, it remained there until 500 CE."

"And then?"

Daniella smiled. "Ah, that is the question: Are the holy vessels really buried deep within the Vatican vaults or do they lie somewhere else?"

Jeff replied, half joking, "Maybe someone should ask the pope."

"They already did, but so far there's been no response."

"Why not? Surely we live in a more ecumenical age."

"I can think of two reasons. The first is based on the Jewish belief that when the menorah is returned to Jerusalem, the Messiah is to appear."

Jeff's eyes widened in surprise. "You mean the Church is concerned that the Jewish Messiah is the true one? Then I don't blame them for being concerned."

"Why's that?"

"Because when the Messiah arrives we'll ask if it's his first or second visit."

Daniella smiled. "Or there may be a second reason."

She opened her desk drawer and removed a copy of the new journal. "This article is based largely on my father's research. It seems to have caused quite a sensation in the academic community. Your assignment is to read it. It provides an alternate explanation as to why the Vatican is not releasing the treasure."

"And that is?"

"Because it's no longer in Rome!"

* * *

They returned to the car in silence. Zvulen read the bewilderment on Jeff's face. "You look like you have more questions now than before."

"This woman has led me on an expedition from one end of the world to the other. I'm afraid I know as much now as when I began."

Daniella responded sympathetically. "Welcome to Find the Temple Treasure Club. But for now, I need some rest. We're scheduled to have dinner at eight at the King David."

Jeff laughed. "I think we'd find more answers dining with King David than at the King David."

* * *

5:00 p.m., Rome

Bronislaw Dunajski walked stoically along the Via dei Corridori to his modest apartment on the Via Erba and sat pensively at his desk and looked out at the city. Events seemed to be running out of control, and he tried to reassess. A young priest murdered in the cardinal's residence in New York—could this be the same young priest who . . .? He pushed the thread of thoughts away to deal with another troubling issue, one that he could not get out of his mind. It had been two days since his confrontation with Cardinal Jarogniew following the cabinet meeting, and he had chosen not to respond, realizing how different their positions were theologically and knowing well that the word "compromise" was not in his vocabulary. And yet, they had much in common.

Bronislaw recalled how he and his younger brother, Michael, were children in a small village in Poland. His parents were involved in the labor movement, and after Germany invaded the country the Nazis began rounding up anyone even indirectly involved, whether communist or not, and sent them to concentration camps. When his parents were warned that they were to be arrested, they arranged for the boys to be given to suitable families until they could be reunited. Bronislaw was given to a family in Warsaw, but when they refused to take both boys, Michael was given to a family in the countryside.

Bronislaw often had dreams of the day his mother delivered him to his new family, how she whispered he should be strong, have faith in God, and always remember his little brother. How often he remembered her final kiss as she left him standing in his new home, tears flooding her eyes before the sound of the door locked him into his new life. The reunion with his parents never came, nor did he ever see his brother again, but he always knew that the memory of that kiss would stay with him forever. That kiss, those words, her tears—it was all that remained of his past.

After the war, Bronislaw was placed in a Catholic orphanage and sent to a Catholic school, where he met Ludvik Jarogniew. The two boys grew up together. They were the same age, lived in the same orphanage, shared the same grade. They became fast friends, both were bright and both excelled in sports. But as they grew into their teens, their personalities and interests diverged, and their friendship faltered. Bronislaw's scholarly aptitude made him top in his class, a situation that Jarogniew's increasing competitiveness could not deal with.

Bronislaw was a modest, soft-spoken boy as he grew into a lanky six-foot-four frame. He had a gaunt face with sharp features and an aquiline nose, with a high forehead that receded back to a shock of dark hair that reminded one of a beleaguered Abraham Lincoln sans beard. But perhaps his most defining feature was a birthmark in the form of a port wine nevus that extended for several centimeters down the left side of his neck, hidden from view under his clothing. He was always the scholar, never without an open book, interested in nature, science, and philosophy.

Ludvik Jarogniew was not as tall but broader, with squared shoulders and a full chest. In school, he was motivated to lead, if not by popularity then by intimidation, and he loosely organized a group of students to do his bidding. For different reasons, the two young men found their calling in the Church. To Jarogniew, being a member of the clergy brought the respect and wealth he desired, and the almost military manner in which the Church held sway over its people fit his nature. He insisted on total loyalty, be it to himself or to the institution, demanding adherence to precedent in religious and social attitudes. He could not countenance any questioning of authority, especially his own. Jarogniew instinctively understood the uses of power, and with the help of a senior cleric who saw great potential in the young man, he advanced through the church hierarchy. It was this cleric who trained him to understand that religion could be used as a means to an end, ends that were more concerned about political power than spiritual growth.

Bronislaw's passage to Catholicism came later. His conversion came not from the quest for power but from an inquisitive mind that sought answers from all quarters. As a teenager, he questioned life and death, morality, and man's role within the universe—questions whose answers were not supplied by his Catholic upbringing or the god they proposed; he soon dismissed religion as irrelevant. By the time he went to college he was an agnostic, studying medieval art, philosophy, and theology at universities in Warsaw, Berlin, and Cambridge until, one day, as he walked beside the Thames, he became entranced by a female fish swimming with her young. It was then that he experienced a profound revelation: that all of life followed the same inherent instructions, one force, one universal creator that gave the breath of being to all that existed. That night, for the first time in years, he knelt beside his bed with his rosary beads and prayed. His spiritual conversion followed. He joined the Jesuits and began training for the priesthood, was ordained in Rome, and received a doctorate in theology at the Gregorian University.

The 1960s was a time of great change in theological considerations and sweeping revision resulted from the Second Vatican Council. His writings soon indicated that he would become a major Catholic scholar. He sought new understandings of how the church, after centuries of hostility to modern thought, should relate to other faiths and to religious liberty. His investiture with forty-eight other scarlet-robed cardinals took place in Rome in 1989.

As he sipped a glass of water he was overcome with a sudden yet unusual sense of fatigue, a weariness not resulting from the walk home but from the prospect of the arguments he knew lay ahead with Jarogniew. It would be a long battle, but he understood that its outcome would influence the future of the Church he cared so greatly about. His eyes began to close as fatigue began its effect, and he rose from his chair, removed his outer cloak and shoes, and lay down on his bed, protected overhead by a simple wooden crucifix nailed to the wall. As he napped, his mind recalled the great moment when he climbed the steps to the pope's golden throne to receive his biretta, the red silk hat of office, and embraced the pope. Within moments, he was asleep.

* * *

Pine Bush, New York

The hamlet of Pine Bush lies at the juncture of Orange and Ulster Counties in New York State, about eighty miles north of Manhattan. Monsignor Sean O'Reilly's home was situated several miles outside the village on a seldom-used dirt road that served the few surrounding homes. It was built by his grandfather, who settled there in the early 1900s, and included almost a hundred acres of dense forest and a stream whose banks would fill when the winter snows melted from the Shawangunk Mountains that rose above. It had served as a summer retreat for the O'Reilly clan, but over time the family sold off parcels of the land, and the house was used less and less until O'Reilly bought it outright from his remaining cousins.

On a hot, sunny afternoon a black Esplanade drove slowly up the dry, dusty dirt road surrounded by tree-lined fields. It passed an old barn with decaying walls and perforated roof and came to a stop on a short, somewhat overgrown driveway leading to the house, an edifice faced with an assortment of rocks of varied shapes and shades. A thick-set muscular individual with tinted glasses and a shaved head, wearing a well-tailored dark suit, quietly exited the car, preparing to carry out his instructions. He perused the area before removing a large black duffel bag from the back of the vehicle. The ground was uneven, and the man walked with a noticeable limp as he made his way along the perimeter of the house, waving away the whirling clouds of summer gnats swarming about. As he approached the rear of the house, he could hear the distant sounds of a creek's gurgling waters. He passed a solid wooden door and continued circling the house. He noticed a large picture window through which a direct view of Sam's Point, the highest spot on the Shawangunk Ridge, could be seen. From the cover of a cluster of scrub oaks he saw Monsignor O'Reilly sitting in a lounge chair, reading. A smile crossed the man's lips, and he made his way to the door and knocked gently. Within moments he heard a voice declare, "Coming." O'Reilly opened the door. "Yes, may I help . . ."

It took a moment before fear iced the monsignor's face.

"What are you doing here?"

"*Missit me Dominus*, the Lord has sent me."

"How did you know where I lived?"

"You showed me."

"What are you talking about?"

"I waited outside the bar after you met with the doctor. That was a terrible mistake, talking to him. I followed you across the bridge and up here. Anyway, after such a long trip, you should at least invite me in."

O'Reilly tried to close the door, but it was too late. The man pushed his way in, walked into the living room, and carefully placed his duffel bag on a blue velour-covered sofa.

"What do you want?" The monsignor's voice trembled as he spoke, and drops of perspiration began to form on his forehead.

"Oh, I think you know." He spoke slowly, in an almost soothing manner, and with chilling assurance: the coolness of a professional about to carry out a practiced procedure. He scanned the inside of the house, taking in the unadorned living space with its stone fireplace on one wall and an open kitchen and dining area on the far side.

"I see you're here alone."

"I don't require anyone else."

"I don't blame you. There's a great deal of solace in privacy. Did not Luke write that Jesus went to a mountainside and spent the night alone, praying to God?"

A long silence followed.

"I'd like you to leave. If you don't, I'll call the police."

"I don't think calling the police would be a wise choice."

The monsignor moved to pick up his cell on the table next to the chair, but his visitor knocked the cell to the floor.

"You're not going to need it, and besides, by the time the police arrived it would be far too late. Now please, sit down, I have several things to do before we can get underway."

The monsignor watched as the man unzipped the bag and, with great deliberation, removed a pair of black sweat pants and a black hooded sweatshirt, and changed into them.

"What are you doing?"

"Patience, my friend."

He took out a pair of latex rubber gloves and, like a physician after scrubbing for an operation, carefully pulled them on.

In the silence of the macabre scene, fear spread through the monsignor's body, the front of his trousers already flooding.

"It was you who killed that young priest."

"Yes, you remember. Unfortunate for you that you do, but—no need to worry, they say there's no memory in death."

The monsignor jumped up, trying to run toward the door, but the man threw a punch that landed across the monsignor's chin, throwing him back into the chair. From the bag, the man removed a rope and tied the monsignor's hands behind him, tied his feet together, and bound him to the chair.

O'Reilly shouted, tears flowing down his face. "No, don't! Why are you doing this?"

"I do God's work."

With that he removed a roll of silver tape and placed a strip of it across his victim's mouth, quietly saying, "Silence is the Lord's music, and you are the orchestra."

The man then picked up his knife.

"This may hurt, but only for a moment. Think of Abraham's son, Isaac, as his father lifted the blade."

He made a four-inch cut along the soft underside of O'Reilly's arm, and blood poured out. The monsignor started violently, the chair rocking, his eyes wide, his shouts of terror muffled beneath the tape. His executioner, with the care and precision of a surgeon, dipped his gloved index finger into the bright red liquid and wrote the words *Soli Deo Gloria* on a piece of rotted wood.

"Now, because you have sinned in the eyes of our Lord Jesus Christ and his Church, we will begin your path to atonement."

* * *

King David Hotel, Jerusalem

At ten to eight, Zvulen let Jeff off at the entrance to the King David Hotel, and parked his car along the circular driveway. The hotel was a palatial European-designed pinkish limestone building. Jeff passed the security check in front of the large front doors and entered the expansive lobby with its motifs of past civilizations from Assyrian to Egyptian. As he made his way through the lobby, observing the ambiance and the international nature of its clientele, the words *dignified* and *serene* came to mind—words from a bygone era of grace and charm. It made him wonder if the world was spinning too fast these days for grace and charm.

The evening was drawing on, and he was looking forward to dinner and any further information Ephraim Selzer might provide.

He also found he was looking forward to something else—to something he hadn't felt in a long time.

The La Regence dining room was crowded with families and businessmen, some in suits, most without, some wearing the traditional Jewish head covering, many not. As he was the first of his party to arrive, he went to the bar, ordered a scotch, neat, and walked out onto the veranda that looked out over the well-lit landscaped gardens, green lawns, and pine trees that bordered the long rectangular swimming pool brightened by its underwater beams. As he raised his eyes he was taken in by the sweeping vistas of Jerusalem's minarets, domes, and the walls of the Old City, its stones reflecting the last of the setting sun's rays.

"Beautiful, isn't it?"

Startled, he turned to see Daniella, whom he hadn't heard approach. She was wearing a soft white cotton sleeveless dress that contrasted with her bronze skin and long brunette hair.

"Beautiful," he managed to repeat, not knowing whether he was responding to the view or the woman at his side. "That's a great deal of history."

She looked out across the valley. "Yes, a city on a hill whose streets at one time or another were filled with Canaanites, Hebrews, Greeks, Romans, Crusaders, Muslims, Turks, Brits, and now Israelis. There are untold stories hidden within those old walls." She spoke in a slow, gentle rhythm, part professorial and part woman, which, as the minutes passed, increasingly became more of the latter.

"And the Temple Mount?"

Daniella smiled. "The Bible calls it Mount Moriah. Our sages tell us it's where the creation of the world took place and where Adam was formed. The Torah describes how Abraham was to sacrifice his son on this mountain, where Jacob dreamed of angels going up and down a ladder, and the prophets reveal that this is where the Holy of Holies, the sacred Arks of the First and Second Temples, were built. Yes, a great deal of history."

"It looks different from here than when we were up close this afternoon."

"Isn't that the fate of history, always to be interpreted differently, depending upon the perspective from which you are viewing it? But, as long as the wall stands, it symbolizes the remains of the Second Temple destroyed by the Romans in CE 72. That's why this generation of Jews is so blessed, for it was almost two thousand years since Jews last possessed the land that God had given us, until now. That's how long we've waited to return." She paused, her speech softened. "If only the last generation had been so blessed, six million more would have been here, including my parent's families. Instead, they are all buried in the ashes of Auschwitz, Treblinka, and the other hells that remind us of man's depravity. That is why we must never lose it again."

Jeff felt the anguish in her voice, the determination, and yet the hope. Now he understood why they call someone born in Israel a Sabra—a prickly pear, hard and unyielding on the outside, yet soft and nourishing within.

They walked back to their table as Ephraim Selzer was being seated.

"Ah, my young friends, thank you for joining me."

They ordered drinks and studied the menu. Their host suggested the lamb sweetbreads from the charcoal grill, the green salad with lemon vinaigrette, the beef entrecote, and ordered the best wine in the house. Again, he insisted on dessert, reemphasizing that it was the true purpose of any meal, and ordered the warm chardonnay zabaglione, talking his guests into sharing the apple sorbet.

When the last of the dishes were removed, Selzer ordered an after-dinner liqueur.

"You know, Dr. Moss," Selzer reflected quietly, "in answer to your question as to why the priest was murdered, I recall something you should know." He sat back and clasped his hands around his middle. "He said that what was given to him was more valuable than gold, as if there was something else about the medals and crown that made it so valued. He said he hoped to include his conclusions in his thesis, but there were still clues in the notebook to figure out."

"Clues in a notebook?"

"Yes, clues, which, when understood, would lead to the ultimate prize. It's just that what was written was not what it appeared to be."

"And that was it? What was written was not what it appeared to be?"

"Yes, Dr. Moss, that was it. Nothing else. As I said, he was reticent about giving out information. He was afraid of something."

Daniella leaned forward and spoke in a whisper. "And he never mentioned what it was that he feared?"

"Take it from an old man who's lived a great deal and observed many things, there is one thing to fear more than anything else, more than the worth of any gold treasure."

Jeff looked closely at Selzer. "And that is?"

"Power. Once you have power, everything, even gold, will follow. There is an old Arab saying: 'If power is for sale, sell your mother to buy it. You can always buy her back.'"

"And he never showed the notebook to you?"

"I don't believe he brought it with him. I invited him out for dinner to continue our discussion, but he had a ticket for the opera and said he couldn't miss it."

Daniella seemed confused. "But he came to Israel to see you."

"I believe I gave him all he wished to know."

"But what was so important about an opera that he couldn't miss it?"

"All he told me was that its ending was the beginning. He left the next morning."

"'The ending was the beginning'?" Jeff looked at him, bewildered.

"Those were his precise words. I never understood their meaning. Perhaps someday you will."

"So where do we go from here?" Jeff asked.

Selzer took a thoughtful final sip from his glass. "If I was a betting man, I would wager the answer lies in the relationship between the medals and the crown. Why were they found together, yet concealed? What is so important that is worth murder?"

"Any idea where to find that?"

"I suppose I would start in his notebook. If I had your energy I'd go to Rome with you. But be very careful. What you have and what you are looking for appears to be of great importance to others, and as long as you have it, you will be in a great deal of danger."

Selzer signed for the check, and they rose to leave.

"By the way, Ephraim, what opera was he going to see?"

"Opera? Why, it was the Israeli Opera's production of *Tosca*."

The soft ring of Jeff's cell interrupted the conversation.

"Jeff, its Darlene. The chief wants to know if you can get back here. We have a problem."

"What's going on?"

"Monsignor O'Reilly was murdered."

"Murdered?" The word brought quick glances from those within earshot.

"When?"

"Dr. Gogoli figured about noon, at his upstate home. And . . . with a stake through his heart."

Jeff swallowed hard. "Okay, I'll catch the next flight out." He turned to Selzer. "I'm afraid your warning may have proved prophetic. There's been a murder of a potential witness. I'm afraid I have to leave."

He and Daniella exchanged looks, the kind with a meaning not yet expressed. Hesitantly, they said goodbye. As he walked away he heard her voice.

"If you see Antonio, thank him for the referral."

Jeff smiled. "I'll do that."

* * *

Zvulen drove Jeff to the inn where they found police cars blanketing the street, their red rotating lights adding to the drama of the scene. Alarmed, they quickened their steps through the open front door. Zvulen stopped to speak to several of the policemen gathered at the entrance, while Jeff walked toward the young woman who worked behind the desk. She was sitting on the floor, her back against the wall, knees drawn as if trying to bury her face. When she saw Jeff, she got up and ran to him, tears rolling down her face, and blurted out what had happened. "Dr. Moss, Amir was attacked by a man who wanted to get into your room."

Jeff tried to calm her. "Is he okay?"

"He was hurt. They took him to Hadassah Hospital."

"And you?"

"I'm fine, but the man was looking for you."

"Who was he?"

"Never saw him before. I already told the police, he was a big man with a beard, and he had a large tear-shaped gold earring hanging from one ear. He came in asking if you were here. I told him we don't give out information on our guests, but he grabbed the register to see your room number. He started up to the second floor, and Amir went to stop him, but the man threw him down the stairs. He broke into your room. I called the police, but he got away before they arrived."

Jeff went up the stairs, followed by Zvulen. The room had been ransacked. "You said they'd be back, and you were right."

Jeff threw his few belongings into his overnight bag, went down the stairs, and checked the time. "It's ten o'clock. Can we make one quick stop and still catch the flight out of Ben Gurion?"

Zvulen nodded. "The hospital? Sure, but it will be close."

"I have no choice; I must see how he is."

* * *

11:00 p.m., Rome

The little-used cell phone rang as Cardinal Jarogniew was preparing for bed. "There's been another accident. The witness in New York was visited by the Angel of Death."

* * *

Ben Gurion Airport, midnight

Zvulen parked directly in front of the departure section, flashing his credentials to security. They entered the building as the flight announcement was coming over the loudspeakers. "El Al flight 1, departing from Tel Aviv at 12:20 now final boarding from Terminal 3."

Jeff returned the gun to Zvulen, rushed to purchase a ticket, and led by Zvulen, quickly passed through security, where they said their goodbyes.

The investment in business class for the eleven-hour flight was well worth it. Passenger class, as usual on El Al flights between Israel and the United States, was filled with families, and that inevitably included crying babies. Even in the relative silence, once the plane reached cruising altitude, he found it difficult to sleep. His mind whirled over what he had learned; and now there was the murder of Monsignor O'Reilly. At least Amir would be fine. His wounds consisted of a black eye, superficial contusions, and a slight break in the collarbone that would mend without the need for surgery.

Jeff took out the article that Daniella had given him and read the opening sentence, picturing her as if she was speaking to him.

"You will not find the Temple Treasure in the depths of Vatican City. You will not even find it in Rome."

He ordered a club soda and began to read.

The opening sentence clearly delineated the essence of her thesis, and the article went on to support it with historical references.

She quoted a Christian monk from Constantinople, Theophanes the Confessor, who lived from about 760 to 817 and had written a history of events that spanned the years 284 to 813. In it, he described how, in 455, Geiseric the Lame, king of the Germanic tribe of the Vandals, overran Rome, loaded the treasures on a boat, and took them to Carthage, his North African capital. Jeff paused for a moment as he realized the origin of the word *vandalism*. Then, in 533, the Byzantine general Flavius Belisarius led a crusade to recapture the Roman provinces of North Africa. He seized the Temple Treasure from a Vandal ship fleeing a harbor in Algeria and shipped it to Constantinople, the capital of Byzantium. When Belisarius arrived in Constantinople, the Emperor Justinian rewarded him for his victory with a huge procession and, as with Titus, the spoils of the Temple of Jerusalem were paraded for all to see.

Jeff let the last drops of club soda run onto his tongue. *So, Justinian had the Temple Treasure in Constantinople, today's Istanbul.* He followed Daniella's evidence as she built her argument like a prosecutor arguing a criminal case. Using numerous sources, she disclosed that Justinian was not only a great emperor who ruled over Africa and Byzantium, but also a great believer in signs and spiritual powers. She hypothesized that Justinian saw it as an omen that whenever a great empire took control of the Temple Treasure and removed it from Jerusalem, that empire failed. It happened with Babylonia, then Persia, then Rome, and finally the empire of the Vandals. Daniella deduced that Justinian didn't want the same catastrophe to befall his empire, so he shipped the entire Temple Treasure back to Jerusalem before the wrath of the Hebrew God was brought to bear on him.

But that wasn't all. Following her father's research, Daniella showed that when Jerusalem came under attack by the Persians in 614, Modestus, the new patriarch of the city, saved the Temple Treasure by having it moved to the grounds of the Monastery of Saint Theodosius and buried somewhere in the sands of the Judean Desert. Daniella concluded that Solomon's Treasure remains in those sands, never yet found.

So that was the rest of the story! Jeff was amazed. If she was correct, the Temple Treasure was back in Israel, hidden for the past fourteen hundred years!

Jeff put the journal aside, assessing the new information. If her thesis was accurate, then what treasure remained in Rome?

What was it that Father Fabrizzi had found? His eyes began to close as sleep had its way. He laced his hand over the package of gold in his jacket and shifted his chair back. As his mind began to ratchet down, he realized he was no longer searching for the Temple Treasure in Rome, at least not in terms of priceless gold and silver. The gold medals and crown were leading to something else, but what? What was it that he was supposed to be looking for? What was the murderer looking for? Whatever it was, it was sleep that overcame his mind's search and put all questions to rest.

PART TWO

JULY 7

9:00 a.m., New York

The heat settled like a thermal blanket over New York. The roads were crowded with the usual morning traffic along with the addition of late holiday returnees. Jeff's taxi, driven by the typical harried driver, weaved its way from the airport to DePalma's office in lower Manhattan.

"Just got in." Jeff placed the gold pieces on the desk. "Thanks for the loan, but I have the images on my cell. The real thing is causing a lot of trouble."

"So I heard. Sorry to cut your trip short."

"No, I found everything I needed to know. Tell me about O'Reilly."

The chief leaned back in his swivel chair. "We found him like Father Fabrizzi, tortured, staked, and the sign hanging from a rope around his neck—the same MO. The place is pretty isolated, but one of the neighbors noticed smoke and called for help."

"Evidence?"

"Nothing, no DNA and no security cameras to check. Who knew the two of you had met?"

"No one that I know of, and O'Reilly wouldn't have said anything. He took me to some quiet bar up on the West Side."

"But someone must have known something."

Jeff thought for a moment. "The only time I mentioned it was in the message I left you."

"Well, somehow it got out."

"That's for sure. My briefcase was stolen, my head used for a drum, a few bullets came my way, and a young man at our hotel was attacked when my hotel room was broken into. Who even knew what I was carrying? Zvulen believes there's an informant back here."

"A leak? But who?"

DePalma shifted the chair to the upright position, cupped his hands under his chin and remained silent, until Jeff noticed a change in expression.

"What?"

"This may have been my fault."

"What do you mean?"

"Maybe it's time to have a talk with the commissioner. He's the only one *I* mentioned it to, and I told him to keep it between us and the mayor."

"And you think he would have said something?"

"Who knows, but someone wants those gold pieces and wants them bad. Which means you better let this Danny fellow you met in Jerusalem be aware."

A shot of concern ran through Jeff. "That Danny fellow turned out to be a Daniella, and a very sharp one at that."

DePalma seemed surprised. "Really? Brains or looks?"

"Both."

A slow smile spread across DePalma's face. "Well now, I haven't heard you speak about a woman in those terms recently."

"Yeah, I'm beginning to realize that."

* * *

2:00 p.m.

There was no answer on Siglione's office phone. Jeff called the main number at the Numismatic Building and was told he had suffered a heart attack but was resting comfortably in New York Hospital. Immediately he took a taxi up to Sixty-Eighth Street and York Avenue. Siglione was lying in bed, looking pale and fatigued when Jeff entered the small single room on the cardiac floor. The eyes brightened when he recognized the visitor.

"You're back. How did you know what had happened?"

"I spoke to your office. I heard you had a little episode."

"The doctor says too much stress. He wants me here another day or two."

"You mean you're working too hard?"

"I suppose. He said as long as I take my pills on time I'll be fine." Siglione reached for a glass of water and took a short drink, clearing his throat. "Tell me, Dr. Moss, did you see Daniella?"

"I did, and she was very helpful."

"Good, and she's okay?"

"She's very okay."

A faint smile formed on the old man's lips. "I thought the two of you might enjoy working together."

Jeff saw where Siglione was going. He turned his attention to the framed photo of a young priest next to his bed.

"Whose picture is that?"

"That's my son Angelo. He's a good boy, but I worry about him. I try calling him, but he rarely calls back. He's been very busy these days working at the diocese."

Jeff helped him adjust his pillows.

Signorelli continued. "And what happened with the gold?"

"Daniella took me to meet with Ephraim Selzer. Do you know him?"

"From way back. What did he think?"

"He thought that diadem could actually be Aaron's crown."

Siglione's eyes widened. "If that's true, what you have is priceless."

"He felt its importance was something other than its monetary value."

Siglione put his hand to his chin for a moment. "Then what's worth all this murder?"

Jeff eyed the front page of the *Post* on a cart next to the bed: SECOND PRIEST SLAIN.

"He thought power was more valuable than money. Possibly something to do with ancient mysticism."

Siglione scratched his head as if trying to recall something. "I have an old friend who is quite knowledgeable about those things, also a collector of antiquities, but long since retired. His name is Levy Shemtov, and he lives in a brownstone down on Charles Street in the West Village. If you call him, perhaps he can help."

A nurse entered the room and tried to present a stern face to her patient. "Are you talking? I told you to get some rest."

Jeff apologized, thanked Siglione for the reference, and made his good-byes.

* * *

3:00 p.m., the West Village

The taxi left Jeff off on the corner of Fourth Street and Sixth Avenue, a few blocks from the recently constructed promenade along the Hudson River Piers. It had been a while since he had last

visited this part of the city, and as he walked through the West
Village he was reminded more of a quaint nineteenth-century
European hamlet than the bedlam that occurs in the rest of Manhattan. Gone was the practical planning of streets numbered in
grid-like order that provides the precision-based business foundation that demands speed in the rest of Manhattan. Instead, one
found cobblestoned streets laid out in haphazard fashion that
never made sense to Jeff's scientific mind. Instead of the ubiquitous modern Manhattan skyscrapers, old brownstones shaded
by the diffused branches of elms and oaks predominated. Yet,
he couldn't help but notice the incursion of high-priced shops,
hip pubs, enticing bistros, and luxury apartment buildings with
sweeping vistas of the river already diluting the old nineteenth-
century artistic charm.

Levy Shemtov resided on the first floor of a modest four-story
brownstone. Jeff rang the outer bell, was buzzed in, and walked
through an opened door from which he heard a friendly voice.

"Dr. Moss, I presume. Thank you for calling. Antonio's an old
friend."

Shemtov was a short thin man, with remaining wisps of ashen
hair, a long gray beard, wearing black trousers, a white dress
shirt open at the collar, and a large black skullcap.

"Please, come in."

Jeff entered a narrow hallway filled with old black-and-white
partially discolored photographs in thin dark frames, some of
which were hanging askew. Jeff followed his host into a dimly
lit living room simply furnished with a couch partially covered
with a scarlet silk throw and two high-backed chairs. Along two
of the walls were rows of dark wooden bookshelves. An old glass
chandelier hung overhead and, in the rear, a large single window
overlooked a small garden illuminated by the afternoon sun. A
wooden desk was located beside the window, and on it were two
glasses and a pitcher of iced tea in which floated leaves of mint.
Jeff was directed to sit in an oversized soft chair facing the desk.
Shemtov sat behind it.

"I thought you might like a cold drink. The mint is fresh from
the garden." He filled the two glasses. "How is Antonio? I fear it's
been a while."

"He'll be fine," Jeff replied as he sank uncomfortably into the
soft, bulky seat. "He had a slight heart problem but is recuperat-
ing nicely."

"That's good to know. Now, how can I help?"

"I'm trying to determine if there could be something in Rome that would be of greater value than the Temple Treasure, especially if it's no longer there."

Shemtov smiled. "I see you've been reading the work of the Tellers."

"Yes, sir, I have. But what if someone found a gold piece with Hebraic letters that brought you back to before the First Temple?"

Shemtov studied Jeff's face. "And this piece was protected to the death?"

Jeff looked at the older man as if Shemtov knew more than was spoken. "Then, I would try to find where that piece came from."

"But what could be so valuable if not the Temple Treasure?"

Shemtov leaned back in his chair. "There are many ways to value a treasure."

"Ephraim said the same thing."

"Yes, I know. We're a fraternity of the few. Ephraim called for my opinion before he met you for dinner."

Jeff smiled. "He said power was more valuable than gold."

Shemtov sipped his iced tea. "Fine observation. So you want to know what power could be hidden in Rome that makes even the greatest ancient treasure insignificant?"

He put on his glasses and walked to a row of bookshelves. Selecting several, he placed them on his desk.

"Assuredly the Vatican has vast fortunes in art and their own treasures of gold and silver—but power?"

"Ephraim suggested a mystical power."

Shemtov opened a large book whose cover was well worn and whose pages were yellowed with age and use.

"This is the Gemara, a book that details arguments that discuss and debate Talmudic laws by Jewish sages more than fifteen hundred years ago."

As he perused the pages he stopped at one, and his index finger moved down the lines as he spoke.

> Rabbi Eliezer earned the gratitude of the Roman Emperor
> and was allowed into the royal treasury to choose his
> reward. While inside, he saw many of the Temple vessels
> which had been carried off by the Romans after they
> destroyed the Temple, including the Showbread table,

the Menorah, the veil of the Ark and the vestments of the anointed priest. And Rabbi Eliezer said: I saw the crown in Rome, and the words "*Kodesh Lashem, Holy to the Lord*" were written in one line.

Jeff couldn't believe what he had heard. "The crown? With *Holy to the Lord?*"

Shemtov was equally surprised at his guest's response. "Yes, on Aaron's crown. Is that of interest to you?"

"It's what was written on the gold piece I'm speaking about. It was shaped like a diadem, and was found in Rome."

"A diadem." Shemtov thought for a moment. "Ephraim did not mention that. Are you sure?"

"Take a look." Jeff took out his cell phone and brought up a picture. "Selzer examined the crown and found it exactly as described in the Torah, and made of pure gold."

Shemtov caught his breath. "And found in Rome? Well, my friend, that could be your source of power." He put on his glasses and reread the section rapidly. "That crown was to have been placed into the Ark of the Covenant. If Rabbi Lazer saw the veil that covered the Ark in Rome, then it suggests that the Romans had access to it." He sat back as if seeing a miracle. "And yet it was always thought the Ark was safely hidden beneath the Holy Temple in Jerusalem! And you're saying they found the crown in Rome."

He walked back to his chair, clearly agitated. "Which means somehow the contents of the Ark were compromised. If that is so, then those contents could be the treasure you are speaking of, for it is said that what was held in the Ark was the greatest source of power the ancient world ever knew."

* * *

3:00 p.m.

"Chief, Commissioner Fleck is on the phone." Darlene's voice interrupted DePalma's signing off on several reports. He threw down his pen and picked up the phone, determined to take the offensive.

Without preamble, Fleck said, "Progress?"

"I told you, we're working on it. And Josh, besides the mayor, who else did you speak to about finding a witness?"

There was a brief silence.

"Why, no one."

DePalma persisted. "Josh, you don't sound certain. It's important. Perhaps you might have mentioned it to someone else."

"Well, come to think of it, yes. I did mention it to Monsignor Quinn. After all, the Church needs to be kept up to date."

DePalma knew he was treading on political thin ice. "Of *course*," he said, not bothering to conceal his disgust. "And *I* need to know where, and to whom. Confidential information is being *leaked*."

"Well, sure. But Monsignor Quinn is such a devoted priest. I have the greatest respect for the man, I never thought it would be a problem."

"Yes, he certainly seems like an okay fellow," DePalma said, and hung up.

DePalma walked out to Darlene. "See if you can set up a meeting with Quinn, and while you're at it, Jeff wants a meeting with Cardinal Healy. And find out what the relationship is, if any, between Fleck, Mayor Arroyo, and Quinn. Whatever you can find—back-scratching, influence, favors owed, and especially money."

* * *

4:30 p.m.

With a great deal to consider, Jeff left Shemtov's apartment and walked back to his office, his mind juggling the concept of power and the Ark. On the way, he texted Daniella the three questions for which he needed answers and realized the extent to which he had come to rely on her scholarship:

Is it possible that the treasure we are seeking was in the Ark?

Could it be a reason to murder?

Are you okay?

Then he added:

Saw Antonio. Had a mild heart attack. Resting comfortably.

JULY 8

Jeff awoke from a deep sleep, aware of his cell declaring its message. It was Daniella's response:

> Figured you must be up by now. Thanks for the news on
> Antonio. Send my love. Never thought that anything from
> the Ark could be in Rome. As far as I know, the Ark was
> never found, so never figured that anything was taken from
> it. In regard to your question about if I'm okay—are you
> starting to worry already? Stay safe.

He thought about her last question. Was he? Jeff smiled. Perhaps he was; but of even greater importance: she knew it.

* * *

An unfamiliar sound turned Cardinal Jarogniew's attention from his book. Reluctantly, he removed his reading glasses and turned to see that an envelope had been slid under the door. After placing the aged volume entitled *The Permanent Instruction of the Alta Vendita* on his desk, he picked up the envelope, noticing it remained unaddressed. He checked the hallway but saw no one. Curious, he returned to his chair and read the note:

> There are leaks. The pope is aware of talk about a schism,
> and was informed that Vatican funds are missing. He has
> ordered a full audit to determine the source. Be careful. By
> the way, Bronislaw is leaving for New York.

Jarogniew removed his glasses and realized that he was under assault. Little time remained.

* * *

10:00 a.m. One Police Plaza

Darlene hurried into DePalma's office. "Monsignor Quinn was a major vote getter for the new mayor. They go back a long way! I thought you better know before your meeting."

"Really? Quinn a political henchman? Okay . . . I guess if the Church wants to maintain its tax-exempt status it better stay out of politics. What else?"

"And one of my sources told me that Quinn's relationship with Fleck goes back even further, to when he was a young priest in Queens and Fleck was running for an assembly seat out there."

"And?"

"They say it was Quinn who got him elected by throwing the entire weight of his parish into the race. A few years later, Quinn applied for a city grant to purchase some land for a proposed youth center. It was Fleck who helped arrange it."

"And where's that center?"

"It was never built. Housing and Urban Development said they never received a request for construction of a youth center, even though the grant was given and the land purchased."

"There's the money. Good work! What else have you got?"

Darlene handed him the copy of a real estate title. "The land was bought in the name of Mary Lanahan."

"Who's Mary Lanahan?"

"Quinn's youngest sister!"

"So, Fleck owes Quinn big time, and Quinn keeps collecting."

* * *

11:30 a.m., St. Patrick's Cathedral

The meeting with Quinn took place in a small office on the south side of St. Patrick's. DePalma had been suspicious to begin with, and now he was eager to learn more.

"You mentioned that the only individuals who were present at the time of the young priest's death were you and Father John DeSanto. Is that correct?"

"That's what I recall."

"You recall? That's what you *said* in our interview. And where is Father John?"

"Father John? I called like you asked me to, but there was no answer, and we still haven't heard from him. When he took his leave of absence he left no forwarding address."

"And how long will he be absent?"

"He never informed us. Just said he needed some time off, and I certainly agreed. The poor man was in a state of shock. We've tried contacting him just to see how he was feeling but there was no answer."

"But you just said he left no forwarding address."

"He rented an apartment in the Bronx, but there was no answer there. I assumed he's taking a few weeks somewhere to get over the trauma of the murder."

Quinn's responses troubled DePalma. The answers were too polished, almost scripted, but also vague. He tried a different tack.

"Besides Father John, was it possible that Monsignor O'Reilly was also present that evening?"

There was a silence. Then: "O'Reilly? Why, no. Not that I'm aware of. Certainly, I don't recall."

"You don't recall? Again, in our interview, you were sure on the details. And now, unfortunately, we can't ask him."

"A terrible tragedy. I don't understand what could have happened. God must be delivering some kind of justice."

"Justice, you say?" DePalma wanted to laugh. "Murder is just?"

"Who are we to judge God's ways?"

"That's the eternal question, isn't it? Did O'Reilly not follow God's ways?"

Again, Quinn seemed flustered. "Why . . . no, I mean he was a good priest, totally dedicated."

"So, nothing to suggest that he would be labeled a heretic?"

"A heretic? Why would he be labeled a heretic? Then again, who am I to judge what only God can answer?"

"Yes, very true. Actually, one of my officers had spoken with Monsignor O'Reilly before his death."

"Really."

"He tells me that O'Reilly said he was there the night you found Father Fabrizzi's body."

Quinn's eyes widened. "He did? And who was that officer?"

"What difference does it make? One of my men."

"Yes, but who?"

"Jeffrey Moss. He's in charge of the case."

"I see. Well, perhaps O'Reilly got confused with all that happened."

"He doesn't seem to be the only one feeling confused. By the way, what is your relationship with Commissioner Fleck?"

"Fleck, the police commissioner? I . . . I don't know what you mean by relationship; I know who he is, met him on several social occasions. Any reason you ask?" Sweat lightly beaded the monsignor's forehead.

"Should I have one?"

"I have *no idea*, Chief DePalma. Now, if that's all you wish to speak about, then I need to attend to confessions."

"That's why I'm here."

"*Excuse* me?" Quinn's face was red.

"Nothing. Please attend to your . . . confessions."

They rose from their chairs. Casually, DePalma asked, "Tell me, Father, what did the murderer look like?"

Quinn looked closely at the detective, his face pulsing red. DePalma would later recall how the eyes emitted laser-like beams.

"You know, Chief DePalma, I don't like you and I don't like what you are implying. I've tried to cooperate, but the next time you or your Jeffrey Moss want to talk to me, you will be talking to my lawyer as well. I am a man of the cloth, and I don't take sin lightly."

"None of us do, Father. Especially the dead."

Quinn turned on his heel and walked out of the room, slamming the door. DePalma smiled as he stood listening to the echo sounding like a clap of thunder within the building's cavernous walls.

JULY 9

The Air Italia flight brought Bronislaw Dunajski to a foggy, wet JFK Airport, where he was greeted by a driver displaying his name on a sign. He was immediately driven to meet Patrick Cardinal Healy at St. Patrick's.

It had been a difficult week for the American cardinal. The second death within his bishopric and the loss of Monsignor O'Reilly were devastating, both personally and politically. The newspapers were screaming, and it was going to get louder before it got softer. O'Reilly had been a trusted aide for many years.

When Dunajski arrived, the archbishop was at a news conference on the steps of the cathedral with the mayor and the police commissioner. A few drops of rain had already fallen, and after a brief statement, a few questions from reporters were allowed. The official response was "no further details," followed by the ever-helpful "all possibilities are being explored."

As the press conference wound down, Healy greeted his guest from Rome and accompanied him to his private study.

"I came because the Vatican is concerned. With the Synod of Bishops about to gather, the pope would prefer to have his message of pastoral beneficence on the front page of newspapers rather than reading the details of these gruesome murders. What is happening?"

"I wish I knew. The police are handling this as best they can. I have a meeting with one of the investigators in a few minutes. Perhaps you should join us."

"If you don't think I would be intruding."

"On the contrary, I think Rome needs to be kept up to date. Events here seem to be getting beyond our control. And it's not just the murders." Healy let out a sigh. "The situation in the States is becoming critical, and the reforms the pope's discussing are essential if we are to have a congregation to lead. A new poll showed that most American Catholics want the pope to approve women becoming priests, and priests to marry."

Dunajski sat back in the large dark-leather armchair. "It's not just here. Rome is also going through an unusual time. I had a run-in with Jarogniew. I never realized how opposed he was to the initiatives the pope wishes to undertake. If it was up to him, the gospel would revert back to the sixteenth century and the Council of Trent that decreed, *What was, still is*. And worse, when Cardinal Estevez spoke, it was as if he was reflecting everything Jarogniew believed."

"But I was told it was you who defended the pope's reforms."

"Someone had to. The pope had to know we supported him."

Dunajski stood and walked across the richly colored Persian rug to a window overlooking Madison Avenue. Outside, the day remained dismal and raindrops were landing in a windblown forty-five-degree trajectory, tapping an irregular beat against the windowpanes. As he looked out he continued. "We're facing a world where secularism and other faiths, especially Islam and Pentecostal Christianity, are making inroads on Catholicism. In Europe, many of our flock believe Catholicism has become irrelevant, and even our great cathedrals are considered more like museums than churches."

As Dunajski turned from the window, Healy perceived his friend's heaviness of heart.

"And it's not just the response of our own," Dunajski continued. "The world is changing, the people are angry, and the failure of governments to provide hope for their children to live in a better world is widespread. A radical nationalism, bordering on racism, is becoming the response, and the far right is raising its head to offer its false answers and irrational hopes."

Healy nodded. "I'm afraid it's happening here also."

Dunajski continued. "I feel a schism taking place behind Vatican walls."

"Jarogniew?"

Dunajski nodded. "He can be ruthless in protecting his power."

"Then you know to be careful."

"No need for the reminder—I grew up with him."

A knock on the door interrupted the meeting. "Your Grace, your next appointment, Dr. Jeffrey Moss, has arrived. Shall I bring him in?"

Monsignor Quinn led Jeff into the archbishop's study and quietly closed the door. Indeed, the closure was so quiet that it remained slightly ajar, and the monsignor was certain to remain in the closest proximity should there be anything of interest mentioned inside.

* * *

Patrick Cardinal Healy greeted Jeff, introductions were made, and Jeff identified the reason for his visit.

"The murder of one member of the clergy within these walls is terrible enough, but to have a second murdered in the same sadistic and ritualistic way is more than coincidence. Rather, it appears that these murders were carried out in a way prescribed by the Catholic Inquisition as the punishment for heresy."

The cardinals looked at each other. "Heresy?"

"The autopsies indicated each was tortured first by flagellation and then a wooden stake thrust through the heart, just as the inquisitor of old was instructed."

With the cardinals' faces showing disbelief, Jeff continued. "And the sign hung around the neck, *Soli Deo Gloria*? It's been the calling card of the Inquisition since the thirteenth century, written on machines of torture that would rend the body to extract confessions. And when there was no admission, regardless of whether there even *was* anything to admit, the accused were burned at the stake . . . But I'm sure I don't need to explain all this to you gentlemen."

"So that explains the fire."

"Yes, Cardinal Healy, all as originally carried out by the inquisitor, with the pope's blessing."

Cardinal Dunajski brushed his hand against his chin. "Unfortunately, we are indeed aware of the tragic excesses of some of our Church fathers."

Healy remained silent for a moment. "How do you know all this?"

"Monsignor O'Reilly told me."

"You spoke with O'Reilly?"

"We had a long talk. That's when he explained how the method of murder led him to conclude that Father Fabrizzi had been deemed a heretic and sentenced to death. And I'm afraid the same sentence stood for Father O'Reilly. But too many questions remain, and I need your help in answering them."

The cardinals nodded.

Jeff asked, "Why were they considered heretics? Who in the Church can carry out the sentence? What is the significance of the gold artifacts that were hidden in Fabrizzi's shoe? And why was he to meet you, Cardinal Healy, the next morning?"

Healy looked perplexed. "I wish I had answers."

"So do I." Jeff paused before following up. "Were they heretics?"

Cardinal Healy shook his head slowly. "I can only speak for Monsignor O'Reilly. I've known him for many years as a trusted and devout colleague."

"Then who could have sentenced him?"

"Heresy can only be declared by the pope or someone with the power of the pope, someone very senior in the Church hierarchy."

"But who?"

Healy shrugged his shoulders as if in defeat. "Declare someone a heretic? But why?"

Dunajski walked to the window, seemingly absorbed by the vehicles driving up Madison Avenue. Finally, he turned, took a deep breath, and began to speak. "I'm afraid I may be responsible for all this."

"Bronislaw, what are you talking about?"

The cardinal looked at his friend. "Patrick, I was the one who suggested Father Fabrizzi speak to you in confidence. That is why no one knew why he was to meet with you."

Jeff and Cardinal Healy sat forward in their chairs as the cardinal continued. "Several weeks ago, Father Fabrizzi approached me with a most interesting story. I was his advisor on his dissertation dealing with how the Church responds to extreme crises. In his review of Church history, he presented two such situations that he thought of significance, one spiritual and one physical. The first occurred in 1517, when Martin Luther posted his ninety-five theses at Wittenberg, attacking the Church for the heresies it condoned, accusing it of acting more like a power-hungry nation state than a holy church. Luther's assault, of course, led to the Protestant Reformation and masses of Catholics leaving the Church. In reaction, it led to the strict enforcement, through instruments like the Inquisition, against anyone who spoke out against the Church, first Protestants and soon the Jews. In other words, the Church responded as if in an acute stress response, lashing out at anyone and everything.

"The second crisis, not as well known, was the sacking of Rome in 1627. It was during his research of this incident that

Alonzo made the acquaintance of an older scholar working on a parallel project. This scholar had come upon a most interesting find—two gold coins and a gold band."

Healy leaned forward in his chair to hear the story, and Jeff realized Dunajski was confirming what Ephraim had alluded to; it was the scholar who found the pieces.

Jeff had questions. "Did he say who the scholar was?"

"He never mentioned his name."

"And did he say what the significance of the gold pieces was?"

"No, but the scholar believed they were clues to something so powerful that it could alter the future of the Church, if not the world."

"The scholar must have been elated with his discovery," Healy said.

"On the contrary," Dunajski continued, "Father Fabrizzi confided that the scholar was deeply troubled, concerned that whoever found an object so powerful would never be safe. One day the scholar told Father Fabrizzi that he felt he would never leave Rome alive. That's when he gave Fabrizzi the gold pieces and told him to hide them for at least a year. Following that, he should speak to a certain man in Jerusalem, the only one to be trusted with what had been found. To me, the story of "magic" gold pieces seemed improbable, but Fabrizzi was most serious, and advised me that the year had passed and that he had decided to meet the man."

Jeff paused in his note taking. "What happened to the scholar?"

"He never saw him again."

"And Fabrizzi?"

"He left for Jerusalem. About ten days ago he called and wanted to know if there was someone in the Church who could be trusted—someone who lived outside Vatican walls." He turned to Cardinal Healy. "That's when I gave him your name. That was the last time we spoke."

Jeff said, "But who else knew he was coming to New York?"

"No one," Dunajski said. "This is the first time I've said anything."

"But someone knew." Jeff looked at his notes. "I thought Monsignor Quinn made the arrangements?"

Cardinal Healy nodded. "It's very possible, he's responsible for my schedule."

"I believe Chief DePalma already had a conversation with him. And one more thing, what is the significance of July sixteenth"

The Cardinals looked at each other and Healy answered. "July sixteenth? That will be the opening of the Third Extraordinary General Assembly of the Synod of Bishops in Rome to determine how the church can more compassionately minister to Catholic families."

Jeff said, "But Quinn mentioned that was why Fabrizzi wanted to speak to you. Something about July sixteenth."

Healy looked at Dunajski. "Why would he need to speak to me about the meeting?"

Dunajski shook his head without speaking, so Jeff continued. "Tell me about this meeting."

Dunajski answered. "The meeting is public knowledge, but knowing today's media, it will become a circus. The headlines will not focus on the family as much as magnifying the internal debates going on within Vatican walls."

Jeff sat back in his chair. "Debates?"

The cardinal glanced at his colleague before answering. "There are forces within the Vatican, powerful archconservative forces, trying to prevent the pope from carrying out his mission of modernizing the Church to the new realities of the twenty-first century. That's what this synod is to discuss. How does the Church care for Catholics living in 'irregular unions,' like those who have civilly remarried after divorce, or cohabitating couples who are not married, or dealing with the question of gay Catholics?"

Jeff turned to Cardinal Dunajski. "And tell me again what Father Fabrizzi thought the scholar had found."

"Something so powerful that whoever possessed it could alter the future of the Church and the world."

The statement played like a recording in Jeff's mind. He had heard it before: *something so powerful . . .*

Dunajski continued. "The meeting on the sixteenth could be the most important meeting the Church has ever held. A convention of bishops from around the world will meet and make recommendations to the pope. If the pope agrees, the accords will be considered for inclusion in canon law."

Jeff realized what was happening. "So, whoever controls that meeting could dictate Church policy?"

"True," Healy said, "but there will be great opposition to whatever the agenda produces. I fear that if the forces that divide Church thought cannot be resolved, a schism as great as any that has occurred in Church history will occur."

Jeff stood and walked to the window, then turned back.

"But that's it—a schism! Do you realize what July sixteenth denotes in Church history?"

Without waiting for an answer, he referred to his notes.

"July 16, 1054, was the date of the Great Schism—the permanent separation of the Catholic Church into two parts! Who chose that date for the council meeting?"

Dunajski responded. "I assume the cardinal secretary; he's responsible for the calendar."

"And who would that be?"

The churchmen looked at each other as if suddenly sharing the same thought. "Cardinal Ludvik Jarogniew," Dunajski said.

Jeff nodded. "And what if there was a force that could determine the future of your Church, split it or solidify it?"

The cardinals were taken aback. "You mean a force like Fabrizzi was speaking of?"

"Yes."

Dunajski answered. "Then that force must be found before falling into the wrong hands."

"Yes, and if we can find that force before others do, not only can we save your Church, but I will have found my murderer."

Jeff reviewed his notes, and realizing that he had asked as many questions as needed, rose to thank them for their time. As he turned to leave he felt the vibration on his cell. The message was from DePalma. *Call me now!*

Jeff stepped to the corner of the room and made the call. "What's up, chief?"

"Received a call from the police in Washington, Connecticut. A Phillip DeSantos reported several days ago that his brother had been missing after going out on a walk in the forest behind his house. They found a body. It was id'd as Father John DeSantos."

"That was the only other person present when Fabrizzi was murdered."

DePalma responded. "I understand. He had a crushed skull, as if hit by a rock."

"A fall?"

"No. He was found nailed to the trunk of a tree. It was a crucifixion."

Jeff took a deep breath and ended the call. He turned to the cardinals. "Father John DeSantos was found dead in the woods behind his brother's home in Connecticut. He was crucified."

Jeff waited for the shock to dissipate.

"I have to go to Rome, and I'm going to need your help."

* * *

If anyone had been listening closely, they would have heard a quiet click as the door to the private study was fully closed. Monsignor Quinn returned to his office and left a message on a rarely used cell phone in Vatican City.

"A Judas was found among our brethren. There will be no betrayal. He has met his fate." He paused before adding. "You should know that Dr. Jeffrey Moss, who is responsible for the murder investigation of the young priest, is leaving for Rome to continue that investigation, with help from your old friend, Jarogniew. I think I know how to get him off the case."

JULY 10

Quinn's talk with Fleck was fresh on the commissioner's mind when he stormed into the chief's office, walking past a startled Darlene before she could give out a warning.

"I hear you're losing control of the case."

"What are you talking about?"

Fleck was agitated. "I mean it appears you're getting nowhere. Perhaps it's time to make a change."

"Look, Commissioner, you have something to tell me, then tell me."

"I mean when you start accusing priests of murder it suggests you're nowhere. If you have no leads, then fine, admit it, but to interrogate one of our most prominent clergy as if an inquisition, and stating that this fellow Moss is calling him a liar is as far as I, or the mayor, will allow."

"You're speaking about Quinn? I was doing my job."

"Then leave Quinn alone. And by the way, I want Jeff Moss off the case immediately, and that's an order." With that he strode out the door.

Darlene walked into her boss's office. "What was that all about?"

DePalma looked up from his desk. "I guess his friend Quinn didn't like our little meeting."

JULY 11

"What do you mean you're taking me off the case?"

DePalma signaled for Jeff to be seated. "Commissioner's orders."

"But we're getting answers."

"Jeff, I'm sorry, but my hands are tied on this one. He wants you off."

"What's going on?"

"Politics, Jeff—dirty politics. I'm putting McNamara on it."

"Look, this case is more than it appears to be, much more, and I'm not going to let it go. Give me a few days before you assign it to someone else." He paused before adding, "Maybe it's time for my vacation."

"What do you mean vacation?"

"I always wanted to spend some quiet time in Rome."

"What are you getting at?"

"I'm going to take a few days off, but it doesn't mean I have to stop investigating."

"What are you saying? You're going to become some lone wolf crime fighter?"

"If I have to."

"Great, and you're going to foot the bill yourself?"

"If I have to. And come to think of it, one of my former surgical residents has the largest cardiothoracic practice in Rome. He's been trying to get me to visit for a while."

DePalma rose from his desk and walked to the window, looking out over the river before turning to Jeff. "Look, I know why you're doing this. It's Kate, isn't it?"

Jeff looked at his friend—a look that acknowledged a nerve had been touched. His eyes glazed over, and he kept them focused on the floor. DePalma kept his attention toward the river, watching the wake of a tugboat slowly moving by, aware that he may have probed beyond the limits of friendship. He knew Jeff to be a deeply private person, reticent to talk about his personal life, especially the loss of Kate. He stood and waited, not knowing if Jeff would leave or respond.

"I suppose you're right," Jeff said. "But it's how I feel, like a space within me that has never sealed. In a way, I blame myself for what happened to her and it hurts if I stand by when an injustice occurs. Two priests that may have seen the murderer? Look, if I'm to be honest with myself and you, I can't stop working this case. If I'm ever to look in the mirror again, I've got to bring whoever did this to justice. I failed with her, I'm not going to fail on this."

DePalma answered carefully. "Jeff, there will always be another case, and each time you'll be thinking that finding the perpetrators somehow brings closure to Kate's murder."

DePalma appreciated what Jeff was going through. In some ways, the reenactment of Kate's murder was his greatest strength but also his greatest weakness. The older detective thought long and hard before responding, aware that his own job was on the line.

"Fine, do what you have to do. I'll give you a week, but you do it on your own time. It's completely unofficial."

As Jeff walked out, DePalma added, trying to hide the hint of smile: "And keep me up to date. If you need backup, let me know. These are bad people you're looking for. No unnecessary risks."

Jeff nodded: "Will do."

* * *

4:00 p.m., the Vatican

The second meeting of the papal cabinet took place as scheduled. All eight members were seated as the pope addressed them on the course the Church was to take.

"Dear brother cardinals, God has delivered the world into a new age; one, I fear, that has left the Church behind. It is time to awaken to new truths regarding today's society, time to realize that some of our views no longer reflect those of many of the faithful in the Catholic world. I believe it is time to lead the Church in a new direction."

Jarogniew had known this would happen, and though he disagreed vehemently, he was amazed at the strength of the message:

so decisive, so liberal, so reformative. As he searched the faces of those at the table and watched their nods of agreement, he felt a tightening under his priestly collar. It was pope-ing by poll. With the exception of Estefaz, they were all simpatico with the pope's declaration.

The pope continued. "Is it not time to gather in our flock, wherever they have fled, and return them to the loving and protective arms of their shepherd? Is it not time to repair the devastation to human lives that occurred from our not accepting nonmarital relationships? Is it not time to welcome back the divorced and remarried that we have cast off, and bless them with the sacrament of communion? And by what right must we, in the name of Christ, abandon those Catholics whose marriages have failed or who have chosen a different lifestyle?"

It was beyond Jarogniew's control to remain silent.

"Your Eminence, I might suggest that we think carefully before we revise our doctrine of faith. Surely, it's not possible for violators of church doctrine to be welcomed back into the Church? Is this not against everything the Church had ever conceived?"

The pope realized that Jarogniew was the strictly conservative ideologue who would most prevent him from reaching the needed reforms. He tried to hide any self-doubt, knowing that if he was to succeed, the lines of battle had to be clearly drawn.

"What we are calling for is not in conflict with our tradition; rather, it is extending that tradition. Was it not Pope John the Twenty-third who called for opening the windows of the Church at Vatican Two? We are simply extending his call, not just opening them, but removing them. It is time to allow the winds of change to enter for all to enjoy their sweetness."

Jarogniew refused to condone the argument, startling the others at this rare and most public division between the old and the new.

"Did not the refusal of Pope Clement the Seventh to acknowledge the divorce of Henry the Eighth from Catherine almost four hundred years ago settle the Catholic view on remarriage? And did not that decision, which cost the Catholic Church not only England but the majority of the English-speaking West, not make the Church purer? Do we not recall the old military maxim, 'strength by contraction'?"

Jarogniew looked at the assembled as if sending a final appeal. "No, my fellow cardinals, be wary from which direction those

winds of change originate. Removing windows often allows con-
tamination in, and only sealing them will keep it out."

The silence that followed could have been cut by a knife. The
pope's cabinet members glanced at one another, aware that they
were witnessing a battle of two giants, of two differing ideologies.
They also were aware that if this little-known pope was to prove
his ability to lead, and demonstrate his capacity to be the deft
political operator needed to succeed as shepherd of the Church,
then now was that moment.

The pope rose. He thanked those in attendance, signaled the
close of the meeting, but asked Jarogniew to stay.

"My dear Ludwig, I appreciate your beliefs, but I can no longer
allow them to interfere with an agenda that emphasizes pastoral
inclusion over issues of doctrine. Your mandate to continue as
my secretary is now, as of this moment, over. It is time to revamp
your traditional thinking, and that includes the stultified ortho-
doxy that threatens to divide our body, and to remove the taint
of scandal that permeates this house. I thank you for your past
service. That is all."

Jarogniew was, as before, startled by the pope's resolve, but
he stood firm. "Before I go, let me remind you that I was responsible for your attaining this position. Without me you would have
remained an unknown cardinal. And now, you have made a cru-
cial error when trying to make the church more inclusive."

"Oh, I think not. It is time to invite people into our home. You
and your conservative friends are enjoining a mystical, apoca-
lyptical world view, and there is no room for that. I know how
you think, and I tell you this: your militant approach may seem
attractive to a certain group, but it will not be tolerated as long as
I occupy this chair. Now it is time for you to leave."

Jarogniew tried to control his anger. "Yes, I will leave, for
the moment. But, I promise you, you will soon be asking me to
return."

With that the cardinal walked out, and yet the rage he expected to feel at this impasse did not arise. It was as if a sudden calmness overtook him, not one of defeat but the confidence
of victory. A fleeting smile crossed his face as he thought of the
pope's commitment to winds of change. Yes, there will be change,
thought Jarogniew, but this new pope cannot imagine how much
change is about to take place.

Jarogniew pressed a pre-set number on his cell phone and left a message: "I want that young priest's possessions found. It's time this mystery was solved."

It wasn't long before the message was received.

* * *

The flight to Rome left JFK at 11:35 in the evening and was scheduled to arrive at 1:10 p.m. local time. Stan Galvin had no problem giving Jeff the week off from the ME's office, even paid for it, broadly interpreting the trip to be within the scope of official ME business. After all, a meeting with a brilliant cardiovascular surgeon in Rome to discuss causes of death following ventricular failure was not only important for any medical examiner to be aware of, but out of the province of any police commissioner.

Jeff understood his objectives. As Ephraim Selzer had instructed, *find the notebook, and find the relationship of the medals and the crown.*

As the plane began its descent into Rome's Fiumicino Airport, Jeff could see how far modern Rome had expanded beyond the third-century walls built by the emperor Aurelian, extending north to the Aniene River where it joined the Tiber. But the fact that such large portions of the original walls remained indicated the importance that Rome's past played in today's city planning. As the plane prepared for landing he observed the juxtaposition of modern apartment buildings and gracious office complexes standing next to ancient marble columns and classical ruins. Automobiles, buses, and scooters filled the boulevards, and sidewalks were crowded with Romans and Rome's visitors. Beautiful gardens filled with summer colors dotted the cityscape, and luxurious villas built long ago came into view. Bridges were everywhere, crossing the Tiber River that transected Rome in three lazy curves and outlining the city from above in blue. In a way, its attention to the past, its plans for the future, and its foundation in religion reminded him of Jerusalem.

* * *

Dr. Alessandro Bagetti greeted Jeff at the arrivals gate. "Hey, *dottore*, it's been a long time."

Jeff exchanged a quick hug with his former student.

"So, welcome to Roma. Not a vacation, you say?"

"Officially I'm here to learn your latest findings."

"And unofficially?"

"That's something else."

As they walked to the parking lot, Jeff brought him up to date with his work at the ME's office before turning his attention to Alessandro. "But I'm here to learn about you. I hear you've taken over Italy, even treating the pope."

"He's a new patient and a special person, but with a moderate left ventricular dysfunction. Unless something unusual happens, he'll be fine. We're just monitoring him to prevent any congestive heart failure. Thanks to you, I've become the guru around here in treating it."

Alessandro showed a broad, infectious smile, exposing white teeth that contrasted with his sun-tanned skin and swept-back jet-black hair. He was of medium height and build, closing in on forty years of age, and his dark eyes sparkled with the energy that brightened anyone's day who met him.

"What can I say, you trained me well."

"What else would I expect from my first chief resident. Busy?"

"Terribly, we have to take on someone else. Know anyone finishing their training? We have six surgeons in the group, and I'm still working day and night. I'm lucky I finished the last case to get here on time. Even my girlfriend's getting frustrated."

"Never tied the knot?"

"At least you didn't call it a noose. But, it may be sooner than I realize. She gave me an ultimatum—now or never." He looked at his former professor. "And you? Has the brilliant Jeffrey Moss finally found his match?"

Jeff smiled and put his arm over his friend's shoulder. "Too busy."

"That's what you said the last time."

They reached the parking lot and Alessandro steered them to a gleaming red sports car parked by itself in the far end of the field.

"Still into cars, I see."

"Hey, they expect a successful bachelor surgeon, trained in the best program in the States, to have one of these. Life today is all about appearances."

Jeff nodded. "Perhaps you're right, especially with the world spending half the day looking at the surface of screens that require no delving into."

Alessandro clicked open the locks and placed Jeff's luggage in the small compartment under the hood in the front of the car. Jeff crouched low and eased himself into the contoured leather passenger seat of the Ferrari 458.

"Looks like the cockpit of a new jet. Don't tell me it flies?"

"Just about. I leased it three weeks ago and I'm loving every minute. This baby goes zero to sixty in less than three-point-four seconds. We're talking rocket speed."

It seemed like rocket speed to Jeff as Alessandro raced into the center of the city in less than forty minutes and turned off the broad Via dei Fori Imperiali, motored slowly through a few narrow streets, and slowed to a crawl on the Via degli Ibernesi. It was more of an alley than a street, and when he pulled over to park, there was no suggestion that he was in front of a hotel.

"You're going to love this place, very special. The owner's name is Stefano. When I told him you trained me, he promised to take good care of you. And by the way, with Europe the way it is, your dollar is worth more than ever."

"Welcome to the Inn at the Roman Forum." A young bellman, tall and thin in a sparkling white uniform with gold trim, opened Alessandro's door. "Aha, Dr. Bagetti, *buongiorno*. I see you delivered your guest."

"Mario, meet Dr. Moss."

Mario walked in front of the car and opened Jeff's door. "*Dottore*, we've been expecting you."

Alessandro pressed a button on the dashboard to open the hood, and Mario removed the single piece of luggage from the trunk.

"Let's meet for dinner one evening and catch up. And by the way, if you have any questions about Rome or the rest of the world's history, ask Mario. In a few years he will also be a professor."

Alessandro gave him a hug and drove off.

Mario noticed how Jeff was fixed on the buildings across the way. "Feels like you're a part of ancient Rome, no? That's why the hotel is called the Inn at the Roman Forum because that large rectangular plaza you're looking at across the way is the Roman Forum. Those ruins that surround the plaza are all that remain of what was the center of civic and community life for centuries, surrounded by the most majestic buildings." Mario pointed to the building just east of the Forum. "And I'm sure you recognize the Coliseum, the greatest symbol of Imperial Rome, built by the emperor Vespasian in AD 70 and paid for by the treasures taken from the Jewish Temple after the Siege of Jerusalem."

Jeff looked at Mario as if he was clairvoyant. "The Temple Treasure?"

"*Si*, taken back to Rome by Titus. Does the treasure interest you?"

Jeff smiled. "Treasure always interests me."

"Up to eighty thousand people crowded in to the Coliseum to watch the gladiator contests, like your Super Bowl—no? Same thing: people trying to kill each other. You must go visit, it's only a five-minute walk."

Jeff turned his attention back to the young man. "So, Mario, you're going to be a professor?"

Mario smiled. "I'm a doctoral student writing my dissertation. Stefano likes to hire grad students who speak several languages and know their history."

Carrying Jeff's bag, Mario escorted him through a narrow stone cryptoporticus, an old concealed passageway housing ancient engravings and ruins that, Mario explained, could be traced back two thousand years.

"Doctor Moss, welcome." A pretty young receptionist wearing a similarly coordinated color scheme of white skirt and blouse with gold trim welcomed him. "Your room is ready. Stefano gave you the best room in the house."

Jeff was surprised. "Why, that's very kind of him."

The receptionist smiled. "Perhaps you are not aware that Dr. Bagetti was Stefano's surgeon and saved his life two years ago when he had a massive heart attack. No one thought he would live, so a teacher of Dr. Bagetti is Stefano's friend."

She made a copy of his passport, as the law required, and Mario accompanied Jeff to his room. It wasn't spacious, but it was spotless and attractively decorated in a white modern décor, furnished in white leather and dark stained floors. Jeff walked onto a small terrace that overlooked a beautiful rear garden filled with palm and fig trees. A red message light was blinking: Cardinal Dunajski would meet him at the Santa Maria Sopra Minerva Church at eleven in the morning.

The search had begun.

JULY 12

It took the taxi fifteen minutes on the Via Vicour to drop Jeff off at the entrance to the Church of the Santa Maria Sopra Minerva. Mario had given Jeff the lowdown while he waited for the cab.

"It's the only Gothic church in Rome and belongs to the Dominicans. It was built in 1280 over a temple named for the Greco-Roman goddess Minerva, thus the name, *sopra* meaning over."

The exterior of the church looked rather plain, but a playful statue of a baby elephant carrying a miniature Egyptian obelisk on its back was set in a side courtyard. To Bernini, the sculptor, it suggested the ideal that strength supports wisdom.

As Jeff entered his eyes were drawn to the bright blue vaulted ceiling surrounded by striking stained glass windows. Suddenly he heard shouting from a recess adjacent to the pews, and then a ringing crash that echoed through the hallowed structure, as if coins had been thrown onto the floor. As Jeff turned toward the disturbance, a man rushed down the side aisle, shouting in a language Jeff didn't understand, but he would recall the anger, the accent, and the man's long white hair. He dismissed the incident and explored the art that adorned the church, calling on his two semesters of Italian Renaissance Art History to make sense of it. He stopped at a fresco of *St. Thomas Condemning the Heretics* by Filippino Lippi, thinking, five hundred years later and they're still condemning heretics! The narrative noted that one of the boys in the fresco was a portrait of Giulio de' Medici, later to become Pope Clement VII.

Clement VII? The Pope on the Cellini coin!

"Welcome."

Jeff turned to see the tall figure of Cardinal Dunajski as he spread his arms.

"I pray here at times. Beautiful in its simplicity, dignified in its demeanor and a sense of piety that connects you to the presence of God. But please, you've come a long way to solve a murder." He began to walk toward the far side. "Behind the gift shop is Father Fabrizzi's office that you wished to see. What are we looking for?"

"A notebook."

The cardinal knocked on Fabrizzi's door before opening it. The room was small and windowless, with only a plain wooden desk, chair, and a simple bookcase.

"What happened?" Dunajski asked.

The room was in disarray, with the desk's central drawer turned over on the floor, the remaining drawers thrown open, and books from the shelves strewn about.

Jeff realized the situation. "Someone was here before us."

"But why?"

"Because the people who murdered Father Fabrizzi are looking for the same thing we are."

Jeff surveyed the chaos, still hoping to find the notebook that Ephraim Selzer mentioned, but it was nowhere to be found. Had it been taken, or was it not here to begin with?

The cardinal seemed confounded. "Someone must have seen something."

They closed the door and walked to the gift counter where they found a wiry old gray-haired woman. She seemed to be examining the floor, bending every now and then to pick up a coin. The cardinal almost had to shout for the woman to hear. She looked up when she realized she was being spoken to, and recognized the cardinal.

"Why yes, Your Eminence. There was a man who asked for Father Fabrizzi's office, said he was a friend and wanted to leave a gift for him. He must have been in there about fifteen minutes or so and just left."

"Can you describe him? What did he look like?"

"He was big, like a bull, a head full of white hair and a foreign accent. He was in a real hurry, asked if I knew where Father Fabrizzi lived. I have a card from the building where Father Fabrizzi stays, but I wouldn't tell the man. He got angry, threw the charity box on the floor, and strode out. I thought that if he was really a friend of Father Fabrizzi, he would have never done that."

The cardinal looked at Jeff, then spoke to the woman. "I agree, Christina. Perhaps you can give me that card."

* * *

3:00 p.m.

Jeff realized he had to hurry. The intruder was already trying to find where Fabrizzi lived, suggesting he had not found what he was looking for. Jeff quickly helped retrieve the last of the coins from the floor, and thanked the cardinal for his help. He telephoned the number on the card, asking the landlady if he could see the apartment. He took a cab into the city when a call from Alessandro reached him. "You're in luck. My last patient had to cancel, some kind of infection, so best to put the procedure off. Are you free?"

"I'm just entering the Banca del Fucino on the Via Nazionale. Need to change dollars into euros, and then I have to search an apartment. Want to join me?"

"No prob, I'll pick you up in fifteen minutes."

* * *

The Via Ferdinando Palasciano was a busy street in an old residential district of Monteverde. Alessandro knew all the shortcuts and reached it in record time, finding a parking space in front of a small store selling Italian-made handbags.

"What's the assignment?"

"You're about to become a detective."

"So, you are teaching me another profession!"

"Always good to have a backup. We're going to check out a young priest's apartment, number 192A."

As they walked up the wide sidewalk, Jeff explained the case, sticking to the murder side of the mystery. They passed a number of small businesses serving the local community—a supermarket, a small store selling fresh fish, several trade shops for shoe and watch repairs, a barber, and a café—before stopping at number 192A, a small apartment building.

They rang the bell and after a short wait were greeted by a middle-aged woman. "So you're the gentleman who called about subletting the apartment. Another man also called about subletting. I didn't realize Father Fabrizzi wanted to leave. You said you have some identification?"

Jeff gave the woman his card. "So, you're a friend of Father Fabrizzi from New York, a detective. I like to know who might be moving in if you are going to be staying with us."

She brought the two men into a small and sparsely furnished studio apartment painted in a dull but neat yellow tone and an old wooden floor. "I haven't seen Father Fabrizzi recently, but he's a good tenant, quiet and neat and pays on time. Wish I had more like him."

Jeff asked, "When's the other man coming?"

"I told him you were scheduled to see it first. When he heard that he hung up. Seemed angry. Father Fabrizzi has a two-year lease with about six months remaining before he has to renew." Jeff was thinking there would be no renewal.

"He liked it because it's within walking distance to the Vatican. Of course, if you are looking for something bigger, I have something on the third floor you may like."

Jeff started to look around. "No, I think this is fine."

"I hope so. I gave the place a good cleaning yesterday, so everything should be in order." When Jeff didn't respond to her further questions, the woman got the clue. "Anyway, I see you're busy, so I'll leave you alone. How long will you need?"

"Not more than fifteen minutes." As the woman was about to leave, Jeff asked a final question. "Tell me, when you cleaned up, did you find any loose papers or a notebook lying around?"

"Notebook, no. Anything that was here I left exactly in place. Father Fabrizzi doesn't like me to move any of his books. So, if that's all, just close the front door and it will lock."

* * *

"So we're looking for a notebook?" asked Alesandro.

"I was told that Fabrizzi kept one, and it's possible he kept it here."

The living space accessed a back door and a small yard where several garbage cans were lined up. The space included a sofa bed and a chest of drawers, a bathroom with a compact shower, and a kitchenette with electric stove, fridge, and microwave. There was a small table that appeared to serve for both dining and desk work. On it were placed several books and a copy of the current issue of *Archaeology Review*.

They divided up the search. Jeff began by opening the archaeology journal on the kitchen table. A postcard of Rome bookmarked Daniella's article, which was heavily outlined with yellow marker. He placed the journal aside and perused the remaining books, which mainly dealt with the history of the Church. One was entitled *The Sack of Rome* and another a paperback edition of *The Autobiography of Benvenuto Cellini.*

When Jeff saw that he thought, Cellini again?

While Alessandro examined the kitchen area, Jeff inspected the chest of drawers, carefully moving aside some underwear, a few pairs of socks, three white shirts still in the cleaner's plastic wrap, and two sweaters. The vanity over the sink in the small bathroom contained only an unopened bottle of aspirin, a fresh bar of soap, and a tube of toothpaste. The rest of the bathroom contained nothing remarkable, nor did the area under the bed and behind the chest.

"Find anything?"

Alesandro answered, "*Nada,* I searched the kitchen cabinets and drawers. This priest lived a sparse life."

Jeff nodded. "But he apparently was fearful of what he had discovered, so we may be looking for a hiding place that's out of the box."

Jeff walked through the short hallway entrance and slid open the closet pocket door, but aside from a blue spring jacket and a heavier brown woolen winter coat whose pockets contained a pair of inexpensive woolen gloves, there was nothing to be found. A shelf above held two hats, one a baseball cap that read *NY Yankees*, and the other a warm Russian faux fur with ear flaps Frustrated, Jeff sat down on one of the two chairs at the small table and surveyed the apartment. What had he missed? He had double-checked everything.

"Guess it's not here. Let's go."

"One second, I need to use the toilet."

Minutes later Jeff heard the universal anguished shout. "The damn toilet's broken!"

"What's wrong?"

"It won't flush. Hold on, maybe it's the chain."

Within a minute Alessandro yelled out: "Hey, Jeff, I think we caught a fish."

Jeff heard the toilet flush, and Alessandro walked out with a dripping white, plastic bag labeled Julio's Market. He handed it to Jeff.

"Is this what you're looking for?"

Jeff removed a thin spiral notebook and thumbed through the dozen or so pages that contained writing. "Voila! You just graduated as a full detective." He placed the journal and notebook into a dry plastic bag from a kitchen drawer.

As they prepared to leave they heard heavy knocking on the front door.

"*C'è nessuno?*"

Jeff put his finger over his lips. The banging on the front door grew louder, and the message was repeated several times in English: "Anyone in there? Open the door!" Jeff had heard the accent before. It was the voice from the Church.

Alessandro pointed to the back door. As they made their way out they heard the sound of the front door being forced. Jeff looked back as the door was thrown open and the man with white hair, the one who almost ran into him at the church, burst in. Jeff and Alessandro made their way along the back of the building and entered an alley that brought them to the street. By the time Alesandro drove away, sirens were heard and police cars stopped in front of the building.

* * *

4:15 p.m.

Cardinal Jarogniew got the expected call later that afternoon.

"Yes, Tirshov."

"I'm sorry, Your Eminence, but I check Fabrizzi's apartment like you tell me, and then I arrested for trespassing. The lady landlord call police. They want to know why I there. They took passport and keep me in police station."

"I see. You were not very careful, were you?"

"No, Your Eminence, but there was other man in apartment and got out as I come in."

"Another man before you?" Jarogniew thought for a moment. "Alright, my friend, I'll see what I can do."

* * *

Not more than a few minutes had passed before the call to the headquarters of the Polizia di Stato in Rome was forwarded directly to the Capo della Polizia.

"Yes, Your Eminence."

"Giuliani, so kind of you to take my call directly. I know how busy you are."

"For you, Your Eminence, any time."

"I was pleased to see you at the last meeting."

"Finding the Final Mystery is most important."

"It's the Lord's work, and that is the reason for this call. I just received word that a messenger, named Tirshov, was sent to pick up a few personals from the apartment of one of our priests. I believe there was a misunderstanding when he entered. Would you look into that for me? He was only carrying out the instructions of the Church, and perhaps became too assertive. He is of great importance to our cause, and I would be most appreciative if you'd intervene."

"Of course, Your Eminence, I'm sure, as you say, it was only a misunderstanding. Is there anything else I can do for you?"

"Actually, there is. I understand there was another man who entered the apartment prior to our messenger. Can you find out his name and where I can reach him?"

"I will look into it immediately."

* * *

It did not take long for the cardinal's phone to ring. "The landlady identified the person who entered the apartment before your messenger as a Jeffrey Moss, and his card states that he is a New York medical examiner and detective in the New York Police Department. The hotel database that we collect each day indicates he checked into The Inn of the Roman Forum yesterday afternoon. He was supposedly there about a rental, but he had also asked the landlady if she had seen a notebook. And by the way, regarding that fellow from the Church, Tirshov, you were correct, it was a misunderstanding. We're letting him go as we speak."

* * *

5:00 p.m.

Once again the phone rang in Jarogniew's apartment. "Ah, Tirshov. I am pleased to see that they let you out so quickly, but tell me, when you searched the apartment, did you see a notebook?"

"Some books, but no notebook."

"You're sure."

"I'm sure. I look everywhere, nothing there."

Jarogniew thought for a moment. "I see. Then, I must ask one more favor of you, but you must be more careful this time."

"Of course, Your Eminence. I promise."

"Good. A Jeffrey Moss has checked into the Inn at the Roman Forum. I need to know everything that he does. And be careful, he's a New York detective."

* * *

The Inn, 5:00 p.m.

Jeff was let off at the inn and hurried to his room to examine the notebook. As he opened the cover a photo of the three gold pieces fell out with a question mark next to it. There were a series of notations consisting of single words or phrases. Jeff assumed that these were the clues that Ephraim Selzer had been told about. On one page was written: *No way is the Temple Treasure in Rome! Written on a second page was Ark of the Covenant;* and on a third the phrase, *E non ho amato mai tanto la vita, tanto la vita!* Some of the notations were in English, some in Latin, and others in Hebrew. Jeff closed the book. Hebrew? Latin? No Temple Treasure? Ark of the Covenant? Jeff had no idea what it all meant, but he knew someone who might. He made the call.

JULY 13

Jeff slept well, ate a late breakfast, and returned to his room to ponder the notebook when his cell rang.

"Hey, Moss, just got in. Great place. You must have pulled some strings for this."

Jeff recognized the voice and tried a stern response. "You're late."

"Thanks for the greeting. You didn't give me much notice, but I did take the first flight out."

"Okay, you're forgiven."

"What's this all about?"

He smiled. "I'll tell you over lunch."

"Fine. Meet you downstairs."

* * *

1:30 p.m., Vatican City

Ludvik Jarogniew sat in his office, his left hand curled around a small glass of his favorite claret, reading the day's headline in *L'Osservatore Romano*, the church's official paper.

"New Setback for Vatican Conservatives as Pope Ousts Jarogniew."

One would have thought that the classic Bottega del Vino crystal would have shattered from the man's clenched fist, but the cardinal's only response was a subtle smile. Events were moving his way as the pope's agenda toward modernity was creating turmoil, a situation that always advanced insurgency. To Jarogniew, the pope's introduction of measures so contradictory to Church policy would soon beget untold suspicions and fears among the bishops, raising immense questions and uncertainties of which Church doctrine to follow. What were the bishops to do, return to their churches and announce that everything they'd been teaching was wrong? But he had only four days to carry out his plan, for once the synod was over and the pope announced his position, the doctrine of papal infallibility would end all attempts at revision. Church precedent was clear: The declaration in 1870 of the First Vatican Council specifically stated that when the pope defined a doctrine concerning faith or morals, it was to be accepted as if given by God himself. Such acceptance had to be prevented at all costs, and Jarogniew realized the time had come to assume the role of protector of Church law as originally declared. He would turn the pope's reinterpretation of canon law to his advantage.

* * *

Daniella Teller looked more beautiful than Jeff had remembered. Few patrons were present when she walked into the dimly lit café. Jeff rose to meet her, aware that his heart had skipped a beat. It had been a long time since he had felt that skip, and though a world-renowned heart specialist, he was almost afraid to admit the etiology of this arrhythmia. After an awkward moment of indecision, they exchanged friendly kisses on both cheeks.

"So, you couldn't do without me?" She smiled, and he feigned distress.

The waiter filled their water glasses, and they each ordered a salad.

"I never realized that I was so inadequate without your help."

They laughed, and relaxed. He brought her up to date on the schism within the Church over doctrine, the search for the source of power, the books found in Fabrizzi's apartment, and the clues found in the notebook.

Daniella was surprised at the progress he had made. "And the first clue stated *no way is the Temple Treasure in Rome?*"

Jeff nodded. "Yes, and when I searched Fabrizzi's apartment a copy of your article was on the table and underlined."

Daniella frowned. "So we're back to the Treasure. Then there's something I need to show you."

The road from the inn was undergoing extensive repairs, and Daniella led him down the steep hill and crossed the busy Via dei Fori Imperiali. The temperature had already climbed to 29 degrees Celsius, which Jeff quickly converted to 85 degrees Fahrenheit, and the humidity was settling in. Before them lay the Roman Forum, and they stood on the long line of tourists to pay the entrance fee to view the massive Arch of Titus. They did not notice the large man with white hair, face partially hidden behind an intermittently browsed magazine outside the exit gate.

"The Arch of Titus is the one piece of direct evidence that still exists showing how the Romans pillaged the sacred Temple after crushing the Jewish revolt." They walked under the arch and examined the bas relief sculpture carved into the interior of one side of the stone arch.

"Remember, this depiction of Titus' triumphal ride into Rome on his chariot was completed back in 81 CE."

They walked to the other side of the arch and Jeff examined the abutment. The bas relief clearly depicted a procession into Rome with the menorah, sacred table, and trumpets being carried on men's shoulders, but Jeff was seeking something else.

"The Ark. What did it look like?"

"According to the Bible it was built out of acacia wood, approximately four feet long, two and a half feet wide, and two and a half feet high, and covered in gold, with two gold rings on each side through which staves of wood overlaid with gold were placed to carry it."

Jeff took several steps back from the huge abutment, looking at the arch from a different perspective. "I don't see it."

"It's not here."

"But they made an image of everything else they took."

"Perhaps they weren't able to take it."

Jeff was surprised. "Why's that? Seems small enough to carry."

Daniella smiled. "I can think of two reasons. One, is that it's written that as King David was taking the Ark to his new capital in Jerusalem, Uzzah, one of the drivers, thought the Ark was about to fall off the cart. When he placed his hand on the Ark to steady it, he was struck dead."

"Magic?"

"Faith. Our sages say the Ark did not need to be carried because God caused it to float. If you have complete faith in God, there is never a need to interfere with his plan. Even two of Aaron's sons were struck down when they approached the Ark without the proper faith."

"You mean whoever touches the Ark will die?"

"Not if they have total faith in the omnipotence of the Lord. That is why the Israelites carried it with them into battle. When the people truly believed that God would hand them victory, they won."

As they walked back to the inn, Jeff thought about the consequences. "So, when the Romans tried to move the Ark, they were struck down."

"Possibly, but what if the Romans never found it? You see, when Josiah, King of Judah, feared that Jerusalem was to be conquered, he buried the Ark somewhere on the Temple Mount. That was almost seven hundred years before the Roman conquest."

"And no one's ever found it?"

"With one possible exception. It is written that a priest, working on the Temple Mount, noticed that one of the floor stones was loose. Thinking he uncovered Josiah's hiding place, he went to report his finding. Before he could tell of his discovery, he fell dead. That is why our sages believed the Ark remained hidden somewhere on the Temple Mount."

"Which is what Levy Shemtov, a scholar that Siglione sent me to, explained. When I mentioned that Aaron's crown was found in Rome, he felt the only explanation was that the Ark must have been broken into and some of its contents stolen. What else was in it besides the crown?"

"As far as I know, the Ark contained the stone tablets of the Ten Commandments, Aaron's Rod, a jar of manna, the first Torah scroll, and the eight vestments of the high priest's clothing, which includes the crown."

Jeff seemed perplexed. "So you're saying that whatever was removed from the Ark was removed long before King Josiah hid it. But when?"

"I have no idea. The last time the Ark and its contents were seen was when King Solomon placed it into a separate room within his new temple, to be entered only by the high priest on Yom Kippur, the Day of Atonement. Reports of its finding are always arising throughout the world, Ethiopia, France, even Canada, but independent confirmation has never been made. Even with detailed instructions written in the Dead Sea and Copper Scrolls, it remains a mystery. But it is of great importance to many Jews, for according to our sages, when the Ark is found, redemption is at hand, and that will be followed by the third and final temple."

Jeff was in deep thought as they continued their walk. "So, it's never been found."

As they entered the inn, Daniella responded. "Jeff, let me tell you what my father, who was not a religious man, used to say. He called it in Hebrew, *Hashgachah Pratit*. It means that no one finds anything he's not deemed to find, and no one finds what is being sought before it's time. So, whatever you are searching for, this source of power, it will only be found because the time of your discovering it has arrived."

"So it wasn't Father Fabrizzi's time."

"Nor, I suppose, my father's."

"But perhaps it will be ours."

*　*　*

New York

At noon, the door of the director's office at the Numismatics Society opened. Siglione was at his desk, a half-empty carton of Chinese takeout at his elbow, reading a manuscript.

"You never stop working, do you?"

Siglione looked up. At first, he didn't recognize the man. He was thickset, muscular, had a shaved head, and wore a well-tailored dark suit with a red power tie. He walked with a decided limp, but only when he removed his dark glasses, revealing eyes as black as midnight, did Siglione identify him.

"So, you've decided to visit me. You look different, successful even. But you're limping. What happened?"

The visitor's face reddened. "An unfortunate accident."

"I'm sorry to hear that. Where have you been? I've tried to reach you."

"I've been busy, but I heard you were ill and wanted to make sure you were feeling better."

Siglione looked at his visitor with suspicion. "Yes, I'm feeling much better."

"Good to hear."

"Monsignor Quinn tells me that you are working for him."

The visitor responded with pride. "Yes, there are assignments the Church believes that only I am qualified to carry out."

"That's wonderful."

The man's tone became dark. "But this is not a social call. Any chance of that was lost a long time ago. You told the monsignor that the gold pieces you examined for the police were worthless and that you didn't know where they were."

Siglione hesitated before responding. "Yes, that's true. I assume the police have them."

"You wouldn't have a copy of those images on your computer, would you?"

"Why so interested in my work, all of a sudden? You've never taken notice before."

"Coins have become my new hobby, just like you. Now let me see them."

The old man saw the hatred in the constricted pupils of the midnight eyes, an intensity of disdain that raised the pounding of his heart to a point where he feared it would burst through his chest wall.

"Fine, I'll show you."

He opened the file and the younger man walked behind the desk and looked at the images of the gold pieces that filled the screen.

"Is this everything?"

"Yes."

"Thank you."

The young man shoved Siglione aside. Working quickly, he forwarded the file to an e-mail address he had memorized.

"That's all. Just wanted to share that with a friend."

Siglione could no longer hide the tremors of his hands. "Now get out of here and don't let me see you again!"

The intruder slammed his fist onto the desk, knocking over the food container and throwing papers onto the floor. Siglione jumped back at the sudden display of violence and turned red, trying to breathe and clutching his heart. "Please, my pills, my pills."

The man picked up the prescription bottle from the desk. "You mean these."

Siglione gasped, "Please."

The man looked at Siglione, opened the bottle, and emptied its contents into the wastebasket next to the desk. "Pray, padre, that the Lord will forgive you. But your wish has been granted—you will never see me again."

Siglione reached for the wastebasket but fell to the floor, clutching his heart, his face turning ashen, eyes calling for help. It wasn't long before the forced gasping came to an end.

* * *

Rome, 5:15 p.m.

The transmitted file was received, printed, read, and placed in a drawer. As he poured a second glass of claret, Cardinal Jarogniew smiled, knowing he had just seen what he needed to know: two medals and a gold band. *So this is what they hid. But why?*

He forwarded the received files to a curator at a museum in Rome with the message: *This is what the priest was carrying. What does it mean?*

It didn't take long for the reply. *The medals were fabricated by Cellini for Pope Clement VII. The gold band looks like a diadem, an old royal crown. You should know that I've seen them before. I was told it could be related to the Temple Treasure.*

Jarogniew stood, contemplating the significance of what Fabrizzi had hidden. Was it true that the gold coins really led to the treasure, and was that treasure truly the source of power he had been searching for? Jarogniew now realized that the key to solving the Final Mystery was the notebook. It was unfortunate that he was unable to obtain it, but he knew who could.

Jarogniew sat back in his chair and sipped his wine, sensing a settling relaxation as the dark red Bordeaux diffused through the channels of mind and body. A subtle smile appeared on his face as he recalled Corinthians 1, 10:13: "When you're in a difficult trial, just remember that you're only visiting there for a short time." He had been through such struggles before and always survived. He would do so again, this time with the triumph of power, overwhelming power. Hadn't his strength always been appreciating what real authority was and how to use it? Only three days remained, but Jarogniew was confident that he was getting closer to revealing the Final Mystery, and with it, it would not matter what the pope and his church, nor all the bishops on earth, declared.

A feeling of confidence descended over him, and it was at times like these, working as hard as he had for so long, that his desire for moments of relaxation overtook him. He picked up his private cell and made a call.

"Yes, my dear. I know how desperate you are for me to speak to your young son again. Please send him to my private apartment this evening, and I will spend as much time as needed, teaching him how to fall on his knees and praise his Maker."

* * *

5:30 p.m.

Daniella sat with Jeff in his room, turning the pages of the notebook. "OK, I've listed all the clues:

> The *Alta Vendita*
> *unde eo omnia cioe*
> Hiram the Widow's Son
> A square and compass
> E non ho amato mai tanto la vita, tanto la vita
> A picture of the gold pieces
> Psalm 118
> ChVRM ABIV
> Ohr Ganuz

Notice how, after each item, there is a check mark, and two notes written in the margin: *Advised to see ES* and *Speak to Francesco*. Any idea what they mean?"

"None."

Daniella reexamined the clues. "Notice how the clues are written in pen, but the check marks and the two notes are written in pencil, almost as if someone was checking off what the inked clues meant."

Jeff studied the page, then turned to several others. "One of the items we analyze in the medical examiner's office is handwriting. Notice the capitals S and A and the small o's in the inked and penciled portions. They are different, as if written by two different people."

Daniella said, "That confirms what Ephraim said, that the scholar wrote the original and Fabrizzi reviewed it." For the moment, she sensed something familiar about the small sample of words, something about the way the penned t's were crossed, but she was fatigued from the early morning plane ride, and her mind passed over it. She needed to get outside.

They walked down the stairs and through the back door where a sign read, "Welcome to the Secret Garden." Secluded and tranquil, the garden was laid out around a fountain with flowing water surrounded by green shrubs and colorful flowers. They sat on a stone bench under the shade of a dark green umbrella pine tree, concentrating on the clues, trying to understand their meaning.

Jeff interrupted the thought process. "The priest told Ephraim that the notes were not what they appeared to be."

Daniella nodded. "That's for sure." She took out the list of clues. "What's the *Alta Vendita*?"

Jeff shook his head. "No idea."

"And 'E non ho amato mai tanto la vita, tanto la vita.'"

Jeff tried to place the phrase. "That sounds awfully familiar, but I can't recall it." He looked at the list and pointed to Hiram the Widow's Son. "What about this?"

Daniella thought for a moment. "There was a King Hiram of Tyre, a city in Lebanon, who sent workers to help Solomon build the temple in Jerusalem."

"Was he a widow's son?"

"I don't recall anything about that."

Daniella pointed to the next clue. "Ever see this before?"

Jeff stared at the page. "I think I have. When I was young, at my Uncle Bernie's house. I was there for the weekend and saw a pamphlet lying on the table opened to this picture. I remember it because when my uncle saw me looking at it he got angry and took it from me, told me I was too young to know about it. Later, my Aunt Molly told me Uncle Bernie was a member of a secret club, with their own passwords and signs, but it was just a bunch of friends who got together every month to play cards. I remember thinking that was cool."

"What kind of secret club?"

"My uncle was a Mason."

"It was the Masons who built Solomon's Temple." She read the penciled note in the margin. "'Advised to see ES. Speak to Francesco.' Who's ES and who's Francesco?"

"It doesn't say." Jeff looked down the list of clues. Any idea what *unde eo omnia cioe* means?"

Daniella shook her head. "The Latin's too complicated for me."

Jeff walked over to the fountain and dipped his hand into the cool water. "Look, we're getting nowhere. We need to find someone who can help us, but someone we can trust. Know anyone?"

"Here in Rome? Maybe I do."

She browsed through her cell phone. "There's a rabbi who lives here, was a friend of my father's. I'll check it out."

* * *

7:00 p.m.

Tirshov sat in a shaded area behind the construction works at the end of the Via degli Ibernesi, occasionally sipping from a plastic bottle of cold water and using it to wipe the perspiration from his forehead. Suddenly he became alert as Jeff and Daniella walked out of the inn.

"Mario, can you get us a taxi?" Jeff said.

"Si, *dottore*, where to?"

"The Great Synagogue."

"Why not walk? It's a beautiful evening, and it's on Lungotevere Dè Cenci in the old Jewish quarter, only one and a half kilometers from here. Shouldn't take us more than twenty minutes."

Jeff looked bemused. "Us?"

Mario glanced at his cell phone. "*Si*, I finish work in five minutes, so if you wait you can walk with me. "I live near there, and that means you will get an excellent tour."

In less than five minutes Mario had changed clothes and reappeared, ready to begin the walk.

"Do you know a Rabbi Meir Elimelech?" Daniella asked.

"Of course. He's the rabbi at the Great Synagogue and was one of my teachers. A fine gentleman. My area of interest is the history of the Jews in Italy in the Middle Ages."

"Why that subject?"

"It's my family's heritage. We lived here for over five hundred years, at least that's as far back as our family tree recounts."

Jeff explained to Daniella that Mario was getting his doctorate.

"*Si*, that's what my dissertation is on."

"So you know Latin?"

"I better. Part of my exams."

Daniella removed the notebook from her pocketbook and pointed to the clue.

"Know what this means?"

"*Unde eo omnia cioe*? Not only do I know what it means, but I know where you can find it. It means, 'Where things come from, where they all go.'"

Daniella said, "'The beginning and end of everything.'"

"*Si*, and it's found on a house built in the 1500s, known as the Teodoro Ameyden home, after a famous Flemish scholar. It's located on Via di Monte Giordano, and if you look carefully you can still make out the inscription over the door."

"How do you know all this?"

Mario gave a broad smile. "I used to have a side job as a guide, and it was part of my walking tour. It's not that far from where we're going, so we can pass by."

He led them through a series of side streets until they reached the narrow, cobblestoned Via di Monte Giordano. At a distance, out of sight, Tirshov followed the trio, stopping suddenly at the corner when he recognized the street they were entering.

As they walked up the street, Mario directed their attention. "It's the soot-covered building with the arched windows and carved travertine." As they approached he pointed to the faded writing over the front door. "It's been neglected for years, but if you look closely you can still make out the words."

Jeff read the Latin phrase and regarded the building. "Anybody live here?"

"I've never seen anyone use the main door, but every now and then I've seen people walking down the steps to the side entrance below. Not sure what it's used for . . . maybe a theater."

"Why do you say that?"

"Because one evening the downstairs door was open, and I saw people wearing costumes."

They continued on to the Teatro Marcelo, then down a series of time-smoothed stone stairs, passing ancient excavations, and then onto the Via del Portico D'Ottavia.

"Welcome to the Jewish ghetto, the district of Sant'Angelo."

Jeff took in the view, busy with colorful lights and crowds. "I thought it would be a walled section in complete disrepair. This place looks like Soho on a warm summer night."

Mario smiled. "Actually, there remains one piece of the ghetto wall built into a courtyard off the Piazza delle Cinque Scole as a memorial, but otherwise, it's a busy spot for tourists."

Indeed, the cobblestoned streets were lined with kosher restaurants and outdoor cafes busy with waiters serving customers grilled meats, fried artichokes, hummus, couscous, and glasses filled with wine.

"Don't be fooled by the glitter and glamour, it's but a moment in a long and difficult history of the Jews in Rome."

"What do you mean?"

Mario's voice turned serious. "To truly understand what's happened here you need to know what the Church did to my people."

They walked together, slowed by the crowd in the street.

"Jews lived here over two hundred years before Jesus, longer than any other European city and hundreds of years before the origin of Christianity. Originally, the Jews came as honored diplomats from Judea, and business flourished. But after the war with Rome and the destruction of the Holy Temple, thousands of Jewish captives were exiled here and sold into slavery. With the growth of Christianity, the popes began to enforce laws to prevent Judaism from spreading. Laws were declared prohibiting Jews from marrying outside their religion and barring the building of new synagogues.

"Even then, Rome's Jews were often held in high regard as physicians, businessmen, and confidants of popes. However, this changed in the eighth century, when a growing tide of anti-Semitism spread throughout Europe. In 1290, King Edward the First expelled the few thousand Jews living in England, and in 1492, the Church forced all Jews in Spain, under the threat of the Inquisition, to be either baptized, banished, or killed as heretics, decrees that soon spread throughout Europe. Many of the Jews who were forced to leave their homes came to Italy, and Rome's Jewish population doubled.

"Life was tolerable, at least until the mid-1500s. That was when the Catholic Counter-Reformation, responding to the challenge of Calvin and Luther, fought the rise of other religions, including Judaism. In 1555, Pope Paul the Fourth declared a Papal bull, *Cum nimis absurdum*, forcing the four thousand Jews of Rome to move into this walled-off ghetto of less than seven acres, an area where the Tiber would continuously flood, destroying the surrounding wooden buildings. The pope assumed that such conditions would be so oppressive that the Jews would be forced to convert, but it had the opposite effect."

Jeff pursued. "How was that?"

"Because the ghetto walls resulted in an even closer community by forcing Jews to marry Jews, as well as removing any outside influences. However, as the community grew, the space within the ghetto walls became so congested that the only possible expansion was up, blocking sunlight from the narrow streets. This combination of overcrowding, severe poverty, and frequent flooding from the Tiber resulted in the rapid spread of disease. During the plague of 1656, eight hundred of the four thousand inhabitants died."

Daniella mentioned the work restrictions.

"That's true, a papal edict canceled all rights that Jews had as citizens, permitting them to be employed at only unskilled jobs, such as ragmen, secondhand dealers or fishmongers. Even the great Jewish physicians were no longer allowed to treat Christians, although the popes continued to ask for their help. Jews could not own property, and the only professions allowed were pawnbrokers and moneylenders, which Christians were prohibited from doing."

"Mario!"

The call came from a friend, and Mario waved as he continued speaking. "The walled-off ghetto had gates that were locked at night and opened at dawn. Whenever Jews left the ghetto the men had to wear a yellow cloth, the *sciamanno*. Every Saturday the entire Jewish community was forced to hear sermons in front of the small church of San Gregorio just outside the ghetto wall, and during Carnevale, a festival like your Mardi Gras, Jews were forced to parade down the Via del Corso, amusing the Christians who lined the streets shouting insults. The Jews were forced to compete in humiliating games, like running naked with ropes around their necks, or with their legs closed into sacks, or even being ridden by soldiers. In addition, each year the Jews had to petition for permission to live here, vow allegiance to the pope at the Arch of Titus, pay a tax and then the rabbi himself had to swear homage to the chief of the city councilors, the Caporione. If permission was granted for the Jews to stay for another year the contract would be finalized by the Caporione kicking the rabbi on his derrière.

"It was only after the Papal States were incorporated into the Kingdom of Italy in 1870 that freedom became permanent. In 1888, the ghetto was demolished and the synagogue was built."

Jeff said, "Sounds like Germany in the 30s."

"Where do you think the Nazis learned it from? The wearing of the yellow badge, forcing the Jews to be denigrated in front of their neighbors, all came from the papal edict. The Roman ghetto was the last remaining ghetto in Western Europe until the Nazis came to power. But if you want to know about that, ask Rabbi Elimelech. That's a whole other story."

* * *

Rome, 7:45 PM

As the sun began its slow descent, its rays reflected off the square aluminum dome of the Great Synagogue called the Tempio

Maggiore, rising high over the surrounding streets. Built in memory of the ghetto, the synagogue has been under constant police surveillance since 1982, when five Palestinian terrorists entered the building during Sabbath services and sprayed the congregation with bullets.

Following at a distance, Tirshov observed Jeff and Daniella being checked by two armed security guards as they passed through the large wooden front doors. After waiting for twenty minutes he dialed a private mobile number.

"Yes."

"I follow them to Via di Monte Giordano. They stop outside building."

"Really, that's very interesting."

"How they know about that?"

"I'm not certain. Where are you now?"

"Outside Great Synagogue. They've been inside for while."

A smile of great satisfaction crossed Jarogniew's face. "The Great Synagogue? Then, I believe you've told me everything I need to know. You've done an excellent job, excellent, and Tirshov, there's no further reason to follow them."

* * *

The presence of armed security made Jeff aware of the reality of the new millennium: one could not even petition one's own God without protection for fear that others felt they were praying to the wrong heaven. Had anyone learned anything from history? The truth of what Santayana had written in 1905 was apparent. *Those who cannot remember the past are condemned to repeat it.* Once again there were forces in the world that insisted the world only pray their way.

They were directed to the rabbi's office and entered the sanctuary, its soaring height supported by massive square fluted stone columns. Pews filled the main space, and long aisles led to steps that rose to a wide pulpit holding an ark, draped with rich scarlet cloth, behind which would be hidden the sacred Torahs.

They walked to the right of the pulpit and through a door that led to the rabbi's study. It was a comfortable room, painted in a muted green, lined with books, a desk, a small round table and several chairs. Rabbi Meir Elimelech stood to welcome them with a smile. He was a tall man in his early seventies, with broad shoulders, deep blue eyes, an aquiline nose and a full head of silver hair that flowed down to a long gray beard. For a moment, he reminded Jeff of someone else, but he quickly put the thought away. The rabbi wore a dark suit over a white shirt, dark tie, and wore a skullcap. He spoke softly in fluent English.

"Please sit."

They sat together at the table.

"So you're the Danny your father spoke of. Well, a pleasure to finally meet you. Your father and I were close when he was working in Rome. A brilliant mind. I miss him."

Daniella introduced Jeff and the purpose of their visit. She glanced at the list of clues she had copied before beginning.

"Would you know someone called Hiram, the widow's son?"

The rabbi seemed surprised. "May I ask why you wish to know?"

"We're wondering if it may have something to do with some type of hidden treasure."

"I see." A slight smile passed across his lips at the mention of treasure. "Perhaps you would like some cold tea."

The rabbi poured out three cups of tea from an ice-filled pitcher and returned to the table.

"Yes, I'm familiar with Hiram, the widow's son, but there's a biblical Hiram and a legendary Hiram. Which do you wish to know?"

"Better make it both," Jeff said.

The rabbi nodded. "Hiram is mentioned in the Bible in relation to the building of King Solomon's Temple in Jerusalem. Solomon asked King Hiram of Tyre for help in the building, so in exchange for corn, wine, and oil, King Hiram sent Solomon cedar trees cut from the forests of Lebanon and thousands of masons and stonecutters. More than eighty-five thousand workmen were employed in the building of the temple which took over seven years to complete. This can all be found in Scripture, especially in the seventh chapter of the First Book of Kings and the second chapter of Chronicles. There it relates that King Hiram wrote a letter to King Solomon advising that he was also sending a particularly skilled worker, a man named Huram-Abi, to help in the construction. According to the Scripture, Huram-Abi was the son of a widow of the tribe of Naphtali. Her husband had come from Tyre."

Jeff said, "So, he was a key figure in building the Temple."

The rabbi nodded. "Yes, apparently Huram-Abi was well known as a master craftsman whose job was to cast the metallic ornaments for Solomon's Temple."

"Is there a relationship between this Huram, or Hiram, and the Temple Treasure?" Daniella asked.

The rabbi replied, "For that we need to delve into who Hiram the craftsman was, his relationship to the Freemasons and their ritual of becoming a master Mason—known as the Legend of the Third Degree."

Daniella removed the clue sheet from her bag and showed it to the rabbi. "And this?"

The rabbi studied the image. "You are leading us into some very interesting areas. May I ask how you know about this?"

"My uncle was a Mason."

"Well, this image is of the Masonic square, or the square and compass, the most recognized symbol of Freemasonry. Just as the first Masons used squares and compasses to build Solomon's Temple, so future Masons were to use these tools metaphorically to reach higher ethical standards. For example, Masons should square their actions by the square of virtue and circumscribe their desires to keep their passions within proper limits to their fellow man."

The rabbi took a sip of tea and continued. "According to Masonic tradition, Hiram-Abi, also known as Abiff, was not just a craftsman of bronze, but the grand master, the chief architect in the building of the entire temple. The legend relates that following the completion of its construction, a number of skilled workers were promised the rank of Master Workman or Mason, elevating them to receiving the secrets reserved for Master Masons and earning a master's increased wages. But three of the workmen insisted they be promoted before the building was completed, and when Abiff refused, they tried to steal from the Temple Treasure. When Abiff stopped them, he was murdered, and the theft was carried out. The conspirators were apprehended and executed, but the legend states that not all of the treasure was recovered."

"What remained missing?" Daniella asked.

Rabbi Elimelech leaned forward. "It is said, objects from the Ark."

"And that might include Aaron's crown?"

"Yes, it's possible. But remember, this is only legend, and Abiff's assassination is not mentioned in either Kings or Chronicles, where the narrative ends by simply saying: 'So Hiram finished all the work he did for King Solomon on the House of the Lord.'"

"But if it's only a legend, why would it be taken seriously?"

"Because of its supreme importance in Masonry. But tell me, Dr. Moss, why do you need to know?"

Jeff handed him his card. "Because I'm investigating the murder of a young priest who, like Hiram Abiff, also refused to reveal a secret about a treasure and died for his silence."

The rabbi seemed to dwell on Jeff's response. "You are asking me to reveal the deepest secrets of the Masonic Brotherhood."

The two guests glanced at each other. "How would you know these secrets?"

The rabbi hesitated. "Because I am, or at least was, a member for a very long time. So, let me answer you this way. The essence of freemasonry is the search for light, the same metaphysical quest that all people have undertaken from the beginning of time—what the Greeks called gnosis, self-discovery. It is the message written over their Temple of Delphi, 'gnothi seauton'—know thyself. This search of self seeks the meaning of existence and leads back to comprehending creation, man's role on earth, and appreciating God's words. Many believe that it is through Kabbalah that one can find the deepest meaning of God's message hidden in the mystical interpretation of ancient Hebrew.

"I do not wish to review its origins, how purportedly Kabbalah was taught by God to a group of angels in Paradise. Rather, it is enough to say that after the sin of the apple, or more precisely, the fig, Adam was taught God's most sacred teachings, which were then passed on to Noah, then Abraham, and then Moses. But greatest was the knowledge gained by David and Solomon. That is why the Masonic Brotherhood use of symbols and words have their basis in Kabbalah.

"Two things you need to know. First, the major symbol in Masonry is the triple tau, which relates to a concealed treasure or hidden truth."

When Jeff heard the words *hidden treasure* he glanced at Daniella.

"And second, King Solomon and King Hiram each had knowledge of one of three syllables or words of a secret phrase, and Hiram Abiff had the third. The three men were to contribute each of their syllables, enabling them to pronounce this secret phrase within the Holy of Holies after the temple was completed. But, with Abiff dead, the third syllable was forever lost. The two known syllables have been passed on through the generations to the most eminent Masons, Masons who continue to covertly search for the third syllable."

"And what will pronouncing that lost phrase allow?"

"The unleashing of a most awesome power."

Daniella spoke with a scholar's skepticism. "And you believe this to be true?"

The rabbi read her expression. "Please understand that our sages were fully aware of the power of letters and syllables. Did not the Bible relate that the Lord said, 'Your name shall no longer be called Abram, but your name shall be Abraham,' and is it not written that 'As for Sarai your wife, do not call her name Sarai for Sarah is her name. I will bless her.' Even the addition of a single letter can change one's destiny. Abraham became the leader of a great nation, and Sarah gave birth to Isaac at age ninety-nine. Yes, letters and syllables can alter the natural course of events."

Daniella considered this. "So, you're suggesting the Bible was steeped in belief in the occult."

"I'm not, but the legend does. King Solomon, King Hiram, and Hiram Abiff were all practicing occultists. It was to be those three sounds that together would form the lost word that Freemasons are still seeking. When they are uttered in proper pitch, duration, order, timing, and intensity, the word will summon down an awesome power."

"Like a prayer, calling for God to respond?"

"No, doctor, it wasn't God's power they were hoping to call for, but a different power, one so dark and of such magnitude that whoever possessed it could rule the world—but a world ruled by evil. It was this lost word, this power of darkness found through the occult, that even Hitler was searching for."

Jeff sat back, as if trying to believe that all the satanic movies he had seen had a basis in reality. "So, you're saying that there is a force of evil that counters God's power of righteousness?"

"What I am saying is that when God creates something, he must also create the antithesis, if there's good then there must be evil, if there's a blessing then there must be a curse, and man must choose which path he elects to follow. That, my friends, is the basis of how God created the world. From Adam and Eve's encounter with the tree in the Garden of Eden, man always had the freedom to choose. Perhaps that is the greatest gift God has given to us, free will, the ability to pursue our own destiny, and God refuses to amend it."

"Even if the world chooses to destroy itself."

"Even then."

Daniella added. "But, you say it's only legend."

The Rabbi gave a subtle smile. "Yes, Daniella, but then again we have the choice to believe it or not."

Elimelech glanced at his watch. "Unfortunately, it's getting late and I must leave for evening prayers, but we should continue our conversation another time."

The rabbi rose to escort his guests to the door. "Of course, most Masonic lodges are more like service organizations, like the Rotary Club, as was probably your uncle's, but there still remain a few who continue to seek the forces of darkness."

Jeff seemed surprised. "But why?"

The rabbi opened the door for his guests. "Because they plan to conquer the world."

The guests looked at each other in silence before Daniella read another clue.

"Rabbi, before you leave, do the words *unde eo omnia cioe* have any significance?"

A shadow of fear seemed to pass across the rabbi's face, like a cloud that momentarily conceals the sun before it drifts on. "How do you know these words?"

"On an old building, not far from here."

"It is best that you stay away from there."

Jeff was surprised with the response. "Why is that?"

"That is where the forces of darkness are sought."

* * *

7:00 p.m.

Jeff and Daniella wandered the streets in thought, looking but not seeing.

"Suppose all he said was true . . ." Daniella seemed to speak for both of them.

Jeff completed the assumption. "Is that the power we're up against? Forces of darkness? Is that why Fabrizzi gave up his life, concerned that such a power could be unleashed and fall into the wrong hands?"

"And the rabbi said something else," Daniella observed. "As the Temple was being completed, the Ark was broken into, and not everything was recovered."

She paused before completing the thought. "Of course, it's only legend."

Jeff smiled. "I'm beginning to believe there is little to distinguish legend from fact."

Daniella responded with a wide grin. "Then I guess it's your choice."

They continued on in silence until Jeff felt his cell vibrate and read the message:

Dinner? 10:00? Ristorante Peppone, 60 Via Emilia - Alessandro.

He turned to Daniella. "Hungry?"

"Getting there."

"Good, we have an invite for ten o'clock." Jeff messaged back to accept.

They walked into a small, empty bistro and sat at the bar and ordered wine. With the drinks the bartender included a small box.

"What's this?"

"Your gift. Go ahead, open it."

Daniella opened the box to find a corkscrew with the name Dante's Roma on it with the address.

"It's a promotion." The bartender waved his arm over the empty tables. "As you can see, we need to do something."

"Thanks, hope it works."

They finished their wine, Jeff paid the check, and Daniella put the gift in her pocketbook. As they walked out into the sun's final hour, Jeff checked the time.

"We have two hours till dinner. What do you want to do?"

Daniella removed the list of clues from her pocketbook and pointed to one of them.

Jeff seemed surprised. "You want to go back? But you were warned. Have you no fear?"

It took twenty minutes to retrace their steps and find the narrow cobblestoned Via di Monte Giordano and the old soot-covered building. The sun was almost completely lost behind the taller buildings, creating an effect of light and shadow, radiating the mystery of chiaroscuro practiced by centuries of Italian painters. The street seemed as deserted as when Mario had brought them there, but this time Daniella walked confidently down the steps below street level.

"Where are you going?"

"Mario said it could be a theater. Anyway, the clue was in the notebook, which must mean something."

"Yeah, it means, do not enter, what lies in here are the forces of darkness."

Daniella replied with a smile on her face. "But, Jeff, it's only legend."

She knocked at the entry, but the only response was the creaking sound of a door left ajar. When there was no reply, they entered a short, narrow hallway lit only by the fading sunlight through the doorway.

Daniella shouted out, *"Ciao c'è qualcuno qui?"* but again, no answer.

"Jeff, there's no one here. Let's check it out."

They made their way into the darkened hallway, using the light from their cell phones to orient themselves. Off the hallway was a coatroom lined with black hooded cloaks hung on hangers.

"It sure has a lot of costumes. Maybe it *is* a theater," Daniella ventured.

Jeff remained skeptical. "Then why would the rabbi warn us to stay away?"

They walked to the room's far end where a narrow, unlocked door groaned open to a small musty windowless storage room partially filled with piles of empty mildewed cartons.

Jeff read the labels. "Commedia delle Arte. I guess you're right about a theater."

As they walked back into the cloakroom, Daniella said, "It doesn't seem to be so sinister as—"

Suddenly, Jeff placed his hand over her mouth. They heard voices approaching, increasing in volume. Men were descending the outer stairs. Jeff led the way back to the rear storage room. As they stepped in they heard a voice call out. *"Salve?"*

A light beam bounced off the cloakroom walls. "Someone here? Why is the door unlocked?"

A second voice replied. "Giorgio must have left it open."

"That's careless. He knows no one unauthorized is allowed in."

Jeff quietly pulled the narrow door shut, enclosing them within the staleness of the space, where they waited in silence. Soon more voices were heard. Many people were entering the building, each one admitted following the same response: *"Alta vendita."* The sounds of whispers entered the cloakroom, followed by the clashing of metal hangers and trailing voices as the visitors exited. When all was quiet, Jeff checked his cell: 8:15. He opened the door enough to observe that the cloakroom was empty. As he and Daniella crept out, they heard a persistent low hum from an adjacent room—a meditative resonance or incantation of some kind.

"We better get out of here," Jeff whispered.

They walked quietly into the narrow hallway, keeping to the wall. Looking to their right they saw a large room filled with seated figures wrapped in black robes. Candles gave an eerie glow. They looked at each other warily, then made their way toward the entry. As Jeff reached for the handle they heard a knock from outside. Quickly they withdrew back into the cloakroom as someone from the meeting walked to open the outer door.

Jeff whispered. "We can't leave."

"What can we do?"

"Try this."

Jeff reached for two hanging cloaks and gave one to Daniella, each drawing the capes and hoods tightly about them. The man who had just arrived entered the cloakroom, put on his cloak and hood, and walked directly into the meeting room. The other man locked the outer door and then stopped at the cloakroom entrance, looking suspiciously at the two caped figures. Daniella gripped Jeff's hand. They kept their eyes locked on the man, who momentarily seemed taken aback.

"Time to go inside. The Master is to speak."

The thick Slavic accent startled Jeff, stirring a recent memory: it was the voice of the man who searched Fabrizzi's office and broke into his apartment. But, to Daniella, it wasn't the sound of the command that brought horror, but the sight of his face: chalk-white cheeks, a long, narrow, twisted hawkish nose, a face without a mouth, and a pointed chin. The sole signs of life were the sunken moving eyes.

"Wait! You forget something!"

They looked at each other, and he continued: "The masks. Where your masks? The Master says must be masks to know who you are."

He left for a moment and returned holding two masks. "These for you."

They put the masks on. Jeff's was made of leather, with a long beak and eye openings covered with crystals. Daniella's was a full mask of a female face, painted gold with bright red lips, heavily lined dark eyebrows and eyelashes, and a single tear under each eye.

"Now you come with me."

As he led them into the large room, faces turned in silence: faces personifying slander and vanity, faces of savages prepared to destroy civilization itself. Jeff and Daniella followed, drawn to the seated forms, mesmerized. There were no human faces, only masks, masks of multiple appearances, of insult, of evil, of death. Some were half-masks painted green with short, wide noses, arching eyebrows with short horned foreheads, and muted eyes. Others were white, covering only the eyes but with long Pinocchio-shaped noses, while others covered the orbits and cheeks that were decorated with silver and gold feathers. Daniella felt as if she had walked into an eighteenth-century insane asylum with the inmates fixed forever in a life of emotional stultification. The speaker watched from the front of the room with interest, waiting for the three latecomers to find their seats.

"Welcome, brother Tirshov, I see you brought guests!" The word *guests* echoed as if reverberating within a canyon of ice.

* * *

Jeff and Daniella glanced at the surrounding figures. When the speaker rapped the table, all eyes turned forward, as if in awe of his commanding presence. The Master stood as straight as a steel beam behind a dark wooden pedestal about five feet high and three feet wide. On it rested two large books with four candles rising from silver holders attached to each corner. The flickering of the flames gave an unnatural appearance to the erect, black-hooded figure with his frightening white face. Black vertical lines extended above and below his mask's eye holes, each marking a single red teardrop.

"My brothers, before me rests the Masonic altar, which in ancient times was a place of sacrifice, atonement, and communion with God. Today, our Masonic brothers from around the globe have lost the true meaning of who we are and where we came from. They no longer understand the essence of sacrifice, nor do they understand the significance of faith or atonement. Indeed, they have lost all means of intimacy with their God. But, we here today understand what that commitment means. On this altar rests our two holiest books, the Bible and the *Alta Vendita*—all the guides we need to live a life of wisdom and truth.

"To aid us in such a life we were given signs and symbols, just as Moses and Aaron offered the Pharaoh in Egypt. First, is the square and compass, representing the symbol of freemasonry, and within which you will observe the letter 'G'. In Hebrew, the language in which our Bible was originally written, the letter 'G' is called *gimel*, with a numerical value of three. In freemasonry, 'G' stands for both God and geometry, for geometry defines limits, limits placed on man by God. We call those limits, tradition. There is no room for modernity here, there is no room for inclusion here, and there is certainly no room for change. He who believes anything else blasphemes the godliness from whence we came and of whom we represent.

"Then there is the symbol of the eye. To those who understand, the Masonic eye represents the eye of God, helping us to appreciate God's continual presence in and care for his universe. A God who, our scripture teaches, is without beginning or end, who always is, always was, and always will be. It is the Masonic eye of God that assures us he will continue to watch over us and guide us and reminds us that he will always be in our daily lives.

"And yet, one symbol remains, one that represents why we are here today. It is known as the Final Mystery, ignorance of which prevents us from achieving our full potential. That unknown is the Ark of the Covenant, its contents lost to us since the destruction of Solomon's Temple, revealing God's promise to David and through which we receive God's continued mercy for our transgressions today. Was not Solomon's Temple built only to house those holy contents? Are we not the descendants of the builders of that house, and, by right, does not the Ark and what is in it belong to us? My brothers, once we possess those holy relics, we will gain the power to complete our mission on earth."

Jeff squeezed Daniella's hand and they glanced at each other. A voice arose from behind a mask not far from where they were sitting. "You told us that mystery was about to be solved."

"And so it will be. We've been given the map. Now all we need to do is follow it to uncover its treasure, the absolute power to achieve absolute dominion." He waited for a response, but when there was only silence, the Master called out, "Then let it be so!" and the room responded, "amen."

Slowly the participants stood. Jeff realized this was their opportunity to exit and he led Daniella through the crowd to the short hallway. As he reached the door a strong hand grasped Daniella's wrist from behind. It was Tirshov.

"Leaving so soon. There's so much to learn."

Daniella tried to pull her arm free, but Tirshov tightened his grip.

"Jeff!"

Jeff turned back to see her being pulled away. He reached out, but the strength of men intervened and forced both back into the large room. Shouts of "Who are they?" arose as the masked faces turned. The words "intruders" and "imposters" rang out.

"The masks! Remove their masks!"

Men reached out, throwing off the couple's hoods and ripping off their masks. Tirshov, still wearing his hideous disguise, approached with a large candle, allowing their faces to be revealed in its sulfurous glow. He turned to the leader. "It is them, Most Worshipful Grand Master, the two you had me follow."

Voices cried out:

"A woman!"

"Blasphemy!"

"Sacrifice her!"

The men started to drag Daniella toward the altar when a voice from behind the alter bellowed: "Let them go!"

"But they are guilty of trespassing our sacred—"

"I said let them go!" the voice commanded.

Hands fell, rapacious eyes turned aside, and angry bodies were forced to withdraw as the Master approached. He held a candle before their faces, his twisted mask staring at them, scarcely a hair's breadth separating their physical beings.

"Leave now and do not return, or you will not leave again."

* * *

9:15 p.m.

The hot shower removed the superficial evidence of her experience, the fresh air revived her lungs, the evening attire altered her appearance, but the memory of what had occurred would not as easily be erased.

The moon was full in the evening sky when Daniella met Jeff in the garden. They held each other, allowing the negatively charged energy to dissipate.

"You're shaking," he said.

"I know." Daniella spoke softly and held him tighter. "They became a mob. I can't get their faces out of my mind. Thank God he stopped them."

He nodded slowly. "But only after he saw who we were."

She looked into his eyes. "Why?"

"I don't know, it was as if he knew who we were."

Daniella sat down on a garden bench. "That big guy, Tirshov?" she said as if realizing what had happened. "Didn't he say he was following us?"

Jeff picked up on her thinking. "If that's the case, then they've known about us for a while. But we learned one thing: They're looking for the same treasure we are."

"You mean the Ark?"

Jeff replied. "And the power it holds."

He glanced at his watch. "Still want to go to dinner?"

She stepped back and took a deep breath. "You promised your friend. I'll be fine."

* * *

10:00 p.m.

The taxi dropped them off at 60 Via Emilia, a quiet, dimly lit street. The interior of the Ristorante Peppone had an air of simple elegance and fastidious care. Alessandro was seated at a corner table wearing a bright red silk dress shirt unbuttoned at the neck, and sipping a glass of red wine. His face broadly brightened and he stood when he saw Jeff and Daniella enter.

"Ah, *dottore*, glad you could make it." Alessandro introduced himself to Daniella, and the three sat for dinner. "I want you to know that this gentleman made me into who I am today."

Daniella smiled. Alessandro's cheerful disposition was an antidote to what they had been through. "You mean a heart surgeon?"

"No, a race car driver."

She found the laughter soothing, and the change in subject a needed remedy. Alessandro filled each of their glasses with wine and offered a toast.

"To Rome—may it bring out the best in each of us."

The glasses rang out in response. "You know," Alessandro continued, "the reason that we touch our glasses is to fulfill the purpose of a toast—that all our senses be stimulated. We see the clarity of the red grape, smell its bouquet, feel its caress on our tongue, and taste the fullness of its fruit, but what of the sense of sound? That, my friends, comes from the touch of welcoming glasses."

They laughed and held out their glasses, this time with greater meaning.

"But, enough sermons. How was your day?"

Daniella looked at Jeff and smiled. "Stressful is a good way to describe it."

Alessandro motioned for the waiter. "In that case, let's eat. If you don't have anything in mind, I have some suggestions."

They looked at each other and smiled. "Absolutely."

"Wonderful, you see the Peppones have been here for generations, and their recipes continue to delight the most consummate food aficionados. But, this may be the last of them because Signore Peppone's son is now my chief surgical resident, and I give him no time to practice his cooking." Alessandro ordered several courses for the table and when finished, Daniella interjected with a sly smile, "I hope all that food is not going to stop Jeff from doing his work."

Alessandro responded, "What do you mean, work? Haven't I been helping him solve his mystery?"

A new bottle was uncorked. "We have a saying here in Italy: 'Lavorare soltanto e non giocare rende Vito un ragazzo noioso.' Too much work makes Vito a dull boy. Remember, you're in Roma. Jeff, at least take this beautiful woman to see the castel. The view in the evening, looking out above the city lights, is unforgettable."

"You mean the Castel Sant'Angelo?"

"What else?" Alessandro looked at Daniella. "Jeff's an opera buff and knows that Tosca's final scene takes place at Sant'Angelo, including the ringing of the castel's bells. Isn't that right?"

"Actually, the orchestration calls for numerous bells to be rung to give the feeling you are in Rome, but what very few know is that Puccini himself came here to determine the pitch and pattern of those bells. He even climbed to the top of Sant'Angelo just to hear the matin bells ring every morning by all the churches in concert."

Alessandro smiled. "See, I told you, he knows everything, especially *Tosca*. Bravo, *dottore*."

"It's true. Tosca is my favorite opera."

"It's not just his favorite, he can sing the entire libretto. Unfortunately, that often occurs during surgery."

Daniella was impressed. "Really?"

Jeff tried to hide his embarrassment. "I suppose. I've seen it many times."

Daniella turned to Jeff. "I would love to hear a few bars."

Jeff was abashed. "What do you mean? Here? Now?"

The voice of the imbibed wine answered. "Why not?"

Alessandro left his chair and spoke to Signore Peppone. It was already late, but the proprietor nodded then quietly spoke to the remaining two tables finishing their dinners. He then tapped a knife on a half-filled glass of water.

"My friends, we are most fortunate this evening, to have a special guest, not only a great surgeon from New York, but a true opera lover. I was just informed that he will sing an aria from his favorite opera, Pucinni's *Tosca*."

Jeff looked around, not certain how to respond, as the patrons and staff joined in applause. It certainly wasn't in his nature to be drawn to the spotlight, but he rose and faced his audience.

"Thank you, Signore Peppone, for your gracious words. Though unprepared, I see I have no choice." He held his handkerchief to his lips, ala Pavarotti, and with great seriouness announced: "'E lucevan le stelle' from act three of Puccini's *Tosca.*"

To those present, the transformation was palpable as he stepped into the role of Cavaradossi and began to sing the opening lines. It wasn't so much the serviceable tenor voice that rendered the opera's most famous aria so captivating; it was the warmth and passion with which it was delivered.

E lucevan le stelle,
olezzava la terra stridea l'uscio dell'orto . . .
e un passo sfiorava la rena
Entrava ella fragrante, mi cadea fra le braccia.
O! dolci baci, o languide carezze,
mentr'io fremente le belle forme disciogliea dai veli!
Svanì per sempre il sogno mio d'amore.
L'ora è fuggita,
e muoio disperato! E muoio disperato!
E non ho amato mai tanto la vita, tanto la vita!

Passersbys paused at the open doorway to listen, several couples edging inside. When the final note was sung, Jeff remained in tragic character, and silence reigned for several moments, followed by a burst of applause. As Jeff bowed, shouts of approval rang throughout the restaurant. Jeff seemed dazed, then bowed again to his audience and sat down. He turned to Daniella for her critique, but she was reflecting on the lyric.

"Jeff, the final words."

"What about them?"

"Do you realize what they are?"

Jeff thought for a moment. "'E non ho amato mai tanto la vita, tanto la vita'?"

"The words from the notebook!"

He played the words back in his mind. "Of course! Without the music, I didn't realize."

"And that's what Fabrizzi meant when he told Ephraim that 'its ending was the beginning.' If Tosca ends in the castle, then that's where we must begin to look!"

Alessandro was mystified. "Am I missing something?"

Jeff patted him on the back. "No, you're back on the case. What can you tell me about the castle?"

"Well, it's probably Italy's most famous, with a long history, but if you really want to know about it, speak to my friend Francesco at the museum. If he knows I sent you, he—"

Almost in unison they exclaimed, "Francesco!?"

Alessandro was startled at their response. "Yes, Francesco Marzoti, the curator at the Museo Nazionale de Castel Sant'Angelo, and a patient of mine. Do you know him?"

"No, but we need to speak to him."

"But of course . . . when?"

They looked at each other. "Tomorrow?"

Alessandro searched his cell, pressed a button, and spoke in Italian for less than two minutes. "It's arranged. Tomorrow morning, eleven o'clock, and that gives you plenty of time for a leisurely stroll along one of the most beautiful streets in Roma, the Via Gulia, all the way to the Tiber. If you leave by nine you'll easily make it."

A cell rang, and the entire restaurant looked to see if it was theirs. Alessandro took the call. "Dr. Bagetti. . . . si . . . si." He put his phone back in his pocket and looked at his guests. "I'm afraid I have to run. Want to do some surgery?"

Jeff smiled. "I'm retired."

Alessandro rose from his chair. "Just wanted to see if you remembered anything. Anyway, we must do this again."

* * *

The cool breeze and full moon presented a beautiful evening as they left the restaurant.

"Feel like walking?"

Daniella looked at Jeff and took a deep breath, her long exhalation suggesting that relaxation was setting in. "I'd like that."

They walked on, listening to the sounds of music from the restaurants and hotels along the Via Veneto.

"You sang that aria with such feeling."

"Thanks. I've always admired Cavaradossi, so brave and young, but as he is about to be executed he wishes he could tell his beloved, Tosca, how much he cared for her and how difficult it is to lose someone you love."

He paused, as if a weight had made it difficult to go on, but he felt he had to express something kept hidden. Daniella sensed that his hesitation ran deeper than a simple explanation. For the first time in a long time, she wished she could reach out and help. As they walked along the elegant boulevard, the streetlights of Rome lit the city warmly, and their hands found each other's.

"To be honest, it declares what I feel."

> The stars were shining,
> And the earth was scented. The gate of the garden creaked
> And a footstep grazed the sand . . .
> Fragrant, she entered and fell into my arms.
> Oh, sweet kisses and languorous caresses
> While feverishly I stripped the beautiful form of its veils!
> Forever, my dream of love has vanished.
> That moment has fled,
> and I die in desperation. And I die in desperation!
> And I never before loved life so much, Loved life so much!

They looked into each other's eyes, searching for the meaning that had been missing for both of them.

"You see, I was once engaged to be married to a young woman, a physician. We were attending *Tosca* at the Met when she was called to the hospital for an emergency. I never saw her again."

"What happened?"

"On the way, she was murdered for the few dollars in her wallet. They never found the killer."

"I'm so sorry."

Daniella clasped his hand in hers, and they walked on in silence.

JULY 14

They slept late, dressed quickly, and had a brief breakfast before their meeting at the castle.

"I had a scary dream; it was the masks, but I got through it."

"He held her hand. If it happens again, wake me up."

They walked the Via Giulia, built in the early sixteenth century and named for Pope Julius II. It was a wide street cobbled with ancient stones, bounded along its length by finely designed churches, elegant buildings, and some of Rome's most luxurious *palazzi*, reminding Jeff of the Audrey Hepburn and Gregory Peck movie, *Roman Holiday*. It was a picture-perfect morning, the sun hanging solo in the bright blue sky, and the day's heat starting to replace the cooler night air. Ahead, rising high, was the towering cylindrical Castel Sant'Angelo, crowned with the bronze statue of the Archangel Michael grasping his sword.

Jeff voiced his thought. "I'm surprised the Vandals left anything from the Ark in the castle. Didn't you write that the Temple Treasure was taken away?"

"Perhaps they weren't able."

"What?"

"To take anything from the Ark."

Jeff searched for the answer. "Am I missing something?"

"Remember what happened to Uzzah when he thought the Ark was falling."

Jeff remembered, "I see what you mean. When he touched it, he was struck dead!"

* * *

11:00 a.m.

They reached the street's end that met the river and crossed the Ponte Sant'Angelo, its balustrade bordered by ten baroque statues of angels holding features of the Passion of Christ said to have been sculpted by pupils of Bernini. They entered the castle and Francesco Marzoti met them in his small stone-walled office three flights above the entrance at eleven o'clock. The curator's appearance suggested precision and punctuality. He was a thin, modest-looking individual in his early fifties, impeccably groomed, wearing gold wire-rimmed glasses underlined with dark shadows that suggested long nights or longer worries.

They introduced themselves.

"A pleasure, I'm sure." He spoke a lyrical English, spiced with a light Italian accent, a reflection of his schooling at Eton and Cambridge.

"Alessandro tells me you were his teacher, which means I owe you a great deal. He saved my life, so any friend of the doctor's is a friend of mine. How may I help?"

Jeff handed him his card. "Actually, we're here to investigate a murder that occurred in New York."

Francesco studied the card and then the faces of his visitors. "So, you're a detective, also. What murder might that be?"

"A young priest, a Father Fabrizzi. He mentioned your name in a note."

There was a silence. Jeff sensed a strain of caution in Marzoti's voice.

"Yes, of course. It's still a shock to all of us. Who would do such a thing?"

"So, you knew him?"

"Of course, he spent many hours here working on his thesis."

"Perhaps you can tell us the nature of his work."

"Sure. Alonzo came here about eighteen months ago. He is, I should say *was*, a pious and sincere young man with two great passions, music and history. At first, he was interested in focusing his dissertation on the development of church music, beginning with the Gregorian chants of the monks during the Middle Ages and how they influenced the generations of music leading to Bach. But he also loved history, and I believe that Cardinal Dunajski, his advisor, felt his work might have greater value if it delved into questions that related to the current problems of the Catholic Church. As a result, Father Fabrizzi chose the topic of how the Church responded to crises throughout its history.

"He did an incredible amount of research in libraries and museums throughout Italy and determined to his satisfaction that the sacking of Rome in 1527 was one of the most significant events in Church history. That's when I first met him. He was seeking information stored in the castle's archives. While here, he befriended an older scholar also interested in the castle's history."

Daniella said, "An older scholar?"

"Yes. In a way, the scholar became the young man's mentor. That was about a year past. Several weeks ago, Alonzo showed me a bag of gold pieces. He wouldn't say how or where he obtained them but thought that one of the pieces, it looked like a diadem, might be related to the treasure Titus brought back from Jerusalem. If so, that would be a truly historic find. He mentioned that the older man had given him a name to contact and asked if I had heard of such a man. Knowing little of the subject, I called a friend knowledgeable in those things, and he affirmed that the gentleman in question was one of the great experts in the area, an Israeli antiquity specialist living in Jerusalem."

"Was the name Ephraim Selzer?"

"Yes, I believe that was the name. And that was the last time I saw Alonzo. He said he was leaving for Jerusalem the next day."

"I see." Jeff was taking notes. "Do you have a picture of the pieces?"

"No, I only saw them briefly."

"Where did Father Fabrizzi do his work?"

"A great deal of it was in the lower levels, first with his mentor and later by himself, although they had free access to all the floors."

"How many floors are there?"

"You mean you haven't taken a tour?"

"I'm afraid we know very little."

"Then you must. There's an excellent tour that Arturo will be giving at four this afternoon, the last of the day."

"We will try to make it." Jeff thought for a moment before getting back on subject. "Did Father Fabrizzi have any place where he may have kept notes?"

"If he did, it would have been in the desk where he worked, but I don't think you'll find anything. It's already been thoroughly searched."

"Searched? By whom?" Daniella asked.

"The cardinal."

"You mean Cardinal Dunajski?"

"No, Cardinal Jarogniew."

"Jarogniew?" Jeff looked surprised but continued his questioning. "Getting back to Father Fabrizzi, you say you never spoke to him again?"

"I said I never saw him again. He had called from Jerusalem and left a message saying he was even more certain of the power of what he had found."

Daniella responded to the word. "Power?"

"Yes, that was the word he used, though he wanted his work to be kept confidential until he returned to Rome."

"And did you?"

Marzoti returned Jeff's regard. "Did I what?"

"Did you keep it confidential?"

The curator looked down at Jeff's card, and again hesitated. "Is this an official inquiry?"

"We're trying to keep this friendly, but yes, it is."

Marzoti seemed to weigh his answer. "I believe I mentioned it to one other person."

"I see." Jeff and Daniella looked at each other. "And did you infer the possible significance of what Fabrizzi had found?"

"As I said, the word Fabrizzi used was power, and I believe I did."

"And who was this other person?"

"Cardinal Jarogniew."

"Jarogniew again?"

Marzoti's tone grew sharp. "Cardinal Jarogniew is one of the most influential clergymen in the Vatican, some say second only to the pope. He was most interested in Fabrizzi's work."

"Why would Cardinal Jarogniew be interested in Fabrizzi's work?"

"The cardinal is interested in many things, including the history of the Vatican treasures. It's even been rumored that the cardinal recently arranged for a search, unofficially, of what lies deep down in the Vatican Vault, but I know little about that. I even recall suggesting that he discuss his interests with the older scholar who had befriended Father Fabrizzi."

"And did he?"

"Absolutely. A year ago. I introduced them."

Jeff made a note. "One more question. Did Father Fabrizzi ever involve himself in the occult?"

The curator's answers were getting short and Jeff observed he was beginning to perspire, though the room was well air conditioned.

"Father Fabrizzi was fascinated with many subjects, including philosophy, metaphysics, anything that related to theology or theosophy, and he wasn't afraid to go outside conventional church parameters if he felt it could lead to the truth. That's an attitude that can cause turbulence within the staid walls of the faith."

Daniella interjected. "Is that what happened? Did Father Fabrizzi cause any turbulence, as you say?"

"No! I'm just saying that Alonzo took every opportunity to learn new things."

Suddenly the curator stood, excused himself, and strode out of the office.

Daniella looked at Jeff. "I'm afraid Mr. Marzoti has suddenly become sensitive in speaking about his friend, Father Fabrizzi."

Jeff stood and walked around the cramped room, taking in the few pieces of art on the walls, artifacts displayed on shelves, and the various brochures announcing museum programs.

"Jeff, take a look at this."

Jeff read the yellow sticky note Daniella was pointing to that was attached to an old manuscript lying on Marzoti's desk. "For Cardinal Jarogniew." The title of the text was *The Permanent Instruction Of The Alta Vendita: A Masonic Blueprint for the Subversion of the Catholic Church.*

They looked at each other: "The *Alta Vendita*—one of the clues in the notebook," Daniella said. "And the password to enter the Masonic meeting."

Jeff opened the manuscript to a page and read, "In our ranks the soldier dies, and the struggle goes on. In time, this mind-set would be so pervasive that priests would be ordained, bishops consecrated, and cardinals nominated whose thinking was in step with modern thought."

Daniella was confused. "What's that all about?"

"No idea, but it seems important." As Jeff took out his iPhone and was taking an image of the page, Marzoti reentered.

"Please excuse me, I needed to check on another appointment." He stopped cold when he saw what Jeff was doing.

"I hope you don't mind, but I saw this manuscript. Looks quite fascinating—and I see it's for Cardinal Jarogniew."

"That's correct."

"Why would the cardinal be interested in *A Masonic Blueprint for the Subversion of the Catholic Church*?"

The curator glared at Jeff as he reached for the manuscript. "Perhaps to protect it."

"From what?"

"The manuscript was a secret document written in the early nineteenth century that describes how to gain control of the Church through subversive means. Rather absurd. It is said that a single copy was made of the original manuscript, and the cardinal was most interested in finding it. Apparently, it was the older scholar who had secured that copy and entrusted it with Alonzo. Just before Alonzo left for Jerusalem, he asked me to keep it safe for him. When I heard about Alonzo's death, I put it aside for the cardinal." As he talked, he carefully placed the manuscript in his desk drawer, locked it, then checked his watch.

"Well now, I didn't realize how quickly time has flown, but I fear my lunch meeting with the board is starting," he said coldly. "It was a pleasure to meet you."

With that Marzoti accompanied his guests out. As they walked down the steep steps to the outer courtyard, Jeff asked a final question: "Tell me, please. Fabrizzi's friend, the scholar, what was his name?"

"I believe it was Teller, yes, Shimon Teller."

* * *

Noon

The name ripped through Daniella as if a bomb had exploded within her mind. As they left their meeting with Marzoti her body went into an autonomic response, not fully aware of her surroundings, just following Jeff without thought. He held her hand, aware of the shock she was dealing with, and guided her to the museum's entrance. It was only after they exited the castle and walked deep into the heat of the day that her thought processes began to respond. She turned to Jeff.

"My father? What was my father doing with Fabrizzi? . . . And what's the connection between my father, Fabrizzi, and Jarogniew?"

Jeff chose not to answer, giving her the freedom to ponder the thoughts that rushed through her mind. The streets had lost their crowds, the tourists preferring to keep within air-conditioned attractions. The mention of Shimon Teller seemed to prevent further communication until Daniella stopped in front of a bistro just off Piazza Navona. Two old men in colorful berets were in deep discussion, drinking wine, eating bread dipped in oil, and playing chess, seemingly oblivious to the heat. Through the large windows, displays of baskets full of home-baked breads and cakes sent an invitation that Daniella could not refuse.

"My mind is reeling with conjecture and confusion . . . and I'm hungry."

The interior was cool and crowded, filled with the cacophonous sounds of global languages. They were led to one of the few available tables, handed menus, and a waiter brought glasses of ice water. He ordered the fixed price lunch for both of them, which included bruschetta, lasagna, and the ubiquitous glass of red wine.

She took a long drink of the ice water, then quietly spoke. "Look, I'm not sure where this is going, but it appears that somehow the search for your murderer involves my father, and I need to know how."

"Then why don't we start by piecing together what we know."

Daniella took out the notebook and slowly began to review. "The aria identifies the castle, Hiram Abiff relates to the Masonic Brotherhood, the Triple Tau relates to a hidden treasure, and the Latin script relates to the building that houses the force of darkness and the search for the Final Mystery."

"And that mystery," Jeff added, "was to find a source of power in the Ark of the Covenant."

"And now a relationship between Fabrizzi and my father. What do you make of it?"

Jeff rested his head on his cupped hands. "Could the answer lie somewhere in the castle, and involves the *Alta Vendita*, which is predicated upon the secret overthrow of the Catholic Church?"

"Maybe that's part of the whole thing. Maybe it's the power within the Ark that's needed to overthrow the Church."

The food was served and Jeff washed down a forkful of pasta with his wine as Daniella continued. "Then how does that relate to my father?"

"What if the clues were written by your father and it was your father who put this all together. He was the one who found the copy of the *Alta Vendita*, knew *Tosca*, and was aware of the Masonic secrets and Kabbalah."

Now Daniella understood why the crossed *t* looked so familiar. It was her father's handwriting. "And Fabrizzi?"

"His student. Didn't Ephraim tell us that an older scholar gave Fabrizzi the notebook? And when Fabrizzi understood the clue's meaning, he checked it off. Fabrizzi did exactly what we are doing, trying to understand where your father was leading us."

Daniella took a last look at the notes and put them back in her bag. "But why would my father give Fabrizzi the clues to his life's work?"

Jeff gently put his hands over hers. "What if he knew he wouldn't be able to finish?"

"You mean because he realized he was in danger . . . which is why the clues were so oblique. He didn't want them to be deciphered by the wrong people."

Daniella sat back and slowly sipped her wine but left her food untouched. "So, my suspicions were correct from the beginning. He didn't die by drowning, did he?"

Jeff studied her face as she struggled in vain to prevent the tears from clouding her eyes. The emotions spread like ink on a blotter: anger, love, helplessness, vulnerability; a torrent of feelings at the realization that she had been right after all. Her father *had* been murdered.

"So, it was my father who figured out the location of the stolen contents of the Ark. But if it wasn't the treasure, why was he murdered?"

"Because he was caught in the middle of a conspiracy to prevent the pope from modernizing the Church."

Daniella played with the fork in her hand, making small circles on her plate. "But who would want to do that?"

"Maybe we should start by asking, who is Cardinal Jarogniew?"

Daniella shook her head. "I wouldn't know whom to ask."

Jeff took out his cell. "But I do."

* * *

1:30 p.m.

The meeting with Cardinal Dunajski took place at the inn, which provided a private conference room for Jeff and Daniella.

"I hope we haven't put you out of your way."

"On the contrary, it sounded like you've made progress, and I needed a break from the politics of this week's synod."

"We're finding numerous pieces of the puzzle, and we're trying to fit them together."

"How can I help?"

"You mentioned the tension in the Church."

Dunajski spoke diplomatically.

"All I meant was that these are difficult times. Many are critical of the views that our new pope holds on a number of issues. There are those in high position who believe that changing Church doctrine will corrupt the basic pillars that the Church rests on."

"Is that what you believe?"

The cardinal continued to avoid disparaging others.

"I believe it important for the pope to raise these concerns. If the Church is our shepherd, then who else should care for those who are living in relationships that are in apparent defiance of Church doctrine? Who else but the Church, through our Lord Jesus Christ, should let them know that God still loves them, that unless we minister and provide comfort and shelter, they will be lost?"

Jeff considered the implications. "Are you suggesting that the Church condone their personal choices?"

"I am only suggesting that the Church follow Christ's teaching to serve his people. However, there are those who are adamantly against even a suggestion of change."

"How adamantly?"

Dunajski spoke with gravitas. "Very."

"What do you know about Cardinal Jarogniew?"

Dunajski seemed surprised at the question. "Why do you ask?"

"You brought up his name when we met in New York, and his name continues to come up. We wanted to get an idea of who he was."

"I know him well, perhaps better than anyone. We grew up together. However, he doesn't agree with all of my positions."

"What do you mean?"

"Cardinal Jarogniew is the most prominent Church leader against the pope's actions. He believes the Church must remain strict in teaching the original Gospel of Christ, not a reinterpretation." Dunajski paused, then said, "And he believes this, as you say, adamantly."

"So, he's very conservative on these issues."

"Perhaps regressive is a better term, even reactionary, and threatening the unity of the Church."

The cardinal looked down at his clasped hands and spoke softly. "I fear that the possibility of a schism over Church doctrine is becoming a reality."

Jeff said, "Would there be any reason for Jarogniew to be interested in the work of Father Fabrizzi?"

Dunajski's eyes widened in puzzlement. "I had no idea Jarogniew had any relationship with Father Fabrizzi."

"Are you familiar with *The Permanent Instruction of The Alta Vendita?*

Again the cardinal appeared surprised.

"How do you know about that?"

Jeff summarized how he had seen the book in the curator's office, that it was found by a friend of Fabrizzi, and that it was to be given to Jarogniew. He chose not to mention the drama of the day before.

"Jarogniew? With a copy of the original *Alta Vendita*? I thought the Church had long ago destroyed whatever copies there were. I remember hearing about it when I was a student, we even discussed it briefly in one of my classes. It was one of those things the Church wished to keep hidden, I suppose, because it called for liberalization."

Jeff said, "Liberalization? But isn't that what Jarogniew is so adamantly against?"

"Yes."

"Then why would he be interested in it?"

Dunajski seemed to look for an answer. "I would have no idea. It's a Masonic document, and the Masons have long been enemies of the Church."

"We were told that it was written in the early 1800s, and that it describes how to gain control of the Catholic Church through subversion."

"Yes," the cardinal replied, "if I recall, the *Alta Vendita* was the highest lodge of the Carbonari, an Italian clandestine society linked to freemasonry. Both were condemned by the Church. Apparently, it declared that open war against the Church was hopeless, but it could be destroyed by secretly placing Masons within the church hierarchy, which would eventually lead to taking over its leadership. In other words, redirecting Church objectives for its own purposes to remove, as they believe, 'the hateful influence of the Catholic Church in society.'"

Daniella had been listening intently.

"Is it possible that Cardinal Jarogniew is using the same strategy as that outlined in the *Alta Vendita*, but instead of liberalizing the Church, he plans to, as you say, take over its leadership for his own purposes?"

The cardinal rose to his feet, his tall, lanky frame slightly stooped. "Jarogniew wishing to take over the Church? I never thought of it like that. I know the *Alta Vendita* involved a long-term strategy leading to gradual control of the church over many generations. I just never believed it was possible."

"Yes," Jeff said. "The manuscript counsels a slow but steady inculcation of brilliant young minds that would gain acceptance into leadership positions until a time when the balance of power shifted, followed by a new order." He opened his iPhone and read the text. "This comes from a page that I copied in the *Alta Vendita*. It says: 'In our ranks the soldier dies, and the struggle goes on. In time, this mind-set would be so pervasive that priests would be ordained, bishops consecrated, and cardinals nominated whose philosophy was in step with modern thought.'"

Daniella looked up at the tall figure of the cardinal.

"Is that possible, an internal benign revolution?"

Dunajski nodded. "Yes, I suppose it's possible, and eventually a pope would be elected from those ranks and lead the Church on this new path of enlightenment."

"But in this case, the path of enlightenment leads to the past." Jeff hesitated, realizing his next question would be a difficult one to answer.

"Is Cardinal Jarogniew an enemy of the Church?"

Dunajski cupped his right hand under his chin as if considering a view that he had not thought of previously.

"It would be quite clever, wouldn't it? There would be no need for Ludvik to assume the Chair of Peter once there were enough bishops and cardinals leading the Church backward. All he'd need to do was influence the pope to his thinking, all the while the Catholic world would assume they were marching under the banner of the apostolic keys."

Jeff followed up. "Is that what's happening?"

"Perhaps. He can be very persuasive. It was Jarogniew who stage-managed the election of this pope, a cardinal who very few knew about."

"And whom he thought he could manipulate to his way of thinking?"

"Knowing him, I would think so. All his life he sought power and complete control of whatever he was engaged in. Indeed, over the years he had reached a position of power almost as great as the past popes and obtained almost complete control of Vatican finances. Nothing happened without his approval. Perhaps that was his plan all along." The cardinal paused for a moment. "I assume that will no longer be possible."

"What do you mean?"

"Jarogniew is no longer Cardinal Secretary. The pope has re-lieved him of his position."

Jeff looked at Daniella with surprise. "We weren't aware of that."

"Assuming that what you say is true, it would appear that without that position, Jarogniew will no longer have the power to lead the Church backward."

"Unless he has another source of power," Daniella interjected.

Dunajski realized what Daniella was alluding to. "And that's what you've been searching for?"

"Yes, but Jarogniew is also seeking it."

The cardinal remained silent for a moment, then nodded as if he understood the full implications. Then he walked over to Jeff, shook his hand, and made a slight bow to Daniella. "My friends, I found this to be a most interesting discussion, something I must think about. I now see where the two of you are heading. I have an audience with the Holy Father this afternoon, and I will present your case to him. Thank you for your help."

"Cardinal, one last question," Jeff said. "When you said Jar-ogniew was adamant, were you implying that nothing would get in his way?"

"That is precisely what I implied."

"Not even if murder was required?"

The cardinal bowed again and left the room.

* * *

1:45 p.m.

Ludvik Jarogniew looked out his window overlooking St. Peter's Square. To the cardinal, it appeared that the throngs of visitors from around the world were praying for a leader to guide them away from the spiritual poverty that the new world, and its modernity, had created. That leadership, he believed, was miss-ing. Even as the invited bishops gathered in Rome for the synod, Jarogniew was already receiving reports of how divisive a new liberal interpretation of Church practice could be.

The thought of his being replaced as Cardinal Secretary brought a smile to Jarogniew. How would the pope address the issue, or would he? Surely, he knew that there would be a reac-tion to his removal. He checked the time. The answer would be arriving momentarily.

A rustle at the door suggested the afternoon post had arrived. He sifted through the notices until he came to the large white envelope with the papal imprint. Would his name even be mentioned? He sat down, poured a claret, adjusted his reading glasses, and unsealed the dispatch. As presumed, it contained the "Instrumentum Laboris," the copy of the pope's approved agenda. It read: "According to Church Law, the Third Extraordinary General Assembly will thoroughly examine and analyze the information, testimonies, and recommendations received from the particular Churches to respond to the new challenges of the family."

That was all, short and to the point. His eyes shifted to the list of committees, eagerly reading through the long lists. It was as he expected. His name was not included, nor those he had put into positions of power. The Church hierarchy had been packed with liberal, revisionist bishops.

He had to admit that his expulsion from the seat of power was a smart political move by the new pope. As if anticipating what he was to find, his eyes shifted to the bottom of the page: it was signed by Bronislaw Dunajski, Cardinal Secretary of the Vatican and Secretary of the Synod of Bishops. He had been replaced by his old enemy. He couldn't help but appreciate the irony. Two boys growing up together, almost brothers, competing from the moment they met, like the biblical Jacob and Esau. This, however, would be the final competition. There would be no need for further conflict, no need to have the majority backing of the synod nor of the pope, for the church of man had only so much power. Jarogniew would soon have a much greater power.

Jarogniew appreciated that it was Shimon Teller's genius that solved the millennia-old mystery. And yet, he also believed it was his destiny, not Teller's, to reap the final reward. Teller only sought the Ark for the history, Jarogniew sought it for the future. How unfortunate that the Israeli didn't understand that Jarogniew was the one chosen to possess it. He had offered him great sums of money, but Teller refused to cooperate. What else was there to do when the archeologist preferred torture rather than handing over the power of the Ark? Surely there was little choice but to carry out the death sentence.

The cardinal had to admit one thing: Teller was one tough Jew, loyal to his values regardless of the consequences, a testimony to what had kept his people alive. But then, destiny presented a second opportunity when he was informed that Teller had passed the answers to a young, innocent priest. And yet, he also refused to cooperate. To what purpose? Another life needlessly wasted.

Jarogniew sat back with pride in his accomplishments, as if years of planning were about to come to fruition. He emptied his glass in one long satisfying swallow.

* * *

2:30 p.m.

Cardinal Emanelle Estefaz knocked gently on the apartment door and Jarogniew rose to greet his visitor.

"So, it's true. He fired you."

"It is. From now on, *we'll* do the firing."

"What can I do?"

Jarogniew went to his desk drawer and removed two sheets of paper. "This is a list of names of the two hundred senior prelates attending the synod. Fifty are members of the Brotherhood, all waiting for the signal. I'd like you to deliver that signal."

"How shall that be done?"

"Simply say, 'The schism has arrived, Sistine Chapel, July 16, 1:00 p.m.'"

"But that is the hour of the synod."

"I prefer to call it what it will be."

Estefaz looked at Jarogniew, understanding his meaning. "So, that was why you chose that date. The anniversary of the Great Schism."

Jarogniew smiled. "Yes, the hour when we will reorient the Church to our way of thinking. I want the bishops to witness the moment that salvation arrives."

* * *

2:30 p.m., The Inn at the Roman Forum

"If it's in the castle, then where?" Daniella said. "Do we start breaking stone walls? It's not like my father to leave out details."

"Then the details must remain in the clues we have yet to figure out." Jeff reexamined the notebook. "Let's start with Psalm 118. Why would your father mention it?"

Daniella thought for a moment. "Not sure, but Google will know." She took out her cell and brought up the psalm. "Listen to this: 'The stone which the builders refused is become the head stone of the corner.'"

"The cornerstone! Your father's telling us which stone it is."

Jeff continued to the next unanswered clue. "And 'ChVRM ABIV'?"

Daniella responded within seconds. "That's an easy one. Hiram Abiff!"

Jeff raised his glass. "You're on a roll. That means one clue remains unsolved. What's 'Ohr Ganuz'?"

"In Hebrew it means a hidden light, but I have no idea what it's referring to."

"So, what do we do?"

"My father taught me that if I don't understand something, the numbers will provide the revelation. Check the sums to understand the meaning, he would tell me."

"You mean Gematria?"

"Yes, Jewish numerology. Are you familiar with it?"

"Only that its some kind of mystical system, like Kabbalah."

"It's used to find hidden meanings, where each Hebrew letter equates to a number and allows us to compare words or phrases with the same numerical value. When the sum of two words or phrases equal each other, it discloses a concealed meaning that connects them."

"And is there a relationship between the cornerstone, the Ohr Ganuz, and Hiram Abiff?"

"We can check by adding the numerical values of the Hebrew letters, using the order of the Hebrew alphabet. The first letter, *aleph*, equals one, *bet* equals two, *gimel* equals three, and so on."

Daniella sat at the desk and wrote out the entire twenty-two letters of the Hebrew alphabet with their numerical equivalents on a piece of the inn's stationery.

100 = ק	10 = י	1 = א
200 = ר	20 = כ	2 = ב
300 = ש	30 = ל	3 = ג
400 = ת	40 = מ	4 = ד
	50 = נ	5 = ה
	60 = ס	6 = ו
	70 = ע	7 = ז
	80 = פ	8 = ח
	90 = צ	9 = ט

"OK, let's add up the letters of the name Hiram Abiff, which in Hebrew is חִירָם.אֲבִי and we get . . . 273."

Jeff checked the addition. "And if you add up the reference to the stone from the psalm?"

Daniella repeated the exercise, "אֶבֶן מָאֲסוּ הַבּוֹנִי 273!"

Jeff seemed startled. "That's amazing. The same total as Hiram Abiff. And what about the word 'ohr ganuz'?"

Daniella wrote it in Hebrew and added the letters up: אוֹר גָנוּז "273!"

Jeff smiled as when uncovering a new discovery. "Then a cornerstone, Hiram Abiff, and this Ohr Ganuz are all connected. But how?"

* * *

The call to Rabbi Elimelech was followed by a taxi ride to the Great Synagogue.

"I see," the rabbi said after being brought up to date. "You equate the reference of the Triple Tau to a hidden treasure of an ancient and mystical power, and you believe it's located in the Castel Sant'Angelo?"

"Yes," Jeff said. "And under a rejected cornerstone, as mentioned in Psalm 118, similar to the loose stone in the temple floor where they believed the Ark was hidden."

Elimelech stood up. His face wore a perplexed smile. "So, you believe the Masonic legend?"

Jeff said, "It's hard to say. But we believe it makes the most sense. Something was taken from the Ark, and, we believe, is hidden here in Rome and is a great source of power."

"I warned you it was legend."

"We think it's more than legend. You see," Jeff added, "Daniella's father left a notebook with clues that relate a stone and a treasure, and when Daniella used Gematria, she found the stone and Hiram Abiff each added up to 273."

The rabbi considered for a moment, and Daniella said, "But my father left a final clue that equals 273, but we don't know what it means."

"And what is the clue?"

"The Ohr Ganuz."

Elimelech totaled the numbers in his head. "Indeed, 273, so there could very well be a relationship. Our sages tell us that wherever the Ark or its contents are located, the Ohr Ganuz would also reside. You see, the Ohr Ganuz is not just any light, but a hidden light, a mystical one. When God created the world and said, 'Let there be light,' the intensity that resulted was not what we see today. That original light was, they say, so penetrating that one could see from one end of the world to the other."

"What happened to it?"

"According to Rashi, the great Jewish commentator of the Middle Ages, when God saw how the wicked enjoyed the light as much as the righteous, he hid it, wanting it to be used only to reward the upright in heart. That light will reappear when the Messiah comes. Our holy sages tell us it is stored in the words of the Torah. When one learns Torah, one will find the deepest meanings of God's ways. That is why the perceptions that the Ohr Ganuz gives us are called insights—seeing what others cannot."

Jeff was fascinated. "And no one has seen it since creation?"

The rabbi smiled. "With one exception. According to legend, the Ohr Ganuz is stored in the lights kindled on Chanukah. The thirty-six lights burned during those eight days correspond to the number of hours that the original light filled the universe before God set it aside. That is why we follow the tradition of gazing into the Menorah lights, allowing us a preview of how great that hidden light must be, for it brings into view the length of the universe and the years of history all at once."

Jeff said, "Sounds like Einstein's Theory of Relativity long before he formulated it."

"In what way?"

"Einstein proposed that there's no such thing as absolute time or space, that they are a part of a single continuum, space-time."

Elimelech considered Jeff's thought. "Yes, perhaps that's what gave Einstein the idea, for reflecting on the Chanukah lights allows us to comprehend a universe beyond time and place. It is, in the end, a brief insight into God's design for the destiny of his people and a momentary glimpse into the world to come."

* * *

They walked from the synagogue into the Jewish Quarter, crowded with diners and tourists.

"I'm not certain he completely believed us," Jeff said.

Daniella gave him an understanding smile. "At least we learned that if something from the Ark is found under a cornerstone in the Castle San Angelo, there should also be an intense light."

"But what is that something? You said it's either the stone tablets of the Ten Commandments, the jar of Manne, the priestly clothes, the original Torah, or Aaron's Rod."

They walked on in silence, trying to determine whether their entire hypothesis was simply that—a hypothesis.

* * *

"Mind if I change the subject?" Jeff knew he had to ask the question.

"Not at all. My mind could use a break from Einstein and numbers."

"When I was in your office, I noticed a picture of what must have been your parents and one of a handsome-looking young fellow. Would he be a boyfriend?"

Daniella looked at him, surprised. "Yes, that young man is special, but not a boyfriend. He was my older brother, my only brother, and I worshipped him. He was tall and strong and brilliant and caring. But he and my mother were killed when Palestinian terrorists bombed Sbarro's restaurant in Jerusalem. My brother was a soldier, on leave, a member of the famous Golani Brigade. If he had lived, he would have become a great leader in Israel."

Jeff felt he had intruded. "I'm so sorry. I shouldn't have asked."

She stopped and held his arm for a moment. "I'm glad you did."

Their hands touched, and they instinctively held them together.

"What I mean to ask is, are you seeing anyone?"

Before she replied he felt her gently squeeze his hand and when he looked at her, he saw the sparkle in her eyes and the grin he had come to recognize and enjoy.

"How can I when you're taking up all my time?"

* * *

4:00 p.m.

They entered the castle and bought the last two tickets for the afternoon tour. Already a large group of Evangelical Christians from a Dallas megachurch had gathered inside the entryway. Jeff and Daniella presented their tickets and quickly joined them. The guide was a young man; "Arturo Spanoli" was the name printed on a card in large letters pinned to his white polo shirt. He was tall, in his twenties, and as thin as a rail. He had dark complexion, smooth black hair with a fashionable small beard under his chin, and a long, straight Roman nose.

"Welcome to the Castel Sant'Angelo, one of Rome's top attractions, with more than 900,000 visitors last year. The castle
was originally built in AD 123 as a mausoleum for the emperor
Hadrian, but in the Middle Ages, Emperor Aureliano made it into
a fortified outpost, and by the year 1277, it became the property
of the Vatican. Later, the papal apartments were added as well
as the long *passetto* or passageway, which was built to connect
the castle with the Vatican. The castle today has five floors and
houses a national museum.

"With each succeeding pope alterations were made to the
original mausoleum."

Arturo pointed to the castle's wall.

"Here is the famous winding ramp, which runs about four
hundred feet, built by the Romans. It leads from here on the
ground floor to the terrace on the roof. The castle, therefore, is
built like a cylinder, and the ramp circles the perimeter. It's a
fairly steep circular incline, so as we walk to the floors above, I
need you to stay together.

"Now, before we begin, a little history on one of the most interesting events of the sixteenth century, the Sack of Rome."

Jeff whispered to Daniella. "That's what Fabrizzi was working
on when he met your father."

Arturo was saying, "In the ceaseless battle for power, Charles
the Fifth, the Holy Roman Emperor, was at war with the League of
Cognac, an alliance of France, Milan, Venice, Florence, and Pope
Clement the Seventh."

"Clement the Seventh? That's who's on the gold coin!" Daniella
burst out. The response was a little loud, and Daniella realized
everyone was looking at her.

"Sorry," she said. "Just surprised about Clement."

"That's okay. Glad you're interested. Yes," Arturo continued,
"Clement joined the king of France as did the other city-states, in
an attempt to free themselves from the powerful influence of the
Holy Roman Empire. However, the Holy Roman army defeated the
French and their allies in Italy, but when funds were not available to pay their thirty-five thousand victorious soldiers, they
mutinied and forced their commander to lead them toward Rome
where they and the hordes of bandits and deserters who joined
them could loot the wealthy city.

"On May 6, 1527, Rome, which was only protected by a small
militia of five thousand, was overrun by the mutinous troops,

mainly German mercenaries. Once they broke through the city walls they turned into a mob, pillaging Rome and murdering its citizens. It was reported that by the time the rampage was over, Rome's population fell from fifty-five thousand to ten thousand."

Arturo took a sip of water from the bottle in his man-bag and continued. "Unable to be contained, they went on to attack the Vatican and Pope Clement, who had only 189 of his private Swiss Guards on hand to defend him. It was no match. The mob massacred almost the entire guard, which fought bravely on the steps of St. Peter's Basilica while allowing the pope to make his escape. The Vatican's Swiss Guard still commemorates that heroic rearguard action by choosing that day to initiate new recruits into its ranks."

A heavyset woman from the Dallas group called out: "How did the pope escape?"

Arturo responded. "Good question, and our next stop."

He led them to an outer walkway.

"The pope escaped using this secret passage, called the Passetto de Borgo. You can't see it from below, but it runs from the entrance of the Vatican, over the Tiber River, and into the safety of this castle, a distance of about half a mile. Now picture the year 1527 and the marauding mercenaries of the Holy Roman Emperor closing in on Pope Clement in the Vatican. The pontiff, surrounded by the surviving Swiss Guard, begins his escape to reach the safety of the castle along this secret passage, tucked into the Vatican's high defensive walls. Witnesses described Pope Clement running through the *passetto* to safety carrying what appeared to be a large and cumbersome bundle under his clothing. The bundle slowed him down, but he refused to release it in spite of putting his life at risk. The question then arises, what was he hiding that could be of such importance?

"Scholars suggest that what looked like clothing was only a cover to hide something much more valuable. What that was we can only speculate, but whatever it was, he brought it inside the castle walls."

Jeff whispered to Daniella. "Could he have been carrying . . ."

She finished his sentence. "Something from the Ark?"

Jeff raised his eyebrows for his response.

Arturo continued. "Well, whatever it was, it explains how it was transported from the Vatican to the castle."

Again, the woman from Dallas called out. "What happened to the pope?"

"He was fine. After the rioting, the pope remained isolated in the castle for a month, was forced to pay a ransom, and was held by invading troops for another five months until he escaped. It has been said that the Castel Sant'Angelo represents the earthly power of the popes while St. Peter's Basilica reflects their spiritual power."

Arturo led them up the winding ramp to the second floor.

"Here you will find the prison cells, as well as the large store-rooms for grains and supplies of food and oil for heating and cooking. Understand, the pope was not only the leader of a church but of a political state, which means he had a civil government to run, and many of those jailed here were felons as well as political prisoners. The prison cells were carved out of the mausoleum, so don't expect to see any comforts. Rather, notice how the cells are bare, gloomy, and narrow, and include instruments of torture—among them a nailed collar, handcuffs, and chains. Remember, this was originally a mausoleum, not a prison, and conditions were very severe. They called it the Mouth of Hell."

Jeff was thinking: that's what they call the prison on Rikers Island in New York.

Arturo pointed to another woman in the crowd.

"Madam, please note that you are standing on the spot where the pope blessed the convicted before they were sentenced to death." The woman did a graceful jeté across the stone floor to the delight of the other Texans.

As Jeff and Daniella examined the barren cells of cold, raw stone, Arturo stopped in front of a cell with a wooden door that had two holes for arms and an opening at eye level to see through.

"Now this cell brings up a great trivia question. What great sixteenth-century Florentine artist was kept here in solitary confinement on charges of murder? He even wrote an autobiography describing his imprisonment, calling his cell 'a gloomy dungeon below the level of a garden, which swam with water and was full of big spiders and many venomous worms . . . sleeping on a wretched mattress of coarse hemp which after three days soaked up water like a sponge'?"

When no one in the tour ventured a name, he continued.

"A second clue: he tried to escape, but after climbing out of his bathroom window, using torn bed sheets sewn into long ropes, he jumped and suffered a fractured leg. You should know that bathrooms were a special accommodation given to important prisoners. In almost all cases, that leg would have developed gangrene but, miraculously, it healed. After a year, the pope exiled him to France. Who was this man?"

Again no one ventured an answer.

"Okay, your last clue. This fellow was, perhaps, the most perplexing, larger-than-life figure of the Italian Renaissance: a celebrated sculptor, goldsmith, author and soldier, a hooligan, and a convicted killer."

When no one responded Arturo gave the answer: "Benvenuto Cellini!"

Jeff and Daniella spoke at the same time: "Cellini? Imprisoned here?!"

Arturo smiled at their response. "Absolutely."

Daniella whispered to Jeff. "The coin! Ephraim said Cellini's coin will tell the story!"

Arturo continued. "What is remarkable about Cellini, as we read in his entertaining and most egotistically styled autobiography, was that in 1527, during the sack of Rome, his bravery played a heroic role in defending the pope and the castle. As an expert marksman, Cellini killed Charles the Third, the Duke of Bourbon who led the attack, and later killed Philibert of Chalon, Prince of Orange. The duke was wearing his famous white cloak which identified him to his troops, but made an easy target for Cellini and his rifle.

"It was Cellini's finest hour. But ten years later Cellini was convicted of murder. In fact, he admits to murdering a number of people he didn't like. As a result, he was thrown into this cell, in the same prison that he helped defend. After his attempted escape and the miraculous healing of his broken leg, his autobiography describes that he saw a mysterious magical light, like a halo around his head. He called it an *uno isplendre* that, he claimed, could be seen by others and that continued to be present until his death."

Jeff and Daniella looked at each other. "A light?"

Arturo laughed. "I see the two of you are really into this. May I suggest that you get a copy of Cellini's memoir, which they sell in the museum's gift shop. It was written between 1558 and 1562, and published posthumously under the title, *The Autobiography of Benvenuto Cellini*. Just be cautious in accepting all he says about his exploits, since imagination and ego often distort judgment."

To Jeff and Daniella, the rest of the tour was like a blur, their minds sifting through the information just received. When the tour was over, Daniella led the way into the gift shop.

She picked up a copy of Cellini's autobiography stacked on one of the store tables, glancing through the pages as she waited in line to pay.

"I see you are fascinated with Cellini."

Daniella looked up to see the inquiring face of Francesco Marzoti.

"Signore Marzoti."

"You took the tour. What did you think?"

"It was excellent, and Arturo was wonderful. Thank you for suggesting it."

"Of course, and Cellini, was there something special you wanted to know?"

An uncomfortable feeling laced through her body, telling her to be cautious.

"No, he just sounded extraordinary."

"Yes, he certainly was. Well then, enjoy your evening. Ciao."

* * *

It wasn't long after Marzoti left the book store that he placed a call to Cardinal Jarogniew's private cell.

"Yes, Francesco."

"We had visitors today. They spent a great deal of time in the castle and were most interested in areas that you would appreciate."

"And what would that be?"

"Father Fabrizzi's research, the *Alta Vendita*, and Benvenuto Cellini."

"Very interesting. And would you know who those visitors might be?"

"The same two who intruded on our meeting last evening."

"Ah, the American doctor detective and the woman."

"So you knew who they were?"

"Of course, Francesco, I've had them followed since they arrived in Rome. And you say they were interested in Fabrizzi's research?"

"Yes, they wanted to know if Fabrizzi left any notes."

The cardinal considered the information. "Fascinating, Francesco. The castle and Cellini and the *Alta Vendita*. I see they are making progress, that's very good to know."

"But they're investigating Fabrizzi's death."

"Yes, Francesco, I know."

"But you let them go!"

"Yes, Francesco, and do you know why?" The cardinal didn't wait for the response. "Because they are uncovering the Final Mystery for us, that's why. They are doing our work and mustn't be disturbed, at least not until they find it. And by the way, Francesco, do you know who the woman is?"

"I believe the name was Teller—yes, Daniella Teller."

"And does the name mean anything to you?"

Francesco thought for a moment. "Teller? You mean Shimon Teller?"

"Yes, my friend, it's Teller's daughter, and she is about to deliver to us what her father refused to hand over."

The cardinal clicked off his phone, poured himself a glass of wine, and sat back in his chair: Oh, the irony of it all, he thought. Halfway through the drink, he pressed the call button on his cell. It was received at a gothic residence at 453 Madison Avenue in New York.

"I need both of you here in the morning. The time has come."

* * *

6:00 p.m.

Jeff and Daniella found seats in a crowded trattoria, hungry and tired from the events of the day. By the time the waiter appeared, Jeff had already read through the menu and e-mails twice, and Daniella was deep into her newly purchased Cellini autobiography, stopping now and then to mark certain passages with her pen.

"Sorry to keep you waiting. We're shorthanded tonight so we're a little tight. May I take your order?"

Daniella was too into the book to respond until Jeff put his hand over the page. "I'll have what he's having," she said without interrupting her reading. Jeff ordered the house salad, a pasta special, and sparkling water, figuring this was no time for wine.

Daniella looked up for a moment. "Arturo was right. What an ego Cellini had. I'm not suggesting that he didn't experience everything he wrote about, but he describes things with such vanity that it's difficult to believe that one man could do so much."

She returned to her reading, when Jeff glanced at the cover of her paperback. "Daniella, the book you're reading is the same one I saw in Fabrizzi's apartment."

She looked up from her reading. "Then maybe he also linked Cellini to the treasure. I'll tell you one thing, this fellow Cellini was a genius, and I think we may be close to understanding what the medals are telling us."

She took out her phone, downloaded a file, and they viewed the pictures of the Cellini medals. She pointed to the obverse side of the first one.

"Notice, the inscribed name: CLEMENS VII, PONT. So, the subject is Pope Clement the Seventh, the date is 1534. Arturo said that was seven years after Cellini helped the pope escape to the castle. Notice how the pope wears a full beard."

"Yes," Jeff said. "Arturo mentioned he was the first pope to wear one."

"And look at the embroidered cope he's wearing, fastened at the breast with a morse that Cellini engraved. Reminds me of the high priest's tunic and breast plate."

Jeff gave Daniella a surprised look. "It could very well be the cloak that Arturo told us the pope escaped with, holding a large bundle under it. The question is, what was he holding?"

"Then listen to this. It's about Cellini's escape during the siege of Rome." Daniella opened the book and turned to a marked page and read.

> Pope Clement, wishing to save the tiaras and the whole
> collection of the great jewels of the Apostolic Camera, had
> me called, and shut himself up together with me and the
> Cavalierino in a room alone. . . . they laid before me the
> tiaras and jewels of the regalia; and His Holiness ordered

me to take all the gems out of their gold settings. This I accordingly did; afterwards I wrapt them separately up in bits of paper and we sewed them into the linings of the pope's and the Cavaliere's clothes. Then they gave me all the gold, which weighed about two hundred pounds, and bade me melt it down as secretly as I was able. I went up to the Angel, {the castle} here I had my lodging, and could lock the door so as to be free from interruption.

There I built a little draught-furnace of bricks, with a largish pot, shaped like an open dish, at the bottom of it; and throwing the gold upon the coals, it gradually sank through and dropped into the pan. While the furnace was working I never left off watching how to annoy our enemies; and as their trenches were less than a stone's-throw right below us, I was able to inflict considerable damage on them with some useless missiles, of which there were several piles, forming the old munition of the castle. I chose a swivel and a falconet, which were both a little damaged in the muzzle, and filled them with the projectiles I have mentioned. When I fired my guns, they hurtled down like mad, occasioning all sorts of unexpected mischief in the trenches. Accordingly I kept these pieces always going at the same time that the gold was being melted down; and a little before vespers I noticed someone coming along the margin of the trench on muleback. The mule was trotting very quickly, and the man was talking to the soldiers in the trenches. I took the precaution of discharging my artillery just before he came immediately opposite; and so, making a good calculation, I hit my mark. AFTER I had melted down the gold, I took it to the Pope, who thanked me cordially for what I had done, and ordered the Cavalierino to give me twenty-five crowns, apologising to me for his inability to give me more. A few days afterwards the articles of peace were signed. I went with three hundred comrades in the train of Signor Orazio Baglioni toward Perugia.

"Didn't Ephraim tell us the medals would have the answers?"
Jeff snapped his fingers. "It's Ephraim! How simple. Remember Fabrizzi's note in the margin?"
"You mean the one that said, *Advised to see ES?*"
"The only *ES* we know of is Ephraim Selzer."

"What are you saying?"

"That it was your father who advised Fabrizzi to speak to Selzer."

"And my father must have determined that the real meaning of Cellini's medals was to recreate the story of the pope's escape and how he took with him the Vatican's most precious possessions. Yet, nowhere does it mention his carrying anything from the Ark."

"Unless Cellini realized it was too dangerous to write about what the pope was really carrying. What if Cellini understood that the pope was hiding something so important, so powerful, that for security reasons he made sure it wasn't found in his book?"

Daniella studied the pieces, then showed the picture of the coin's reverse to Jeff.

"What do you see?"

"A prison cell found in the lowest level of a large building and a figure holding a sword over a male prisoner bound in chains."

"Yes, and we know that the most secure underground prison was the Castel Sant' Angelo."

She pointed to the second medal's reverse.

"Cellini entitled it, *Moses Holding The Rod That Struck The Rock For Water To Pour Out To Satisfy The People's Thirst*. But if you look closely all you really see is a man with a beard."

Jeff realized where she was going. "Pope Clement."

"Yes," Daniella whispered, "and holding a rod, the rod that Cellini himself identified as the one Moses used, the same rod as Aaron's."

Jeff folded his arms on the table and exhaled as if he had reached a journey's end.

"So, that's it? That's what we've been looking for? Amidst the slaughter and pillage taking place during the siege, and from all the vast treasures that the Vatican held, that's what the pope chose to carry out at the risk of his own life."

They looked at each other, appreciating what they had discovered.

She said, "Aaron's Rod! Taken from the Ark when Solomon first built his temple, and somehow, like the diadem, it ended up in Rome."

Jeff followed up. "And, the most powerful instrument the Vatican held. That's what he carried into the castle under his robe, knowing that if it fell into the hands of the marauders all would be lost."

Daniella stayed in the moment. "And Cellini buried it where it would never be found."

"And it was your father who figured it out. He just never lived to uncover it."

"Correct, and that's what your murderer is after, knowing that Aaron's Rod was so powerful that it could divert rivers, destroy cities, and draw water from rock!"

Jeff nodded. "And bring down the Church. But where in the castle is it?"

Daniella placed her pen on the picture. "I think Cellini answered that. Notice where the rod is pointing."

"To a wall of rock in a prison cell!"

"And not just any cell, but Cellini's cell, where it's been hidden for almost five centuries."

Daniella opened the book to the pages marked by her napkin and handed it to Jeff.

"Read this," she said.

> Still I do not want to leave out one thing, the greatest that
> ever happened to any person—[a thing] which attests to the
> divinity of God and his ineffable ways, which he deemed
> me desrving of being made worthy. Even afgter that vision
> [perhaps the dream jst described] there remained a glow [or
> a halo (uno isplendre)] over my head, a thing marvelous to
> behold. This is visible to every person to whom U wish to
> show it, even if they are few in number.

Jeff's face lit up as if he also was struck by the light. "A glow. The Ohr Ganuz! Buried within his cell, a light so intense that it created a permanent halo on Cellini!"

As they were about to leave, Daniella asked a final question. "But why on the medals? I mean, if Cellini didn't want it in his book, why put the revelation on the medals?"

Jeff recalled what Siglione had said. "Because Cellini made them as a personal gift to Pope Clement seeking favor for other commissions to work on. No one else would see them. What could be more persuasive than to remind the pope of Cellini's finest hour, when he helped the pope escape from the massacre."

"And only my father realized their significance."

"Yes, and now you do also."

They paid the bill and walked out into the heat and humidity that no longer had any effect on them. They were dwelling on the possibilities.

* * *

Jeff stopped short. "One problem."

She looked at him inquisitively. "What?"

"The rod."

"What about it?"

"Who's going to take hold of it?"

Daniella understood the implication. "You mean you prefer not to die. Yes, that could be a problem." Daniella hid the twinkle in her eye. "I guess there's only one way to find out."

"I knew you'd come up with something. What is it?"

"Try it and see what happens."

He didn't know how to reply, not certain if she was serious.

She smiled and put her hand in his. "Just kidding. I suppose we're going to need someone whose ancestor came from the Kohanim, for it is said that only the priestly class can touch the contents of the Ark without being destroyed."

Jeff relaxed. "There's nothing priestly about my family tree."

"Maybe Rabbi Elimelech would know someone."

"Maybe he would. You speak to him and I'll arrange a visit to Cellini's cell. And I better check in with New York. It's been a while."

* * *

1:00 p.m., New York

Darlene answered the call at police headquarters. "Jeff, is everything okay?"

"I think we're getting somewhere. Is the chief in?"

"He's at lunch with Mayor Arroyo."

"Okay. Tell him we're close to finding the meaning of the coins. When we do, the murderer will find us. I'll try and keep you up to date as we go along."

"Need help?"

"Things are getting a little dicey, but this may go down before anyone can get here. It could be as soon as tonight."

"What about the local police?"

"I'm not sure. It seems this has become a political play and a powerful cardinal with a great deal of influence may be in the middle of it. I'm not certain whom to trust. The fact is, the stakes are much greater than any of us were aware."

"Can you handle it?"

"Do I have a choice?"

Darlene paused before adding. "One more thing you should know."

"What's that?"

"They found Father John's body in the woods behind his brother's house in Connecticut. At first, they thought it was an accident, hit in the head by a falling tree limb. But forensics determined that the extent of the trauma could only be inflicted if he was purposely bludgeoned to death."

The silence of the message being understood was broken when Darlene added: "Jeff, be careful."

"Yeah, I'll try."

JULY 15

The Hotel Cassia, a middling but comfortable three-star establishment, lies in a rather isolated area in northern Rome, not far from Lake Bracciano. Monsignor James Quinn entered its *ristorante* with a thickset man who had a shaved head, deep, dark eyes, and a noticeable limp. The two spied the room before walking to a small table in an unlit corner and sat across from an older man in suit and tie, sipping a glass of claret. They exchanged pleasantries until two Glenmorangie eighteen-year-old Scotch whiskeys were served.

"Thanks for getting here so promptly." Ludvik Jarogniew spoke quietly. "There remains a great deal to be done if we are to find what we are looking for." He paused and looked at the man with the shaved head. "Since we failed the first time."

The young Siglione reddened. "Forgive me, Your Eminence, I never thought of the shoes."

The cardinal gave a slight nod and placed his hand consolingly on the young man's arm. "It's understandable. Actually, hiding it there was quite clever, but this time we want to be certain of our task. Thus far we have been most fortunate, as the doctor and his archeologist friend are doing the Lord's work for us, and, I have been informed, have made great progress in uncovering the Final Mystery."

Jarogniew took a sip of the claret. "Your job, gentlemen, will be to help me retrieve their find as soon as they reveal it." He removed an envelope from his pocket. "Here's the location of their hotel and a goodly sum for your efforts. Quinn, I want you to keep your eye on the doctor. Angelo, I want the woman followed. I believe that is your specialty."

Angelo offered a salacious smile as the cardinal continued. "You should also know, Angelo, that we've uncovered a most interesting coincidence. It wasn't Father Fabrizzi who made the discoveries of where the Final Mystery is located, but Shimon Teller. I believe you were last with him about a year ago here in Rome."

As if a reflexive response, Angelo massaged the long scar on his injured leg, attempting to rub out a memory. "Yes, Your Eminence, I cannot forget."

"Then, you will be glad to know that the young lady you are to follow is his daughter, Daniella. I believe you also know her."

Jarogniew studied the response as Angelo's contrite demeanor momentarily disappeared, and he finished his Scotch in one violent swig.

"From long ago. The Tellers were friends of my father."

"Good, then you will have an opportunity to get reacquainted. But remember, I need her to lead us to the treasure. That is our sole objective. After that, you can do as you wish. Is that understood?"

Angelo involuntarily clenched his right hand that had been playing with a metal spoon, bending it as if it were a piece of cheap plastic. "Yes, Your Eminence."

The cardinal handed each a cell phone. "These are prepaid burners, only to be used in an emergency. When you have the information, you are to call me and then dispose of them."

The cardinal rose from the table, leaving a generous number of euros behind. "By the way, Angelo, I was so sorry to hear about the death of your father."

"Thank you, Your Eminence. They say it was another heart attack, and I am deeply pained."

"I can only imagine."

* * *

2:00 p.m., Rome, The Jewish Quarter

Daniella stepped out of a clean white taxi to meet Rabbi Elimelech in a small kosher pastry shop on the Piazza Costaguti, within the old Jewish Quarter. She was not aware of a similar-looking taxi following her from the inn, nor aware of the man exiting that taxi several cars behind.

Angelo Siglione's face was hidden behind smoke-tinted glasses as he walked to a small restaurant opposite the pastry shop. He sat down at one of the outdoor tables, lit a cigarette, opened a newspaper, and ordered a glass of red wine. He buried his head in

the pages, sipped his wine, and intermittently observed the diners across the street, especially the beautiful young woman and
the tall bearded older man wearing a brimmed black hat.

Daniella and the rabbi ordered coffees as she offered her explanation of the coins and the crown and related how she and Jeff
deduced that her father had identified Cellini's treasure.

"And you believe Aaron's Rod is part of the treasure that Cellini helped the pope escape with?"

"We do."

"And you think it will be found in Cellini's prison cell?"

"That is correct."

The rabbi appeared trying to determine if any of this was
even possible. "The idea alone is chilling. Aaron's Rod? It would
be a miracle. Do you realize its power? The Torah teaches that
whenever the rod was raised, God's power would be transmitted
through it, like lightning striking a metal surface and conducted
to where it was pointed. When the Egyptian king asked for a sign
of God's presence, Aaron threw his rod to the ground and it became a serpent, and when the serpent turned back into a rod it
swallowed all the staffs of Egypt's magicians, yet remained as thin
as before."

Daniella nodded. "Yes, Rabbi, I am aware of the plagues the
rod initiated. When Aaron raised his rod, it turned the Nile into
blood, and when Pharaoh refused to let the Israelites go, Aaron
extended his rod and frogs filled the waters and lands of Egypt,
and when Pharaoh still refused their freedom, Aaron smote the
dust of Egypt with the rod and the dust turned into lice, filling
Egypt's borders."

"Yes, the power of Aaron's Rod produced responses that lie
outside the natural physical laws as we know them. That is why
they are called miracles."

Daniella needed to know as much as she could. "Where did
the rod come from?"

"It is said that it was created by God at the end of the sixth
day of creation and given to Adam when he and Eve were expelled from Eden. From Adam, it was given to Enoch, Noah's
great-grandfather, then given to Noah's son, Shem, and passed
on to our fathers Abraham, Isaac, and Jacob until it came into
the possession of Joseph in Egypt. When Joseph died, it is said
that Jethro took possession of the rod and planted it in his garden, where it remained, unable to be removed. Even touching it

was fatal. Jethro declared that the man who could remove the rod would be given his daughter, Zipporah, to wed. That person was Moses, who recognized what no one else was able to see, three words engraved upon it. When Moses called out the words, the rod rose from the ground and came to him.

"And somehow, your father deduced that the rod is here in Rome, hidden in the castle for five hundred years. Amazing! Our tradition believes that rod will be a scepter for the Messiah to rule the world."

Daniella said, "That's why we must find it before anyone else does."

The rabbi raised a finger in warning.

"But it must be held by a member of Aaron's lineage, a priest, and not just any priest, one that has ultimate faith in the Lord, otherwise, our sages say, whoever touches it will die."

"I know," Daniella said, looking concerned. "But are the priests still safe? I mean, it's been thousands of years. What if, with time, the priestly protection is no longer present, or what if their direct lineage, their pure DNA, so to speak, has been lost?"

Elimelech considered the question. "You mean what if the immunity has been diluted to the point that it no longer provides safety, like a vaccine that has lost its potency? This is not a vaccine. If you believe in the Almighty, then you must believe his power never wavers. I'm from the priestly tribe, as was my father and grandfather before him and his father, a lineage that follows directly from Aaron himself, the first high priest."

"Would you take the risk?"

"I would."

"But what if the line was broken?"

"It could never have been broken—it's our tradition. The first thing a Jewish father passes on to his son is to teach him whether he was born into the priestly tribe of Aaron and his sons."

"But weren't Aaron's sons destroyed when they approached the Holy Ark?"

"Yes, for not being pure in their thoughts."

"Then how will you know?"

"I won't."

"And you believe the DNA evidence?"

"I've read the studies confirming that Kohanim have the same sequence of DNA, but I don't need DNA evidence. If you trust in the Lord and our Torah, no further proof is needed."

He hesitated before continuing. "Of course, I will help you. How could I deny the honor of being the first to hold the rod that goes back to the beginning of time? Call me and let me know when."

* * *

2:00 p.m.

Jeff needed permission to search Cellini's prison cell, but he had a feeling that Marzoti would not be sympathetic. However, if Cardinal Dunajski put in the request, it would be difficult to refuse. He called the cardinal, who agreed to make the arrangements, even if he had to be present personally.

The cardinal returned the call within minutes.

"Marzoti agreed. We are to meet this evening at the entrance to the castle at eight o'clock, half an hour after closing."

* * *

The curator ended the call and thought about Cardinal Dunajski's unusual request. Examine Cellini's cell? Why? The cell had been there for almost five centuries and inspected many times. What was left to see? Perhaps another interested party should be notified. He pressed the numbers on his cell.

"Yes, Francesco."

"I thought you should know that Cardinal Dunajski is coming to examine Cellini's cell this evening."

There was a pause. "And when would that be?"

"Eight o'clock, after closing."

Jarogniew smiled. "Dunajski in Cellini's cell?"

"With several others."

"Most interesting. You know, Francesco, I and my associates would also like to be present. Why don't you join us, say, eight-fifteen?"

Francesco smiled. "It will be my pleasure. I will make the arrangements."

"As always this must be kept strictly between us."

"Of course."

Jarogniew ended the call, realizing this was the final step. "So, they found it." He pushed a contact that sent a message to several recipients, all on untraceable cell phones: *8:15 tonight at the Castel Sant'Angelo. The Mystery is ours.*

* * *

3:15 p.m.

Angelo Siglione placed the newspaper on the table, sipped the last of his wine, and read the message on his cell. The meaning was clear: there was no longer a need for the surveillance of Daniella Teller. Rather, he was to meet at the castle at 8:15—the treasure had been found. Angelo reconsidered. No need to follow the woman? Maybe not for the cardinal, but he had other reasons, more personal, and as important to him as any treasure. As old memories flew through his mind, he saw Daniella bid good-bye to the rabbi and walk down the street. He rose from his chair and threw his cell phone into an overfilled trash container. He would not be prevented from carrying out the task he was so looking forward to.

* * *

Daniella strolled along the crowded thoroughfare lined with restaurants, art galleries, and apartments that sold for over a million euros. She felt a sense of comfort as the afternoon sun lent a reassuring warmth, confident that she was on the last leg of one of the greatest discoveries in archeological history: the finding of Aaron's Rod. It would be a day she would celebrate in honor of her father's memory. As she passed the sidewalk benches filled with an older generation discussing the day's news and local rumors, she pictured her future: a husband to share her life with and, with God's help, a child to pass on the hope of a better world. But for now, aware of a rare sense of near completion, she enjoyed the delights along the narrow ways and alluring store windows filled with a variety of fascinating goods.

The restaurants were busy with late lunch diners as she window-shopped the Via del Portico d'Ottavia and inhaled the aromas that flowed from the spice shops and bakeries. She passed the two-hundred-year-old Boccione Jewish Bakery and smelled the freshly baked pizza *ebraica*, a Jewish pizza that was more like a thick cake of fruits and nuts. She continued on, her attention drawn to a large store crowded with shoppers, and entered the Fratelli Bassetti Tessuti, one of Rome's largest fabric stores. She snaked through its aisles filled with rolls of fabrics and knitting accessories in an infinite number of colors and shades. The

scene brought her back to childhood and memories of her mother
knitting on the porch of their home near Netanya, overlooking
the sparkling Mediterranean Sea. She walked through the rooms
filled with different cloths and felt the variety of textures between
her fingers. Soon the vibration of a message interrupted her lei-
sure: *When will you be back? Jeff*

She sent the reply: *Twenty minutes. Enjoying my window
shopping. just left Elimelech, a lot to discuss.*

* * *

Daniella exited the store and made her way along the Via Vittorio
Emanuele II. She heard a commotion from behind and turned
to see a man with a shaved head pushing his way through the
strolling sightseers. For a moment there was a flash of recogni-
tion, but the thought passed, and she continued browsing. Deciding on one last pleasure, she entered a small textile shop on
the Piazza Paganica. Again, she found shelves filled with endless
colors of ribbons, lace, threads, cords, and buttons. She recalled
how she would hold her mother's hand while shopping for these
same items at the variety store on Gordon Street. Those were
such beautiful and safe times, when everything in life was new
and big and waiting to be explored.

As she started to leave, her thoughts were interrupted by the
sight of the bald-headed man peering through the window. Was
this coincidence? Her two years of training in the IDF, Israel's Defense Force, instinctively returned. *Was he looking for her?* When
she looked again, he was gone.

She exited the shop and crossed the street, increasing her
pace while glancing into the reflections of the glass storefronts,
searching for his image. Was he really there? Seeing no one, she
turned into a quiet street, stopping to give a fleeting look behind.
He was there. She was now certain the man was following her.
Who was he? What did he want? She quickened her pace and
turned into a narrow alley that brought her back to the Piazza
Paganica. She looked about, seeking a taxi, a policeman, some
source of safety, but all she saw was the man getting closer. He
had a limp and was dragging his right leg. She tried to orient
herself, not certain as to where she was, until a flash of memory
had her look up to see the aluminum-sheathed dome of the Great
Synagogue. She headed toward it, walking up Lungotevere Cenci
until she saw the two security guards stationed in front of the

sanctuary. She spoke to them, pointing out the man behind her, who slowed his pace when he saw the guards, then hurried to the entrance. As she glanced back she saw one of the guards speaking to her pursuer. She walked to the rear of the synagogue and knocked on the office door. The door opened, and Rabbi Elimelech looked at her in surprise.

"Daniella, did you forget something?"

She glanced back at the entrance. "A man is following me."

"Did he enter the synagogue?"

"I'm not sure. I told the security guards."

"Let me take a look."

The rabbi walked to the entrance and returned immediately.

"Shaved head? He's speaking to a guard now."

Elimelech thought for a moment, then took her by the arm. "Come with me."

They walked into his office where the rabbi removed a framed blue and white map of Israel on the far wall and pushed on a section of dark stained wood. Daniella heard a click, and the panel, the size of a narrow door, swung open.

"Come, quickly. I think I've only used this exit once, but he will never find you in here."

Daniella marveled at the perfect deception. "What is this?"

"A passageway. Last used, as far as I know, during the Nazi roundup of the Jews during World War Two."

"To escape?"

"And to live. Now it leads to the Jewish Museum at the lower level."

There was a loud knocking on the door, and a voice. "Rabbi?"

Elimelech whispered to Daniella, "Stay here." He walked back into his office, closed the secret panel, rehung the map, and opened the outer door. The security guard and the man with the shaved head were waiting.

"Rabbi, this man says he is looking for someone."

"Please, come in."

Elimelech looked closely at the man, who was perspiring heavily.

"Yes, how can I help you?"

"I'm looking for a friend of mine, a woman. I believe she just entered the synagogue. Dark hair, tall, pretty." He looked around the office. "Have you seen her?"

"Not since I've been here."

The man looked puzzled and glanced around the office again. "Fine, thanks."

The security man accompanied him out, and Elimelech locked the outer door, removed a flashlight from his desk, and opened the hidden panel.

"He's gone, but to be safe I'll take you down these stairs that lead to the museum. You can exit there."

Daniella felt her tension ease as the rabbi led her down the dusty concrete stairs.

"Were you here during the war?"

"No. It was nearly seventy years ago and I was a child still living in Poland. My parents had been taken by the Nazis, and I was sent to live with a non-Jewish family. When the war was over, I was told my parents had died in the extermination camps. Following high school, a teacher suggested I study in Italy. I received a doctorate in philosophy and, as if delving back to my roots, studied for the rabbinate at the same time. So, I wasn't here then, but I know the stories. Unfortunately, every year fewer and fewer witnesses remain who lived those years."

They walked down slowly, following the flashlight's beam.

"But it happened. I still have congregants who remember the day the Germans entered Rome. It was in September 1943. They turned the ghetto into a prison and enforced the racial laws that Mussolini had enacted. They were called the Manifesto della razza, which stripped the Jews of their Italian citizenship, banned them from positions in banking, government, and education, confiscated their properties, and eliminated marriages between Jews and Italians. By the end of the month the head of the SS demanded that unless the Jewish community paid fifty kilograms of gold within three days—about fifty-six thousand dollars at the time—a number of Jewish men from the city would be deported. The Jews tried to raise the money, but when it appeared they could not meet the deadline, Rabbi Zolli, Rome's chief rabbi, went to the Vatican for a loan, and they agreed. At the last moment, the Jews were able to meet the demand. That resulted in a temporary relaxation of the anti-Jewish measures, but it lasted less than three weeks. On October 16, German soldiers encircled the ghetto and began the merciless house-by-house hunt for Jews, forcing them into waiting trucks, which would transfer them to their death at Auschwitz. Fear spread throughout the ghetto. Those lucky enough to hide in the homes of good Christian people or in churches and monasteries out in the country escaped."

Daniella listened in horror as the rabbi narrated. "How many survived?"

"Of the twelve hundred and fifty-nine taken to Auschwitz? Sixteen!"

Daniella had heard the stories many times. But each time was as horrifying as the first.

"The museum opened in 1960," the rabbi said. "When the synagogue was built in the early 1900s, it was simply a space under the main building, perhaps to be used should an emergency arise. Well, that emergency came in the early days of the Nazi round-up, and hundreds of Jews were secreted here until the resistance could move them to safety."

"Did Rabbi Zolli stay here with the others?"

"Unfortunately, no. He left as soon as he found a place to hide. When the Germans entered Rome, the rabbi moved. Some say he took refuge in the Vatican, others say the police urged him to go into hiding with the Italian resistance. Regardless, most of the congregation accused him of abandoning the community, and he was not seen again until the city was liberated in June of 1944. He survived, but many accused him of desertion. After the liberation, the Allied forces saw to it that Zolli resumed his position as chief rabbi. In December 1944, he confidentially told the head of the Jewish community that he was in poor health and would be resigning his position. But then the shock: the rabbi and his wife were baptized."

"They converted to Catholicism?"

"Probably not as much from any theological basis as from being shunned by the survivors. It's all in his memoir, *Before the Dawn*. He died in 1956."

They reached the bottom of the stairwell, where they found a closed steel door with a panic bar lock.

"This will take you into the museum."

Together they pushed the stubborn bar until the door creaked open to the dimly lit museum.

"You'll be safe from here. The museum is closed today, but if you walk to your left, through the exhibit rooms, you will see a red exit sign and a door that only opens from inside with no reentry. Once outside, you will be in a narrow alley that is a dead end to your left, but the right will lead you back to the Via Catalana. From there you can find a taxi back to your hotel. Give me five minutes to disengage the security system. Remember, go to the exit sign to your left."

Daniella's cell lit up with a message from Jeff. *Where are you? Meeting tonight at castle entrance 8:00 PM—can rabbi help?*

She explained the situation to the rabbi. "Tonight we're going to examine Cellini's cell. Can you meet us at eight o'clock at the castle entrance?"

"Wouldn't miss it."

She returned the message. *At synagogue, ran into problem, back soon. Rabbi will be there at eight.*

Slowly he closed the door. "Okay, I'll see you tonight, good luck."

* * *

Daniella heard the heavy door lock behind her. She walked to her left and made her way through a series of sparsely lit rooms, each featuring an exhibit. As she entered room four she saw the red illumination of the exit sign on the opposite wall. She reached the exit, waited five minutes to be certain the security system was turned off, then threw her weight onto the steel bar, swinging the door completely open. She waited for the siren's sound, but only silence followed. Sunlight flooded in as she took a step into the alley, reflexively raising her handbag to block the blinding sun.

"There you are!"

Daniella froze, trying to determine where the shout came from, but her eyes were still adapting to the glare. She heard the quickening irregular steps from her right and the calling voice, "Now I've got you." Her heart pounded against her chest wall, and the sense of fear spread over her like oil over water. She looked to her left, but the street ended in front of a high wall. There was nowhere to go. Her mind tried to focus, and she spun around in time to thrust her handbag between the closing door and its frame. She heard the sounds of her pursuer nearing as she rushed into the museum, listening for the click of the panic bar as it locked close.

It never came. She turned back to see the door flung wide. Standing in the sunlight was the man who had followed her.

"Where are you, Daniella?"

Daniella? He knew her name? Who was it? She moved quietly through the passage from room 5 to room 4. Could she reopen the door leading to the rabbi's office?

"Come now, you remember me, its Angelo, Angelo Siglione."

Angelo Siglione? Antonio's son? She hadn't seen him since they were kids. Why would he be following me?

"Please, Daniella, I need to talk to you."

She could hear his footsteps coming closer, the hard and soft irregular sounds of limping steps. She didn't know if it was fear or foresight that prevented her from responding.

"I need to know what you're doing here."

She remained silent, moving through the darkened halls. Again, the rasping voice spoke.

"Just tell me about Fabrizzi and the treasure."

What does Angelo know about Fabrizzi? She moved through the rooms filled with tombstones from the catacombs of Rome. How did he know? Was he involved? Was he working with his father?

"You can't get away, Daniella. I know you know where the treasure is."

Treasure? Is that what he wants? How? She made her way into room one, which she'd first walked through when she left the secret stairs. As she tried to reach the hidden door she collided with one of the display cases, sending a clatter through the room. She backed away and maneuvered past the exhibits, reaching the wall in front of her. Her hands groped to find the door, but there was no marking, no differentiation for an opening. Her heart continued racing as she reached into her bag, fumbling for her cell, and fingered a message to the rabbi.

He's in museum. Please open door ASAP.

From behind there was a sound and she turned toward it. Had he seen the light from her phone? She tried to retrace her steps, but it was too late. She heard his panting behind her, and then his arm around her neck pulled her against his body.

"I found you."

"Angelo, what are you doing? Take your hands off me."

She clenched her fist and shot her elbow backward with all her strength into his groin.

He gave a shout and released his grip. She knew he was much stronger than she was, but her army training had prepared her for bigger assailants. She turned toward him and threw her knee into the same spot, but this time his hand was there, and he grabbed her leg, throwing her down on her back. She kicked him in the face with her other foot, and again he released her as he stumbled backward against an exhibition case, breaking the glass into a million pieces.

"You bitch!"

She scrambled to her feet and with the cover of darkness ran toward the far end of the room. She turned on her cell momentarily, using the light to find the entrance into the next room. There was none; the room had but one entryway, and he was coming through it. Where could she go? The space was filled with glass exhibit cases. The irregular sound of his steps was getting closer. She removed her shoes and walked as carefully and quietly as she could to the far end of the room. She tried to hide, but as she knelt behind one of the cases, she brushed against it. The case moved slightly and then there was a noise—something had fallen to the floor. Looking up, she could make out his movements as he approached.

"I heard that. Now I know where you are."

The bizarre drumbeat of his limping steps came closer as she tried to make herself inconspicuous.

"I'm almost there, Daniella. There's nothing to be afraid of. Remember when we were kids how we had fun together at your birthday party, like brother and sister? We should do that again."

The sound of steps and the volume of the twisted words were increasing. Daniella crouched lower behind the case, trying to control her breathing, when the piercing sound of her cell erupted. She glanced down—it was Jeff. Afraid to speak, she turned her cell off and pushed it deep into her bag.

And then her fingers felt a long, thin object: the bartender's gift, the corkscrew!

"Was that your cell? I bet you did that so I would find you, like when we played hide and seek. But the prize for finding you will be different this time, so start telling me how much you always wanted me. Then, after you show me, you can tell me all about the treasure and where it is. You see, you have to give me a good reason to let you live, which is more than I allowed your father."

Her hand tightened around the corkscrew as a fist came down on her head; she fell backward, stunned, to the floor.

"I found you!"

She tried to get up but couldn't push him off. She smelled the putrid odor of his sweat as he laughed and forced his lips onto hers.

"Come now, my dear, you can do better than that. Don't you realize you owe me? After all, it was your father who made me a cripple, slicing my leg with his knife, almost severing the nerve. He was one tough dude, I'll give him that. Nothing like the others, who begged for mercy. No, your father gave me a real run for my money until his head got in the way of a rock I was holding. It's because of him that wherever I go I'm marked like Cain, a cripple forever."

Daniella felt herself weakening, growing tired from the struggle. Her fingers tightened into a fist around the corkscrew and she wriggled violently to try and free her arm.

"Now, my dearest, you will offer yourself in penitence for what he did to me. You know, the sins of the father? Go ahead, my dear, start begging."

With a burst of desperate strength, she shot her left arm into his face, the coiled rings of the corkscrew finding its mark above her, plunging through the gelatinous substance of his left eye until it reached deep into the orbit's bony socket.

"That's your penitence!" she cried.

Angelo screamed in pain and fell back, his hands clutching his eye, the corkscrew still deep within the socket. As he rolled onto his back, Daniella struggled to her feet and staggered away.

"You bitch! What did you do to me?"

He had found his gun, and fired again and again, blindly, the sounds of shattering glass filling the room. Daniella looked for the exit door. Ahead was a dim light, and she ran toward it. It wasn't the exit sign but the sign for the museum's gift shop. She reached for the door's handle, but it was locked. There was nothing left to do. She shrank down onto the floor, her back against the glass wall, too exhausted to go on. The wild screams, like a bull running amok, calling out her name, were getting closer. She sat huddled, ready to meet her fate, like the ancient Jews at Masada. As she peered up she saw him standing above her, the corkscrew still stuck in his face.

"Daniella, there . . . you . . . are." His voice wheedled in a taunting refrain. "Time to get up and tell me how sorry you are for causing this inconvenience. I'm sure it's just a lover's quarrel."

He dragged her up by the hair, snapping her head back so that she was staring into the horror of his disfigured face.

"Now, my love, tell me how much you miss me."

Suddenly, as if through a dense fog, she sensed the approaching echoes of someone shouting her name.

"Daniella?"

Somehow she responded: "Here. I'm here."

She felt his hand releasing its grip, and sank to the floor, trying to discern the shadowed figure pulling her attacker away, attempting to recall a familiarity of voice, but the exhaustion of consciousness advanced too quickly. And then a gunshot followed by another. Her last memory was the distant sound of a reverberating explosion.

* * *

8:00 p.m.

Jeff paid the six euros taxi fare, removed the gym bag he had purchased, and walked across the bridge. Except for the external security lights and dimmed internals, Sant'Angelo appeared deserted. He heard footsteps behind and turned to see a tall man in black garb with a companion wearing a white hooded cloak. At first, he thought one of the men was the rabbi, but as they approached, he recognized Cardinal Dunajski and a male companion.

"Cardinal, I mistook you for Rabbi Elimelech. Perhaps he's already inside."

"Then we should go in. I hope you don't mind, but Father Esconzo wished to come with me."

"Of course not."

Esconzo's face was partially hidden by the white hood.

Jeff knocked on the door, and the security guard opened it, explaining that no one else had arrived. He led them through the empty corridors to the winding ramp leading down to the level of the prison, and they made their way to Cellini's cell. The door was already open and the cell was empty, except for a chair and a small square wooden table. Jeff put the bag on the stone floor, unzipped it, then removed a mallet, a chisel, a pry bar, three flashlights, several bottles of water, and a stethoscope.

"I stopped at the hardware store, but the stethoscope I borrowed from a doctor's office."

Dunajski smiled. "Looks like a full examination, but I hope you know where to examine. This is a big place."

Jeff looked around the cell. "Cellini's medal pointed to one of the stones on the wall, and we believe it's here in his cell." Jeff removed a paper from his pocket. "It's Psalm 118. We determined the location from the Hebrew which translates as, 'the stone the builders despised has become the cornerstone,' so I'll start there." Jeff placed the stethoscope on a stone making up the rear corners, gently percussing the walls with the mallet. "It's like listening to a heart, sounding for something loose or hollow." After examining several stones, he removed the stethoscope from his ears, as if uncertain, then reexamined the walls again. "Something's wrong, the sounds are all solid."

"Perhaps I can help," said Father Esconzo. He took the paper and read the psalm. "You have interpreted the Hebrew word, *penah*, to mean cornerstone, but it could more precisely suggest an angle where two nonparallel lines meet. That would include the corner floor stones. Why not try that?"

Jeff placed the stethoscope on the floor's cornerstone at the far end of the cell and gently tapped it with the mallet. He repeated the routine, trying to determine the accuracy of his interpretation. "There's no question, the sound is different from the others, it's hollow, the stone's loose."

It took several taps with the mallet and chisel before the stone began to move. Using the pry bar, he levered the stone, revealing a cavity dug into the cell's floor, about twelve inches square and six feet deep.

Jeff flashed the light into the hole.

"Something's down there."

* * *

Two high beams flooded the cell.

"You have saved us a great deal of work," a voice said, and from out of the shadows five men appeared.

"Well now, Dunajski, I see you made it."

The three startled men crouched above the hole turned to see Cardinals Jarogniew and Estefaz, Francesco Marzoti, Monsignor James Quinn, and a broad-shouldered bull of a man with white hair, a short neck, beady black eyes, and a revolver.

Jarogniew flashed the light on Jeff. "Ah, Dr. Moss, so we meet again."

The man with the gun laughed. When he spoke, his words betrayed a thick Slavic accent.

"Dr. Moss, I not recognize you without mask."

Jarogniew focused the light on the others. "And who else, Dunajski, did you invite to our party?"

At that moment, they heard steps behind them. Jarogniew turned the beam to find a tall man with a gray beard and black hat.

"Sorry I'm late, Jeff . . ." Elimelech realized they weren't alone.

"Well, look who's here. The good rabbi," Jarogniew said.

"Is everything OK?" Jeff said.

"It took me longer . . ."

Tirshov pointed his gun at the rabbi. "Shut up, or you dead man."

Jarogniew kept the beam on the rabbi. "Now, Tirshov, let's try to avoid any disturbance, if possible, after all this is an old friend from the Masonic lodge. You know, Rabbi, we haven't seen you at our meetings in years."

Elimelech responded sharply. "When you changed the idea of what Masonry means, I knew it was time to leave."

Jarogniew smiled. "Then you will be especially interested in our little archeologic dig." He focused the light on the man in the white hooded cloak. "And who is this?"

The man called Esconzo lowered his hood and looked intently at the cardinal.

Jarogniew stared at the man, momentarily frozen, his face turning ashen, his smile lost before he was able to regain his demeanor.

"Well, what a pleasant surprise. So nice to see you here. We might as well get this taken care of now."

"What's this all about, Ludvik?" demanded Esconzo.

"Well, Your Eminence, it's quite simple, your Church is being taken over."

"What do you mean 'being taken over'?"

Jarogniew flashed a big grin. "Surely you're aware of the *Alta Vendita*."

The pope looked puzzled. "Should I be?"

"Not important, few Catholics are, but it will be the demise of the Church as you know it. You see, *The Permanent Instruction of the Alta Vendita* is a secret document written in the early nineteenth century by the Masonic Brotherhood that brilliantly mapped a blueprint as to how to annex the Catholic Church. That's exactly what we are doing."

Dunajski couldn't believe what he was hearing. "You mean all these years you've been a Freemason trying to undermine the Church?"

"Not just a member," Elimelech interrupted. "He's the leader, the Most Worshipful Grand Master."

The pope's face hardened, realizing the depth of deception present in his Church.

Jarogniew smiled. "Yes, my friend, all along, under the guise of your Church, while seeking to uncover the Final Mystery."

Jeff realized what was happening. "So, you already found it?"

"No, you did, although credit must be given to the brilliant Shimon Teller and his young friend, Father Fabrizzi."

Jeff continued. "And it was you who had them killed."

Jarogniew's response took a boastful tone. "A necessary evil. I didn't approve of the methods, but that was carried out by an overzealous keeper of the faith. Regardless, what they uncovered was what Freemasons had been seeking for over two thousand years—the Final Mystery, the power of the Ark of the Covenant. When Teller and Fabrizzi refused to cooperate, force had to be used."

The pope was trying to understand what was taking place. "But destroy the Church? How?"

Jarogniew continued. "By following the plan that the *Alta Vendita* outlined: to slowly infiltrate the Church hierarchy until a critical mass of Church leaders could be inserted to change the course of Catholicism."

Dunajski responded. "But the Freemasons wanted to liberalize the Church."

"I prefer to think of it as liberate. We have had enough liberal ideas sprinkled into our beliefs and it can no longer be tolerated. You see, the Church was so fearful of its theological position that it could never tolerate a challenge to its questionable dogma from any group with an alternative tradition. For centuries, the Masons were attacked for wanting to practice its rituals without the intrusion of the Church until it became obvious that to survive, the Church had to be destroyed. But how? Certainly, a direct assault on the Church itself was not feasible, so they arrived at an alternate strategy."

"And that was the *Alta Vendita*?"

"Yes, Esconzo. They knew success would be slow, but the strategy was brilliant, the gradual takeover of the Catholic world by using the Church structure itself to gain its ends. For over half a century we have followed that strategy, spreading a gospel that, in time, would be so pervasive that priests would be ordained, bishops consecrated, and cardinals nominated who would be of one mind. Eventually, it would lead the Church to our path."

"And what path is that?"

Elimelech cut in. "To make Catholicism an instrument of his will, hijacking the Church into a dictatorial governance."

Jarogniew smiled. "I prefer to call it the Gospel of Discipline and Adherence, total subordination to Church doctrine, leading to complete regimentation. The end result would be a Catholic Church following the dictates of a new, stricter papal leader, all the while thinking they are marching under the banner of the Apostolic keys."

Dunajski responded. "They already tried fascism, and it failed."

His grin indicated that Jarogniew was enjoying the discussion. "It failed only because the vehicle was political rather than spiritual. What Hitler didn't realize is that people prefer to blindly follow a god than a human. Has not history taught that the masses prefer being told what to do than to make decisions themselves? What we are offering the people is a more responsive gospel, one that results in a faster route to redemption—blind obedience."

Dunajski's face revealed his amazement. "You're describing a theocracy!"

"Isn't that what the Catholic Church is? God as the supreme ruler with the priests defining God's laws? It's just that things have become a little too lax—or, as you like to say, a little too modern."

Jarogniew spoke to the group as if delivering a lecture. "There was a time in our history when the Church had complete control of a man's life. Remember Galileo? One of the greatest minds on earth charged with crimes against the Church, then begging the Church for a reprieve from his sins. That was a time when the Church was so powerful that it was able to prevent the advance of art and science for hundreds of years. We're just making a few edits, adding an autocratic touch of discipline, returning, as I should say, to that more regulated time."

The pope responded. "But surely you can't overthrow the entire Church. Do you think you can enforce your will on all the bishops assembled for the synod? A majority will never go along with it."

"I'm afraid, dear Esconzo, there is no longer a need for a majority. You see, what we are about to find under that stone is all that is necessary."

"And what is that?"

"Power, my friend, absolute power. But, let's find out, shall we? Now, there might be one little problem that needs to be dealt with, whoever touches the object may die. So, Bronislaw, why don't you bring up what you found?"

"And if I refuse?"

Tirshov waved the gun at Dunajski. "Then you die."

Dunajski realized he had no choice and kneeled on the rough stone floor, turning the spotlight to envision the space left by the missing stone. Reaching down, he withdrew a long, thin object wrapped in an old, dust laden cloth.

"So far so good. Now, Bronislaw, uncover it and put it on the floor."

The eyes of all those present watched with anticipation as Dunajski began to unwrap the bulky material until he uncovered a rod-like implement ornamented on one end.

"You're still alive! The sages had written that whoever touched the rod would die. It appears they were wrong. What do you think, rabbi?"

Elimelech didn't respond. His attention was drawn to Dunajski, for as the tall cardinal stood up, his cloak fell from his shoulders. It was but a moment, and Dunajski quickly covered himself, but Elimelech's eyes were glued on the cardinal as if he were looking at an image from a bygone time.

Jarogniew raised his voice. "Rabbi, know anything about a rod with blossoms and fruit made of sapphires on its head?"

Elimelech hesitated before responding, as if switching gears from his focus on Dunajski to Jarogniew's question. As the rabbi turned his attention to the rod that Dunajski was holding it took a moment before he realized what he was looking at, his face matching the disbelief of the sight. "Is this possible! Could this truly be Aaron's Rod?"

Jarogniew laughed. "Tell me, Rabbi, what makes you think so?"

"It's as described by our sages. Aaron's Rod grew a bud that blossomed into a flower and then an almond."

"As it is here. Now, rabbi, take the rod and turn it over."

Elimelech hesitated.

"Oh, go on, Rabbi, nothing to be afraid of. If the cardinal is still with us, surely you will be."

On the reverse side was an engraved Hebrew inscription.

Jarogniew was unable to control his triumph. "Well, now, look at that, three syllables, each with its own sound. Recognize them, Rabbi?"

"דצ"ך עד"ש באח"ב, Ditzakh, Adash, Biachav." Elimelech pronounced the Hebrew words engraved on the rod, his eyes widening, his body beginning to quiver, his voice starting to shudder. "We read those words at the Seder table every Passover—the abbreviation of the ten plagues."

"Yes, the power of the ten plagues lies in that rod, but it is much more, my friend. It is the three syllables, lost to man since Solomon's Temple three thousand years ago, until this moment." Jarogniew had difficulty containing his excitement. "And when these three words are pronounced, it will call forth the greatest power the ancient world ever knew. But what Solomon failed to do, I will."

Jarogniew turned to the pope. "Now you understand how your Church is to be lost. What you have uncovered is a power that can control the world. That is why the first step is for you to resign your position—you can say for health reasons—and support my election to replace you."

"And what will you do then?"

"By gaining control of the Church, we gain control of its vast resources, financial, political, and spiritual. Liberal thought has been tried and failed, leading only to freedom's abuse. And what are you left with? A world of revolution, terrorism, and disdain of order."

"The people will never go for it."

"The people will do as they are told! Rulers from the Pharaohs to Hitler have taught us that people would rather be enslaved then die. Hasn't the Church been leading them blindly for over two thousand years?"

"And what are you offering them?"

"A respect for law and order, each individual knowing their place in a more perfect society. Of course, it will all be paraded behind the cross, uniting them under one banner, one thought, one objective—but it will be the Lord who guides them to subjugation."

"This time, Ludvik, you've gone too far."

Jarogniew laughed. "Have I, Bronislaw?"

Dunajski read the depth of cruelty in Jarogniew's eyes. "So, you think you can call forth the force of God, just as Aaron and Moses did?"

"Not the force of God. The three syllables call upon a much greater one."

The pope seemed puzzled. "And what force is greater than God's?"

Jarogniew replied, "The forces of darkness. That is why, Esconzo, you will sign the *renuntiatio,* resigning your position, restoring me as cardinal secretary and supporting my election as the next pope."

The pope looked at Jarogniew: "You're mad."

"Once you sign I couldn't care what you call me." Jarogniew placed a sheet of paper on the table.

The pope glanced at the writing. "I will never sign it."

"Oh, I believe you will. A pope cannot be voted out of office, but he can die. Your choice."

"I will sign nothing."

"Sign it or you will be struck down like every first-born male in Egypt."

"Never!"

A sardonic smile appeared on Jarogniew's face. "As you wish."

Jarogniew reached for the rod, hesitantly at first, then realizing there was no reaction, grasped it and extended his arm, pointing the rod at the pope, just as Aaron had over the land of Egypt. Slowly, with irregular melody and cadence, he chanted the three lost syllables: "Ditzak, Adash, Biachav."

For a moment, there was silence, and then the intoned notes reverberated throughout the castle, resonant sounds ricocheting off stone walls. Soon a shadow appeared, growing slowly, filling the prison with a blackness so deep that even a vibration could not escape; a web so dense that not a muscle could flex nor a breath inspire. Once again, the Plague of Darkness had descended, rendering what had been as obscure as the deepest void. Those who had read the Bible understood its meaning; those who read Milton understood hell:

O dark, dark, dark, amid the blaze of noon,
Irrecoverably dark, total eclipse
Without all hope of day!

From the depths of the void arose a wind, so fierce and haunt-ing, it was as if Satan himself was ascending from the deepest pits of the abyss. Jarogniew looked up, his face red, the very ap-pearance of evil itself. "The forces of darkness have been released, and the end of days is upon you and your Church. Now you will sign."

Jarogniew held out the rod, and a radiant glow appeared about the pope, his arm moving spasmodically toward the docu-ment, as if unable to resist. His hand grasped a pen and moved toward the signature line. The others watched in horror as the pope struggled to resist the unseen, his body straining but power-less against the overwhelming force.

Suddenly, Elimelech's attention was drawn away from the scene as he looked up and observed the descent of Hebrew letters falling like drops of rain, holograms of symbols floating randomly into the cell. As they fell, they began to reassemble in an ensem-ble, each knowing their prescribed position. Elimelech retreated, his back pressed against the wall, tears collecting in his eyes as he recognized the order the Hebrew letters were taking: it was the word never to be spoken, the mystical forty-two letters of the name of God.

The letters completed their movement, spelling out the holy name. The darkness evaporated, sound and motion returned, and the rod fell from Jarogniew's gloved grasp, reverberating as it struck the stones below. The pope's hand fell free and the pen and paper dropped to the floor. As quickly as it began, it ended.

Jarogniew was taken aback, then enraged. As the forces of darkness retreated, the laws of nature returned. Jarogniew rec-ognized an emotion he hadn't experienced in decades: fear. He grabbed the rod, repeating the secret words, but to no avail. His eyes burning like glowing coals, Jarogniew struck the stone wall with the rod again and again, shouting the syllables, but there was no response.

"No! This can't be." In the heat of his rage, he swung the rod wildly at the pope, who raised his hands to block the thrust.

"Sign it, you bastard."

Jeff started forward, attempting to stop the brutality, but Tir-shov fired a warning shot that stopped him.

"Nobody move."

The pope tried to defend himself, and for a moment was able to grasp the punishing rod, but to no avail. Clutching his heart, he stood frozen, forcing attempts to fill his lungs and staring at his attacker, as if trying to understand the depth of Jarogniew's hatred. Within moments he fell to the stone floor, face down, without movement. Jarogniew threw the rod across the cell and stood over the fallen body. "Give me that gun!"

Tirshov handed him the pistol, and the cardinal aimed it at the lifeless body, screaming uncontrollably, "Now you'll sign it."

Elimelech flung himself at Jarogniew and tried to wrestle the gun away. They struggled before a shot rang out. All eyes were on Jarogniew as he stumbled backward, the gun in his hand, and then Elimelech fell to the ground, blood seeping through his shirt.

Tirshov laughed, Quinn remained still, Marzoti looked on in horror, and Estefaz made the sign of the cross. Dunajski said, "May the Lord be merciful."

At that moment, unworldly sounds filled the castle, piercing sounds beyond man's tolerance of hearing, sounds heard at Mount Sinai when God read the commandments, sounds that Elimelech realized he had heard before. It was the piercing call of the shofar, heard at the end of the Day of Atonement when Jews make their final petition for forgiveness before the heavens close.

From the stone floor, Aaron's Rod rose and floated through space. Elimelech watched in wonder as it moved toward Cardinal Dunajski, just as it had floated to Moses in Jethro's garden, just as the Ark had floated above its cart.

"Take the rod." The voice came from the fallen Elimelech, looking up at Dunajski. The weakened voice repeated: "Please, Jacob, the rod."

Dunajski hesitated, as if conflicted between the present and an echo from the past. What name had he been called? Jacob? He held out his hand and held the rod.

The rabbi continued, his voice weakening, "Now, Jacob, point the rod at the gun."

Jarogniew laughed maniacally, brandishing the gun. "Go ahead, Bronislaw, point the rod, see what happens. I'll give you a last chance before you and your friends die!"

Dunajski, without understanding why, pointed the rod toward his mortal enemy.

Elimelech's words could barely be heard. "Now read the words."

"But where?"

"Look closely."

Dunajski stared at the rod, and then, as if a cloud were dissipating, the forty-two floating letters appeared, bright and full of energy. From deep in memory he recognized what the letters spelled:

It was: THE NAME.

Jarogniew kept the pistol pointed at Dunajski. "Well, my old friend, I'm afraid that rod is worthless." His hand pulsed on the trigger.

Tears came to Dunajski's eyes as he pronounced the immutable Hebrew name of God that was never to be spoken. There was a flash, and the rod turned a burning red, flames leaped from it, and its furnace of fire entered Jarogniew's body and descended to his very soul.

And then it was over. His clothes lay in a smoking heap on the cold stone floor, his body nowhere to be seen. It was as the Torah had described of Aaron's sons when they brought strange fire before the Ark.

Estefaz and the others fled in fear while Jeff attended to Elimelech, ripping a piece off his shirt and tying it tightly around the rabbi's shoulder to stop the bleeding. "Lucky, it's only a flesh wound. You'll be fine." Then he knelt beside the pope, felt the carotid, and shook his head. "It's too late."

"No, it's not too late." Surprised, they looked at Elimelech, who continued. "Point the rod at the pope, Jacob."

Again, Dunajski followed the command without understanding, pointing the rod at the pope's motionless body. Suddenly an intense white light embraced the dead pope like a blanket of pure snow. Within moments, there was a slight movement. Amazed, Jeff knelt to feel the artery.

"There's a pulse. Call an ambulance."

Dunajski called Rome's emergency number, 118.

"Rabbi . . . how?" Jeff strove to get his bearings.

Elimelech quietly responded, "The power of Aaron's Rod."

Jeff said, "But I thought its power could only be transmitted through the family of Aaron."

"And so it was."

Dunajski bent over the rabbi and studied him closely. "Who are you?"

The rabbi looked up into the cardinal's face and answered softly, "I am Michael, your brother."

Dunajski tried to understand, tried to fit the pieces together, tried to find the key to a locked past. And then tears filled his eyes. "Michael? Is it you? Yes, I remember."

The rabbi turned to Jeff. "Jacob is my brother, though we haven't seen each other since the night my parents gave us away. Each day I've prayed for God to bring him back to me. Now, my prayers have been answered."

Dunajski remained puzzled. "But how did you know?"

"The port wine nevus, the large purple mark that you were born with. When your cloak fell off I saw it. That was something I could never forget. That's why you were the one who had to bring the pope back to life, for you are the eldest, the firstborn son, who, like our father, was a descendent of Aaron the priest. It is the firstborn who is chosen to lead our people. You are Aaron's true successor."

"But what about Jarogniew? You saw the power of God that he called forth."

"It was the wrong god."

"But he held Aaron's Rod. That means he had the power."

The rabbi offered a gentle smile. "No, Jeff, it's not the rod that contains the power, it's the holiness of the person grasping it that gives it the power. That's why he was destroyed. My brother, like Aaron, has that holiness."

* * *

Within minutes sirens were heard, and a white-painted vehicle with an encircled orange reflective stripe and the word *AMBULAN-ZA* arrived at the castle. The guard led the EMTs down the steps to the cell where they bandaged the rabbi's wound and placed him and the pope on stretchers and carried them to their vehicle.

"Take them to Tor Vergata University Hospital. Dr. Alessandro Bagetti is the physician," Jeff instructed.

The ambulance doors closed, and the blue flashing lights pulled away.

* * *

Tor Vergata University Hospital

It was several hours later when Daniella awoke to the feeling of her face being cleansed with a soft moist towel. Through the shadows of her mind, she heard a faint familiar voice calling her name and the warm soft hands of a surgeon gently holding hers.

"Danny?"

She opened her eyes and struggled to focus, trying to recognize the voice. Once more she heard a familiar, "Danny?"

The picture slowly came into view. "Jeff?" She hesitated, then spoke softly. "You called me Danny."

"You did tell me that's what old friends call you."

Her eyes labored to focus. "Where am I?"

"In the hospital. You suffered a concussion and a few bruises, but you'll be fine."

"What happened?"

"Your message said that you had a little problem. When I couldn't reach you, I jumped in a cab and went to the Great Synagogue. The rabbi read your message and we rushed into the museum and heard a gunshot. We ran toward the sound and found a man attacking you."

"What happened?"

"I pulled him off you. He was holding a gun and I tried to get it away from him. In the scuffle, the gun went off and he fell to the floor, soaked in blood, dead, a corkscrew through his eye. Was that your doing?"

"Yes." Daniella tried to fit all the parts together. "It was Professor Signorelli's son, Angelo. He's your murderer, the one who killed my father and the priests in New York." She hesitated: "Are you OK?"

"I'm fine. And you will be to. Alessandro took good care of you."

The shadow of a smile crossed her lips. "Did you find it?"

"In Cellini's cell."

A look of contentment crossed Daniella's bruised face. She whispered, "We figured it was there, didn't we."

"Yes we did. And you were right. It was Aaron's Rod."

A contented smile broadened and small furrows appeared above her brow. "Wow! I wish my father could have been there."

"I have a feeling he was."

"And Jarogniew?"

"Destroyed by his own lust for power, and his friends are under arrest. Case closed."

"Then there's nothing left for us to do."

Jeff smiled, and kissed her gently on the lips. "I have some ideas."

He carefully drew the blanket around her. "But first it's best that you get some rest."

A faint "thank you" was heard as she closed her eyes, sank into her pillow, and fell into a deep sleep.

* * *

July 16, 9:00 a.m., Tor Vergata University Hospital

"He'd like to see you now."

Dr. Alessandro Bagetti motioned for the visitors to enter the pope's second-floor hospital room. Jeff, Cardinal Dunajski, and a bandaged Rabbi Elimelech entered.

The pope looked at Jeff. "Dr. Bagetti tells me you saved my life."

Jeff smiled. "Actually, I had nothing to do with it." He looked at Elimelech. "It was his doing."

The pope looked at the rabbi, puzzled. "It was you?"

Elimelech smiled and put his hand on Dunajski's shoulder. "Actually, it was my brother, Jacob."

"Brother? Jacob?"

"We have a lot to catch up on, but right now you must save your Church."

* * *

1:00 p.m., Vatican City

The pope stood outside the Sistine Chapel where 240 bishops of the synod were gathered.

"So, Bronislaw, are you ready to become my permanent cardinal secretary?"

Cardinal Dunajski looked at those around him before responding. "Your Eminence, I have given your gracious offer a great deal of consideration, but I believe my destiny lies on another path."

"And that is?"

"To resume the beliefs of my father and his father. I am of the priestly class of Israel, a direct descendant of Aaron. The Lord has taken me on a long journey. Now it's time to return home."

The pope smiled, as if pleased with Dunajski's decision. "Then, Jacob, go with the Lord's blessing."

The pope turned to Elimelech. "And, Rabbi, thank you for making me realize the true meaning of what Jesus taught: his message of peace and tolerance for all. It is time for our Church to understand that there are many ways to reach heaven."

JULY 17

The world picked up the early morning printed editions to learn that the pope's agenda had been unanimously approved. Included was his final charge to the bishops attending the closing synod session in which he described the events that had transpired over the past seventeen days. In it, he especially thanked the Chief Rabbi of Rome for his aid, in spite of grave personal danger. The pope added: "It was a rabbi who inspired Peter to found this church, and it was a rabbi who saved it."

JULY 31

New York's Medal of Commendation was awarded to Dr. Jeffrey Moss, citing his exemplary service to the New York and world communities. The ceremony was attended by Mayor Arroyo, Chief DePalma, Dr. Stan Galvin, a host of police and government officials, and Archbishop Patrick Cardinal Healy. Following the festivities, Mayor Arroyo approached Jeff, who was speaking to Chief DePalma and Stan.

"Detective, congratulations on receiving your medal."

"Thank you, Mayor, but to be honest, I feel like I've been involved with too many medals recently."

The group laughed, and the mayor continued. "Just want you to know that Police Commissioner Fleck has been arrested for hindering an investigation, more concerned about the dictates of Quinn than the people of New York."

The mayor stood next to Jeff and posed for the cameras. "By the way, Detective, Chief DePalma advises me that we just received another case for you to take over—one that will demand the greatest scholarly research. I suggested that you take a day or two off before starting."

Jeff smiled and gave a winking glance. "Thank you, but I'm already working on my next case, quite a complicated one, and it may take more than a few days to figure out."

"I see. Well, I had no idea you were already given a new assignment. Good luck."

As the mayor left, DePalma and Stan seemed puzzled. "You're working on a new case?"

"Yes, an expedition, with one of the greatest archeologists in the world."

"Any place in particular?"

"I believe our first stop is Jerusalem."

"That reminds me, this is for you." DePalma reached into the bag he was holding and handed Jeff an elegant square black velvet box with small hinges. "I think you'll know what to do with it."

Jeff carefully opened it and smiled at its contents. "Thanks."

At that moment a tall, tan brunette made her way to the group.

"Hi, love. Hate to interrupt, but we have a plane to catch."

As they walked away, Jeff turned to the surprised trio. "You just met my next case."

EPILOGUE

Jeff held the long, thin Rod wrapped in its time-worn white cloth. "I guess you were right. The only way to know is to hold it and see what happens."

Daniella smiled. "Remember, it's the person who gives it the power, not the rod."

He handed Daniella the black velvet box. "And what shall we do with this?"

"What is it?"

"DePalma gave it to me. Better open it."

Inside was the gold diadem, gleaming in the sunlight.

Jeff looked at her inquiringly. "Now what? The museum?"

"Aaron's rod and crown?" Daniella thought for a moment before responding. "I'm afraid the world's not ready yet."

"Then what?"

"Bury them together under a loose stone where the temple once stood."

"But will they ever be found?"

"As my father said, *Hashgochah pratis*—no one finds anything they are not deemed to find, and no one will find what is being sought before its time."

THE END

AUTHOR'S NOTE

This is a work of fiction. However, in creating the fiction, I have tried to adhere to historical accuracy, including the histories of the Jewish people and the Catholic Church. The discussion on Cellini is factual, and the quotes from his autobiography are authentic. Where a smoother narrative was required, I took the writer's prerogative. For Cellini's autobiography see: *The Autobiography of Benvenuto Cellini*, annotated by George Bull (New York: Penguin Classics, 1999); originally published 1558 under the title *Vita di Benvenuto di Maestro Giovanni Cellini, fiorentino*. ISBN: 9780140447187

I am not aware of any conspiracy to destroy the Catholic Church, although the *Alta Vendita* is a historically accurate manuscript and the conspiracy surrounding it is true. For the full text of the *Permanent Instruction of the Alta Vendita* see Msgr. George E. Dillon's *Grand Orient Freemasonry Unmasked*.

The legends and symbols of the Free Masons that I used in this book are based historically on the secret beliefs of the Masonic Brotherhood, as best as could be gathered. The names of the cardinals, rabbis, and other characters are fictional and are not intended to represent any particular individuals.

The theory of where the Temple Treasure is to be found was adapted from the research of Sean Kingsley and his book *God's Gold: A Quest for the Lost Temple Treasures of Jerusalem* (New York: Harper Collins, 2007).

I also wish to thank Jacob Libin for his insightful interpretation of the death of Aaron's sons.

ABOUT THE AUTHOR

The Vatican's Vault is Barry Libin's second novel. The first, *The Mystery of the Milton Manuscript* discloses the true meaning of Milton's epic poem, *Paradise Lost* (Urim Publications, 2014). *The Vatican's Vault* continues in that genre of historical novels.